WE OWN
Tonight

We Own Tonight

One Last Time

Not Until You

If I Only Knew

WE OWN
Tonight

NEW YORK TIMES BESTSELLING AUTHOR
CORINNE MICHAELS

Editor:
Ashley Williams, AW Editing

Proofreading:
Kara Hildebrand & Janice Owen

Cover Design:
Sommer Stein, Perfect Pear Creative

Cover photo © Perrywinkle Photography

DEDICATION

*To all the girls who dreamed of what could've been while singing along
to your favorite band on your Walkman. This one is for you.*

"Damn it, Heather. We're always late because of you!" Nicole yells from outside the bathroom. She's been my best friend since the sixth grade. You'd think by now she'd know to pad things by twenty minutes if she wants a snowball's chance in hell of getting anywhere on time.

"The peril," I taunt her as I finish putting my hair up.

"You drive me nuts."

"Such is life."

I hear her mutter something under her breath as she walks away. I don't know why she gets so upset. We have plenty of time. With the way Nicole drives, her lead foot will have us at the concert fifteen minutes before the opening act.

Of course, I'm taking my sweet ass time getting ready. I have zero desire to be forced to put on makeup or any version of pants.

Nicole's idea of girls' night out and mine are totally different. I could stay home, drink a martini, and be happy. My best friend wants to paint the town red. I'm too old for that shit. I end up smelling like a garbage can and feeling like I ate a jar of cotton balls. I'd rather be comfy in pajamas than wear these jeans that I had to lie on the bed to shimmy into. I can only imagine what I looked like while I was sucking it in and bending backward to get the damn button closed. Then I did about fifteen lunges to "stretch" the pants, all the while praying I didn't bust a seam. Nothing like a workout just to get dressed.

I make a mental note to call my trainer friend at the boxing ring.

She knocks again. "I'm leaving you."

No, you're not.

I open the door a smidge. "I have the tickets in here. So, you know what? Go ahead." I stick my tongue out and then quickly close the door and lock it. If they hadn't already left me twice before, I wouldn't have to go to such lengths. I learned quickly that I always had to have the upper hand with my three best friends. Then again, if I had let her leave me, I could be watching Netflix and shoveling popcorn into my mouth.

Nicole may not have figured out to pad time, but she has learned I have a spiteful side, so she lets me finish without another interruption. I could stay in here longer just to piss her off, but that would mean more time staring at the pink tiles on the wall that I loathe.

My house isn't bad, but it isn't great, either. When my parents passed away, it was passed down to me. It's old and probably falling apart more than I'd like to admit. Yet, I can't get rid of it. It's the only thing of them I have, and the only place I can afford.

The mortgage is paid off, which allows me to put what little money I have left over after my monthly bills to go toward my sister's medical care.

Once I'm happy with my appearance, I head out with a shit-eating grin.

She looks at her watch as I emerge and shakes her head. "I swear."

The best way to keep Nicole from blowing up is with diversion. "You shouldn't swear, it's unbecoming of you. Are we picking up Danni and Kristin?"

"No, and I'm grateful we aren't, because we would miss the opening band."

She and I are the two most sarcastic and the biggest assholes out of the group. When we start to bicker, it gets bad —quick. Without our two mediators, it's best not to engage.

"Are you sure?" I ask ignoring the jab.

"Yes, I'm sure. They're meeting us there."

Nicole and I walk out and get in her car. I wish she'd buy a normal size vehicle. I'm five-foot-five, and my knees mash my boobs because of how squished I am. Between my already tight jeans and this sardine can, I'm going to bust a gut.

"Please," I say dramatically, "tell me they're not bringing their husbands."

She laughs. "Dickhead One and Jackhole Two aren't coming. They're going for a boys' night." She sticks her finger in her mouth and makes a gagging sound.

Thank God for small miracles. Their husbands are the worst, especially Danielle's.

"Maybe the two loser husbands will fall madly in love with each other," I muse while I shift to get comfortable.

Nicole smirks as she watches me. "And figure out they were never meant to be married to such amazing women like them."

"And then we'll finally build that compound where the four of us can live."

"No. We're going to need penises. There's no way I'm living with you people without having someone to bang. You three will drive me so far up the wall that I'll need the release. Daily."

"You're ridiculous."

"You're damn near celibate."

Here we go again. "Shut your face." She whips out of my driveway so fast that I almost smack my head on the window. "Nic!" I yell as she takes another turn way too fast in this damn death trap. "Jesus! Slow down!"

"Stop being dramatic. I'm with you, and you have a badge. No one is going to ticket me."

"I don't care if you get pulled over." I right myself and grab the edge of the seat. "I care about dying."

"You're going to die from lack of sex if anything." She rolls her eyes and cues the '90s station. "Listen to Four Blocks Down, and get ready to watch the boys shake their delectable asses on stage. After that, you can remove the stick up your ass, maybe then you won't be so miserable."

"I'm not miserable." I slap her arm.

"Okay." She shrugs and ignores me, which is her typical way of blowing me off.

Am I miserable? No. I'm happy . . . for the most part.

I have a great job that keeps me fulfilled. Being a female police officer isn't easy, but I love it.

The only real downside to my job is that I come face to face with my ex-husband every day. Luckily, things didn't end *that* badly. But I'd be full of crap if I didn't admit how much it bothers me. Things with Matt are—weird. Sometimes people just don't work or you realize the person you married isn't what you thought. I wish I could transfer to another town, but my sister Stephanie and the twelve years invested in my pension keep me here.

Nicole belts out another round of lyrics. "Sing it with me, Heather!"

I don't want to, but I'm taken back in time when the four of us had bangs that were so high they could cause whiplash, wore colors that no one should ever wear, and drooled over Four Blocks Down without a smidgen of shame.

Smashed in the tiny death trap posing as a vehicle, I let go a little.

We both sing along, belting out the lyrics of our first crushes. "I wish I still had my Eli pillow case," I grin.

"I had a Randy towel. I would like to wrap myself up with him again." Nicole sighs.

I swear this girl needs sex more than anyone I know. "Does your vibrator ever get a break?"

She looks over at me with her usual you're-an-idiot face. "You're going to realize very soon, my love, if you don't use it . . . you lose it."

"And you're going to overuse it," I say. She's the only one of us who never married. Nicole lives in downtown Tampa. She has to schlep it all the way out to Carrollwood to pick me up, but she knows if she didn't, I wouldn't go.

Sometimes, I envy her life. She has everything she dreamed of. Opening Dupree Designs and then landing her contract with one of the wealthiest developers in the city was pure luck. She slept with him, got a few more jobs, and before she knew it—she was on top.

Then she dumped him.

We park the car at the arena, and Nicole shifts in her seat. "Listen, I know you're hell bent on being the responsible one of us, but tonight," she grabs my hands, "I beg you to let loose. You *need* a break."

I glare at her. "I do let loose."

"Your hair is in a bun," she raises her brow. "You're the definition of tight."

I touch my hair, hating that she has a point. But this is me. I like to make good choices. Other than marrying Matt, which wasn't *bad* per se . . . just hasty. Never mind that he was an asshole. And he sucked in bed.

Okay, so maybe it was a bad choice.

Moving on. "I'm not uptight, Nic."

"I didn't say uptight. But let your hair down. It'll make Danni jealous since she can't get her hair your color blonde no matter how much money she spends. Maybe one day she'll get over herself and stop trying." Nicole and Danielle have a love/hate relationship. This week it seems to be more on the hate side. I wish they'd get over this already and talk it out, but they both claim there's no issues.

From what I can gather, Nicole slept with Danielle's ex three days before she got married. I don't know if it's true or not, but I wouldn't be surprised since it is Nic we're talking about. When I heard the back story, I distanced myself from the entire thing. No way was I getting in the middle of it, but Nicole typically has something snippy to say about her and vice versa.

Feuds aside, Nicole is right. I don't ever go out. If I'm not being a couch potato, I'm with my sister.

I pull my hair out of the bun, allowing my blonde locks to fall around me. Thanks to the twist, it almost has curls. Nicole grabs her bag from the backseat and tosses her makeup pouch onto my lap. "Put some of that on. You know, look hot. Not like a frumpy divorcée."

"I often question why I didn't drop you after high school." I grab some eyeliner and darken my brown eyes. I add a little blush and lip gloss. "Better?"

"Much."

We head into the concert, and I can't stop giggling to myself. Everyone is around our age—all here to see a freaking boy band. The group we all lusted over as teens is now fully grown, but here we are, ready to swoon and scream their songs.

I can't remember how many dreams I had about Eli Walsh or how many notebooks I filled with Mrs. Heather Walsh signatures. I'm sure I'm not alone, either. There are probably a few hundred middle-aged women here tonight who had done the same thing.

Some more scantily clad than others.

"What the hell is she wearing?"

Nicole glances over and makes a disgusted face. "Dear, Lord. Someone needs to tell her that a muffin top and a mini skirt don't mix."

I snort.

"I feel like this is our version of a high school reunion," I cogitate while scanning the crowd for Danni and Kristin. I know we're not spring chickens, but when did we get as old as some of the people standing in line? Sheesh.

"Heather!" Kristin waves as they rush toward us.

Even though we see each other at least every three months, I miss them. We made a promise when we graduated high school we'd have a quarterly date, and so far, we've all made a point of sticking to it. It helps that we all stayed in the greater Tampa area, but I think no matter the distance, we'd always be there for each other.

Some friendships are unbreakable—even if someone sleeps with someone else's ex.

"I've missed you," I say as she wraps her arms around me.

She plants a kiss on my cheek. "I missed you more."

We all stand here, hugging it out. We're dorks, but I couldn't care less. Other than my sister, they're the only family I have.

"How's Steph feeling?" Danielle asks.

"She's doing good, I think. I'm waiting for her to call me." It's so sweet how Danielle always asks about Stephanie.

"I'm glad she's doing okay." She smiles.

"Yeah, she should've called though. I should probably give her a call . . ."

Danni grabs my hand, stopping me from going for my

phone. "I'm sure her nurse would let you know if there were something wrong."

She's right, but the worrier in me can't help myself. I've spent what feels like my entire life making decisions around Stephanie. I don't take any chances when it comes to her.

"I'm just going to check," I explain as I grab my phone from my bra.

Danielle laughs. "I should've known better than to try to stop you."

There are no missed calls or texts.

Breathe. I'm sure she's fine, don't overreact.

I send a quick text because I'll never let it go.

> Hey, you okay? I haven't heard from you today.

She answers right back.

> STEPHANIE
> Yes, Mother.

Brat.

> Have you had any more tremors?

My sister suffers from Huntington's disease. She was diagnosed at nineteen, and it took her independence before she even had time to enjoy it. I tried to care for her. I did everything I could to keep her with me, but when she started suffering from relapsing paralysis and struggling to speak, we knew it was beyond my capability.

Watching your twenty-six-year-old sister battle with early onset dementia is devastating. The last few weeks have been good, though. She's been cognitive, alert, and even happy. Her symptoms are sometimes so mild that I forget how sick she is, but then the disease rears its ugly face again and there's no forgetting.

STEPHANIE

Nope. And aren't you out with the girls? Go have some fun, Heather. Tell them I said hi!

"Is Steph okay?" Nicole asks when she sees me typing away.

"She's fine. I mean, you know . . ." My mood drops immediately as I think about how she'll never experience this. Danielle touches my arm, and I force myself to smile. "She says hi."

"Give her our love," Kristin replies. I type out their message and tell her I love her before tucking my phone away again.

"Okay!" Nicole exclaims. "Let's go see these amazing seats that our super-fan Kristin scored us."

Kristin gives Nic the stink eye, which would be way more effective if she weren't in their fan club. Yup, my thirty-eight-year-old best friend is in a fan club for Four Blocks Down. I'm positive she regretted telling us this piece of information, but it landed us front row seats, so we haven't been too hard on her . . . yet.

"You can sit in the nose bleeds if you want."

Nicole wraps her arm around her shoulder. "You love me too much to deprive me of Randy." She lets out a dreamy sigh.

I laugh. "As if you'll ever get that close to him. And he's married!"

I try to put Stephanie in the back of my mind. My sister's illness is ripping me apart. I wish I could help her, but I can't control any of it. It makes me feel helpless all the time.

Stephanie grew up listening to me blare the music and dance around like a loon, and instead, she's stuck in a damn assisted living facility while I'm out. It isn't fair. None of this is fair. She should be here with me.

"Hey," Danni nudges me. "You look beautiful."

I give her a small smile. "Thanks." I'm no longer feeling carefree. I can't stop thinking about how much I wish I could be doing this with her.

"I'm sorry." Her smile falls slightly.

"For what?"

She shrugs. "I made reality come crashing into our big fun night of no worries."

"Stop! Don't feel that way." I wrap my arm around her shoulder. "My reality never leaves me. My sister is dying. It's just the way it is."

Danielle's smile falls completely now. "I'm so, so sorry, Heather."

I know she didn't mean to bring me down. I wish I could be more like Nicole. No responsibilities, sex with random strangers, nothing to worry about . . . but that isn't how my life goes.

Nope. Mine is a series of tragedies. While my friends were partying in college, I was working full time. My nights and weekends weren't filled with formals or trips to the beach, they were consumed by doing homework with Steph. I'm not bitter. I'm actually grateful in some ways. It forced me to cherish life and the people in it. Every day I have with Stephanie is a gift.

I shake my head. "You have nothing to apologize for. Let's act like idiots and pretend there are no problems in the world."

"You want to party like it's 1999?"

"Yeah, just like that. If only we had our Four Blocks Down dolls."

"They are collectable memorabilia," Kristin corrects before blushing scarlet and mumbling about needing to go find our seats. Nicole, Danielle, and I laugh hysterically as we follow her inside.

I wave to two of the guys in my squad, who are apparently working overtime detail as security as we pass them. Shit. I didn't even think anyone from my squad would be here. Usually, it's the other district that handles the MidFlorida Amphitheater. They look thrilled to be here—not. I make a note to behave so my entire department doesn't find out that I came to see my favorite boy band. However, knowing them, they've already texted everyone. I swear, cops are worse than teenage girls with their gossip.

I'll never live this down.

Music plays from the two opening acts. I sing along because . . . their songs were my jams when I was a teen. I would blare their screw men anthems through my speakers, windows down, singing off key, and belting every note because they were my idols. I owe many of my breakups to them telling me that I didn't need to take it.

"Ah!" Danielle squeals after the second band finishes. "FBD is next! I had the biggest crush on—"

"Shaun," Nicole cuts her off. "We remember you licking his poster."

"Oh my God!" I giggle. "I remember that. She straight made out with it." I guzzle the rest of my beer and shake my hair around.

"I wanted him to be my first kiss," Danielle explains.

We all did. Hell, I may have had multiple fantasies with Eli, but I wouldn't have kicked any of them out of my bed. They were everything when we were younger. I think somewhere in my mind we're all frozen in time.

"Want another beer?" Kristin yells.

I've had three already. I'm halfway to drunk. I shake my head no.

"Yes, she does," Nicole answers for me. I look at her with

my mouth open. "I'm driving. You're having fun." She turns back to Kristin. "She'll be drinking all night."

"Oh," Danni laughs, "this is going to be epic."

"Shut up, I'm a good drunk."

In my mind.

"You're good for a laugh," Danni tacks on.

The lights go out, and the mood shifts. All of us start to scream and hold hands. This is Eli and Randy's hometown, so it's extra special. Their homecoming concerts are always louder and longer.

"Are you ready, Tampa?" PJ's voice booms.

We all yell louder.

"We said," Shaun's voice comes through this time, "are you ready?"

I bounce with Nicole, unable to control myself. I allow the energy of the room to fill me. I'm probably the loudest of the four of us. I don't give a shit, either. "Hell yeah!"

Kristin looks at me with a huge grin. So unlike me.

"That's it, Tampa!" Randy's face flashes on the screen on the side of the stage. "The Walsh brothers are home. And we want to hear you!"

Eli's face. I sigh. "Did you miss us?"

"Fuck yeah I did," I scream.

"Good." The screen displays both Eli and Randy. "We missed you, too. And you're about to see a whole lot of us. FBD is back, and we're ready to blow your minds."

The arena goes black.

And slowly, I see something rise out of the stage.

I stand mesmerized.

The light shines in my eyes, blinding me, but when I can see again, I would swear that Eli Walsh is staring right at me.

Emerald-green eyes pierce through me. His dark brown hair is cut short on the sides and the top falls errantly around his forehead. I take in every ounce of his perfect body. The way his arms pull against the fabric of his shirt, the pants that hug his perfect ass, and the span of his broad shoulders, makes me want to climb him like a tree. Then, with our gaze connected, he winks and throws a wicked grin my way.

Holy shit.

I stand there and gaze back at him like a fish with my eyes wide and mouth open. He looks away, but it happened. Eli Walsh smiled and winked at me. I just died.

"I'm hallucinating," I say to Nicole as I explain what occurred, or at least what I think did. "He wasn't actually looking at me, right? I'm being insane. I must be stupid drunk to be imagining this."

She lets out one of her evil laughs while shaking her head. "You have no idea how pretty you are. I swear. Blonde hair, petite, brown eyes, big tits . . . of course he winked at you. Hell, I'd do you."

I can't tell if this is her typical sarcasm or if she's being honest. Part of me doesn't want to know. I can continue to delude myself that he was zoomed in on me. What mega superstar/sex God who can have any woman he wants would hone in on me?

Sigh, I can't even lie to myself well.

The next song comes on, and he doesn't glance my way once.

Okay, I'm literally certifiable.

I knew I had to be off my rocker. Now I can continue on with my life.

We drink more, sing, and I do everything I can not to stare at him. But . . . I can't help it. He's too beautiful to look away from. I watch the way his chest heaves as he dances around the stage in perfect sync with the other guys. How his eyes scan the crowd but still make every woman think he's looking right at her. It's magnetic. Eli Walsh is ridiculously sexy. Even in his forties. He's aged so well it makes me wish I were a guy. They have it so much easier than women. My boobs were much perkier fifteen years ago.

His smile, though. That hasn't changed one bit. It still brightens every part of him.

"Heather!" Danielle calls to me over the music. "Matt," she jerks her head to the left.

Ugh. Why the hell is he here? I can't escape him.

One night. I wanted one single night with no Matt, Stephanie, bills, crumbling house, or any other issue. Once again, I get screwed, and not in the way that leaves me sated at the end of the night.

I grab Nicole's beer and chug.

"Whoa!" she says, taking the half empty can from me. "Easy there. You're a lightweight on a good day, but I can't remember the last time you drank like this. Pace yourself."

"You said to enjoy myself."

She smirks. "Touché."

I ignore Matt standing off to the side and looking authoritative in his uniform. It used to turn me on when he got ready for his shift. Watching him put on his vest and then take his time to make sure every crease was in line. Once he was sure his uniform was perfect, he would put his gun belt on and stand with his chest puffed out. Now he looks like an old guy who thinks his middle bulge is muscle. Sorry, dude, it's the bulletproof vest making your chest big, not what's under it.

Kristin wraps her arm around my waist, dragging my attention from him. "Ignore all men except those on that stage."

"I just can't seem to get him to disappear."

She touches my cheek. "Try to escape in the music."

I bob my head as we sing to our favorite ballad. "I love this song." I sigh.

"Love me till the end of . . . time," we both sing in harmony.

"I'll love you, Eli!" I scream.

His eyes lock on mine, and my face becomes an inferno. Heat floods my entire body as his lips turn up slightly, and he gazes at me a beat longer than last time. Everything inside me clenches. My breathing halts, and I don't look away. Eli finally turns to do some spin with the rest of the group, breaking our moment.

I just died of humiliation. I cannot believe I yelled that and he heard me.

Kill me now.

Kristin bursts out laughing, almost falling over from her hysterics. "I think I just peed a little."

"Shut up."

"You yelled . . . that you love him . . . and he . . . heard you!" she manages through her fit of laughter. "Only you."

I pretend it didn't affect me. We had a connection. I felt it, and I swear he did, too. My heart raced and not just because it was him. Part of me was mortified, but the other part of me was emboldened. He freaking looked at me. I know I didn't imagine it.

"Maybe he didn't hear."

"Oh, he heard," Kristin shakes her head.

The girls go back to dancing around and singing along while I feel like an asshole. I hate to be the center of attention, and I hate being embarrassed. That moment was as horrifying as it was exhilarating.

I need some air. There's no way I can look at the stage right now. If he isn't looking at me —which I know he's not—

I'll feel stupid. If he is—again I know he's not—I may have a stroke.

"Be right back," I call out to the girls.

"You okay?" Danielle yells.

"I need another beer."

She raises her can and then I head up the stairs. The music plays in the background as I keep moving.

I arrive at the concession stand and grab two more drinks. I'm going to need them. But I decide there's no way I'm going to feel bad. I'm allowed to let loose. Besides, I'm sure he gets this all the time. Everyone here loves him, so why the hell do I care if he happened to hear me? I don't.

Lie.

But, no, this is the first time I've been out in how long? I'm going to enjoy every damn minute. I brush it off, sip my beer, and decide to own my pubescent love of Eli Walsh.

As I turn, I come face to face with Matt.

"Hey," he says.

"Hi." I muster all the enthusiasm I have . . . which is none.

He scans the crowd and looks at the beer in my hand. I can see the judgment in his eyes. God forbid I actually have a life. "I didn't expect to see you here."

"I didn't think I'd see you, either."

Matt puffs out his chest and puts his hand on his gun belt. "Well, I figured I'd get some overtime."

"That's good."

I'm not sure what to say at this point.

"So, how's life? Steph?"

Like you care.

"She's been good. Asked about you the other day."

Matt rakes his fingers through his short brown hair. Seeing him like this makes it hard to forget how good things were for a period of time. Right now, he's just a normal guy, not the asshole who broke my heart. "I'm glad she's doing good. So, Four Blocks Down? Didn't peg you for a groupie."

I'm honestly shocked he's surprised. Four Blocks Down was played at our wedding. He knows how much I love them. My bridesmaids serenaded me to my favorite Eli song.

"Attending a concert doesn't make me a groupie, Matt. I'm enjoying a night out."

His hand touches my shoulder. I wait for a feeling, any feeling, but nothing comes. I used to turn into a puddle when he was near me. He used to make my heart race, now he makes my head hurt.

I don't know if I can pinpoint exactly when it happened, but we fell out of love as quickly as we fell in love. I think I cried more over losing the idea of my marriage than losing him. I wanted a love like my parents had. Instead, I got apathy and a man who was extremely jealous of my sick sister.

Matt's thumb grazes my bare skin. "You deserve it."

The door opens, and Nicole catches my eye. The scowl on her face makes me grin. There's no love lost between these two.

She bumps my hip with hers, causing my beer to slosh over the rim of the cup. "If it isn't Deputy Dickless, or should we say, Captain Kangaroo?" Nicole says before grabbing the cup and taking a drink.

Here we go.

"Hello, Nicole," he says through gritted teeth. "And I'm a lieutenant not a deputy or captain."

"*Sooo* sorry to get that wrong." She touches her chest. "Well, as much as I don't give a shit . . ."

"Nic," I say, hoping to diffuse the situation. Nicole holds grudges, and the fact that Matt hurt me still enrages her.

Thankfully, she takes another swig instead of responding. When she finishes, she links her arm in mine. "On that note. I'm going to steal my best friend so we can enjoy our night without spineless men who leave their wives because they're selfish. Bye now."

She pulls me away.

"Bye," I say.

Nicole squeezes my arm. "I love you and want you to please not spend another second thinking of him."

"I'm fine. He was being really nice."

That was part of the problem. In the beginning, I was happy. Then Steph got sicker, and my attention wasn't directed toward him anymore. I needed to care for her, which meant Matt had to care for me. He either didn't want to or he didn't know how to, and it was the beginning of the end. We fought all the time and barely saw each other. Then, right before he left me, he was ridiculously nice. There wasn't passionate lovemaking or any big grand fights. Everything was even keel.

"Good. Let's go sing and see if you make an ass out of yourself again."

Ugh. I regret this already.

We get back to the front row as the boys are playing one of their older songs. I don't know why they play the new stuff. Really, no one cares. We want to pretend we're still thirteen singing into our hairbrush microphones.

"All right, ladies," Randy croons. "It's that time. We're going to take it down a notch. Maybe find that girl who only comes around once?"

My favorite song ever.

Eli walks around the stage, smiling and pointing to random women. "I feel like I need to sing to someone this time, Ran."

Randy smirks. "You need some inspiration, brother?"

Eli continues to walk around while tapping his chin. "I need a girl who's going to be mine. Are you her?" he asks the crowd.

People scream, jump around, and wave their hands frantically. I move behind Nicole, just in case . . . because I would rather take a bullet than go up there.

He comes around the stage and stands in front of me. His green eyes sparkle with mischief as they land on me.

He points. "You," his voice sizzles as he stares at me.

Fuck my life.

All the blood rushes from my head. No. No way. I vaguely hear the screams around me, but I can't move. I shake my head in protest.

Eli's finger hooks as the bouncer comes around. "Come up here, sweetheart."

"No," I whisper as Nicole pushes my back forward. "I can't."

"You're so going." She thrusts me forward, and the bouncer pulls me over the rail.

I look up as Eli stands with his hand out. "Will you be my once in a lifetime?" he starts to sing the lyrics.

My heart races as I place my fingers against his palm. I pray to God I can keep myself from passing out. I'm on stage with Four Blocks Down.

Breathe, Heather, I tell myself as he walks me around while singing.

"You're the only girl I see." Eli hits each note. His hand doesn't release mine as he begins to sway. This was the song that I always imagined him singing to me. "I want to wake up next to you."

Oh, Eli . . . if only. I feel the heat burn my cheeks. What the hell is wrong with me?

Eli sits me in the chair on stage. Thank God, because I may hit the deck. I say a silent prayer for the bright lights that obstruct my view into the audience. At least I can't see my friends doing who knows what. Or my co-workers. He kneels in front of me, holding my hand as if he were proposing. I can't feel my extremities. I'm shaking, and it isn't from being cold. "Will you be my once in a lifetime?" he asks again.

I know this is the damn routine.

I've seen them in concert at least four times, twice in high school and twice in college, but I'm completely lost to him. There are over twenty thousand fans here, but in this instant . . . it's him and me. A girl can dream.

His hand brushes against my cheek as he hits the final note. He helps me stand and then pulls me close. "Don't go anywhere after the show," he whispers in my ear.

I pull back and look in his deep green eyes waiting to hear: Just kidding. But it doesn't come.

Holy shit. He just asked me to stay? I'm being Punk'd. Seriously, where is the camera crew waiting to jump out at me?

The next song begins as the bouncer helps me back over the rail.

The girls attack me with their screams and flailing arms. I can't speak. I don't even know if I can breathe.

Nicole steps in front of them and holds my shoulders. "In and out, Heather."

I focus on inhaling and shake my head. "What the hell just happened?" My mouth hangs open.

"Well . . ." She grins before continuing, "You were serenaded by the hottest guy ever."

They ask me a million questions about what it felt like. The only thing I can say is: "Surreal." It was freaking surreal. I would never believe that actually happened if they hadn't shown me the video on their phones. Every glorious second is documented. I can see my face is flushed, my eyes wide, and I'm pale. Great. I look up, hoping he hasn't seen me and my friends freaking out, but his back is to us as he sings to the other side of the arena.

I think about what he whispered to me. Did he want me to

wait—for real? And why? Maybe he wants to give me a signed souvenir? It would make sense. Embarrass the fuck out of some girl and then give her an autographed T-shirt.

"Nic," I call her over because there is no way I'm not telling someone.

"Yeah?"

"He wants me to wait after the show," I yell in her ear.

Her face brightens. "No way!"

"It's got to be a misunderstanding, right?" I ask.

"Or he wants you."

"No!" She's on crack. There's no way in hell he "wants" me. That's dumb.

"He already knows you love him." She smirks.

"Whatever. There's no way I am going to wait."

"The hell you aren't!" Nicole crosses her arms. "We're staying. We're going to find out what Eli Walsh wants because you'd be an idiot not to."

Yeah, I'm an idiot all right—not because I don't want to meet him but because I do. Very much.

CHAPTER THREE

"Good show," PJ says as he cracks his neck. "I'm getting too old for this shit."

"You are old."

"You're older than I am," PJ reminds me.

Even though I'm forty-two, I enjoy the rush of performing. I'd just like it not to be so rough on my aging body. I don't remember having to take this many painkillers a few years ago, but between the traveling, shit food, and performing—I feel old as fuck.

Even though I love acting much more than I thought I would, I love the fans more. I don't have this kind of fun when I'm stuck on a set all day.

I look over at my brother, "Randy is older than all of us, so there's that."

"Fuck off," Randy tosses back. "We've got a few weeks before we need to meet up again since the tour is over. I'm going to head home to Savannah. She said the kids are acting up. It's time for Daddy to come lay the smack down."

"Right." I laugh. Those kids have him wrapped around his finger. "We all know Vannah is who they listen to."

"Don't piss in my Cheerios."

"We're heading out to the meet and greet." Shaun slaps my leg. "You coming?"

I gave my manager strict instructions to get that girl back here. I practically drew him a map on how to find her. She better be there or I'm canning his ass. I loved watching her face while I sang to her. She was like a deer in the headlights as I laid it on thick. I almost lost my shit when she yelled out that she loved me. She couldn't cover her face fast enough.

It was cute.

I like cute.

I also haven't gotten laid in about a month, so this seems perfect. Especially if she's good in bed. Plus, since we're done touring and my mother has been up my ass about spending time with her, I'm sticking around Tampa for a few weeks anyway. It may be nice to have a distraction until I start filming the next season of *A Thin Blue Line* in two months.

"Let's go meet the people." I stand, stretching my arms over my head. What I want to say is, "Let's go find the blonde."

We're contractually obligated to attend a meet and greet at every show. I fucking hate it. It's always the same shit. We sit back in the lounge and drink while girls tell us the same things over and over. I'm glad they love us. I'm glad they've been listening to us since they were thirteen, but I don't give a shit. It only reminds me how old I am.

If she's there, though, I'm going to thoroughly enjoy myself. I'm going to watch those brown eyes fill with pleasure while I make her lose her mind.

"You had Mitch bring the blonde back, huh?" Randy asks as he throws shit in his bag.

"Yup."

The guys leave the room while I hang back to talk to Randy.

He chuckles. "You're going to knock up one of these girls someday."

I roll my eyes. "The fuck I am. I learned that lesson on our first world tour. I've been at this for twenty years and haven't had that happen yet. No mini Elis or Eliettes running around here."

"That you know of," Randy retorts.

We could go back and forth, but the one thing is . . . I'm careful. There's no freaking way I'm getting saddled with some kid from a groupie. I know better. Plus, Mitch is a scary prick. We're his bread and butter. No way does he want some stupid shit taking away from his chance to make money. I know firsthand how easy he can make things disappear.

"Don't worry about me."

He stops putting things in the bag and gives me his serious look. "Like that'll ever happen."

Randy is two years older, and since our dad skipped out when we were kids and then died two years later, he thinks it's his job to protect me.

"Seriously, Ran. Stop. Be my fucking brother for once."

He huffs. "Fine. I think you need to grow up, Eli. You're over forty, never married, no kids, not even a serious girl-friend since—"

"Don't say her name." I put my hand up. "I don't want to even think about her tonight."

Randy knows better. I don't talk about her. At all.

"Fine, but Vannah is worried, too."

"Savannah couldn't care less about my love life. What you meant to say is Mom is worried. She's probably chewing Vannah's ear off about it, so she's coming to you."

My mother is the queen of meddling. She's like a damn parakeet, "Eli needs a wife. Eli needs a wife." I hear it all the damn time.

"No, it's not Mom. It's everyone. Stop the partying and

random girls. Find someone who actually has a brain. You can't tell me you're satisfied with your life."

"I can tell you I'm done listening to you." I lean back and cross my arms.

Why do people think I need to be married to be happy? When did that become the definition of success and contentment?

Randy hoists his bag over his shoulder and smirks. I can practically read the thoughts in his mind. He thinks he has me. He has all the answers for why I need to live the life he thinks I should be living.

"And what about when things get tougher for you?"

And he just hit the only sore spot I have.

"Now I'm done."

I flip him off and walk out. As soon as I enter the hallway, I hear the screams. I'm really not in the mood anymore, but I have to at least appear. I wave to the girls who couldn't get in and head to the meet and greet where I hope she's waiting.

There are days when this life is exhausting. I work my ass off and don't get to enjoy it nearly as much as I thought I would. It's all work all the time in my life. This business has a life expectancy, and I'm past it, which is why my focus has shifted to my show and movie projects. That is where I feel normal. I'm surrounded by people who don't care who I was all those years ago. I'm an actor, a friend, a fucking human. When I'm on tour, it's different.

Acting gives me way more freedom than the band ever did, too. I have more days off, no days on the bus, and a nice long break between filming. I don't know how these other musicians constantly tour.

I turn the corner, and the music from the after party fills the air. The bass is loud, and the lights are dimmed, which means the girls are most definitely primed. My mind is set on one thing: convincing the blonde to spend the night with me.

My mind has been consumed by her, and I move quickly, hoping she's there.

I haven't been this excited about a girl in a long time. There is no such thing as normal dating for performers. No woman wants to put up with the tabloids, groupies, and the fact that her man is never around. I sure as fuck wouldn't.

"Eli," a girl I don't know croons. "There you are."

She's hot, but not the girl I'm searching for.

"I'll find you later," I brush her off.

I glance around the dark room, but I don't see her. A few other girls approach me. I give them my customary smile while still scanning the faces for the one I'm looking for. She should be here. That's the one good thing about our manager —he does his damn job.

Finally, a few people move, and I see her. She's standing in the corner with her friend. Her long blonde hair is pulled to the side, showing off the skin on her shoulder, while she's sipping a beer. I love a woman who drinks from a bottle. It's sexy and down to earth. Shows me she isn't all high maintenance and can hang with the boys.

I push my way through the crowd and beeline right toward her. "You made it," I say, scaring her a little.

"Oh—" She clears her throat. "I-I . . . you said? I mean, you did tell me to, right?"

"Since you told me you love me, and I serenaded you, I figured we should meet officially."

Her brown eyes widen as her bashful smile flashes. She's even prettier than I remember. Her body curves in all the right places. Everywhere a man wants to lay his hands is carved to perfection. It's clear she's physically fit, and I'm ready to see what's beneath those clothes.

"I'm Nicole." Her friend extends her hand. She then gives me one of those looks that tells me she's watching me. I see why the blonde brought her. Smart move.

"Eli." I return the gesture with my most sincere smile.

"I'm Heather, by the way."

"Heather," I repeat, allowing her name to roll off my tongue. "Want another beer?" Her face turns red. "Did I say something?"

"No," she says as her hand touches my arm. "I'm sorry. I'm just nervous."

I like that I keep her slightly off kilter. Most of the girls that come back here are almost too sure of themselves. Like we should be so lucky to have chosen them. Then, it's sexual promises and over the top offers. Ninety percent of the time, I never even go there. I guess after this long, I've become picky.

I blame my niece and nephew. I'm not saying I want to settle down, because that's the last thing I need, but it would be nice to have someone to talk to once in a while. I'm surrounded by actresses most of the time, so I've had enough fake relationships.

"Don't be nervous," I try to reassure her.

Heather smiles and tucks her hair behind her ear. Is there anything this girl won't do that I find attractive? I must be losing my mind. "It was a great show."

"I'm glad you thought so." And I am. I sang and danced my ass off. Whenever we come home, we give a little more. "I enjoyed a few parts more than others."

"Me, too." Her eyes brighten.

"Why don't we go somewhere a little more private and talk? The after-show area is always crammed, and I won't be able to avoid everyone."

She looks at Nicole and then back at me. Nicole nudges her a little, and I decide that girl is my new best friend. Of course, I want to do a lot more than talk, but first, I want to get her away from all the noise.

I catch my manager's attention and jerk my head in Nicole's direction. He'll make sure she stays occupied.

"I don't know."

"I promise, this place will become something neither of us want to be a part of." I go for the truth, hoping she'll catch my drift. "I just want to talk, if that's what you want." So, I lie a little.

Nicole smiles, whispers in her ear, and shoves her forward. I extend my hand, hoping that her friend helped me out a little. Heather looks down and then entwines our fingers.

Fuck this is going to be a good night.

Oh my God. Oh my God. I'm going to a private place with Eli. What the hell am I thinking? I'm not. Clearly, I'm having some kind of out-of-body experience. I would never do this. Yet, here I am, holding his hand and walking away from the meet and greet.

"You okay?" His deep voice is laced with concern.

"I'm great." I'm such a liar.

"Yeah? Because you're shaking."

My entire body is trembling. I haven't pinpointed whether it's because I'm excited or scared out of my fucking mind. I'm pretty sure it's the latter. I focus on my breathing. I'm in high stress situations all the time, this should be a cake walk.

This is, as Nicole says, hooking up. Apparently, people do this all the time and it's normal. I can be normal. I can put all this crazy shit aside and be in the moment.

Just let tonight be what it is and enjoy it.

I clear my throat and smile. "This kind of stuff never happens to me."

He chuckles as he comes to a stop in front of the tour bus. "What kind of stuff?"

"This," I say a little high-pitched. "I don't typically drink, scream at random people, get serenaded, get asked backstage, and now . . ." I trail off. There's no way I'm finishing that statement, because I don't know what exactly is happening. Maybe he wants to ask me about something dumb. He may not want sex. I don't know that I want sex.

That's a lie.

I totally want sex. I want to let loose like Nicole told me to. To be completely without fear of consequence for just one night. I'm always responsible. My life is practically a billboard for sensibility. I uphold the law, care for my sister, work to support myself and Steph, volunteer at the youth center, but I never let loose.

I'm going to have fun. Well, if he wants to.

Thank you Jesus for beer. Or whichever person made it.

"What do you want to happen, Heather?" Eli's eyes smolder as he tugs me close.

Oh. Fuck. Me.

"I-I . . ." my mouth goes dry.

His hands move around my hips as he shifts us so my back is against the door of the bus. He's so close. Eli's touch travels up my sides until he stops at my neck. "Well? We can talk or we can do something else."

I think back to what Nicole said. *Let go for one night.* And for tonight, I'm going to fulfill my teenage fantasy. I'm going to sleep with Eli Walsh . . . on a tour bus . . . after an FBD concert.

My back straightens as I muster my inner Nicole. I press my body against his, hooking my hand around his back. "I think we can find something else to do."

His green eyes flash with surprise before his mouth collides against my lips. Every inch of his body is flush with mine. Our lips move in harmony as he fumbles for the door handle. As soon as the door opens, we fall back. He walks me backward up the steps and through the vehicle without missing a beat or stumbling.

I lose myself in his kiss. He isn't soft or gentle. No, he devours me. It's passion unbridled. Neither of us worry about finesse. This is unlike any kiss I ever shared with Matt. He was slow, cold, and perfunctory. There was no *need*.

I need this. I need to escape my mind.

Eli pushes me where he wants me while holding my head in his grip. My fingers roam his body as we continue to move. He opens the door to the bedroom. "Bed," he mutters before his lips find mine again.

I pull at his shirt, breaking the kiss as I tear it off. "Wow," I say as my eyes take in his chest. My fingers move slowly over his pecs and then down toward his abs, rising and falling over each valley and divot. He doesn't have an ounce of fat on him, and I can feel every flex and pulse beneath my fingertips.

"You're beautiful." His soulful eyes lock on mine as he pushes my hair back.

"I'm average."

His gaze rakes over my body before coming back to mine. "There's nothing average about you, Heather."

That's all I need. My hand grasps his neck, and I bring his mouth back to me. No one has ever made me feel like this. And I'm still dressed.

He uses his weight to push me onto the bed. I revel in the feel of him braced above me. It's Eli fucking Walsh. Before I know it, my shirt is coming off, and I'm grabbing for his buckle. I undo it before he rolls me on top of him.

Our lips move in perfect unison, and my heart beats out of my chest. In the back of my mind, I know how out of character this is for me, but I can't stop. I want to be wild and crazy. The fact that I'm going to sleep with Eli is a little overwhelming, but it feels right. Maybe because I've dreamed of him since I was a kid. Maybe it's because I'm drunk as hell. Either way, it's happening.

I sit up, fully on display as I unhook my bra. My blonde hair spills in front of me, giving me a little coverage. Our eyes lock, and I glide the straps down.

Eli grins beneath me as the material falls away. I'm not fully exposed, but it's enough for him to see what he wants. "You have perfect tits," his deep voice is smooth as silk. "Move your hair, baby. I want to see all of you." Eli puts his hands behind his head, watching with rapt attention.

I do as he says. Again, totally out of character. I'm always in charge, but I surrender to him without question and pull my hair back before lowering closer to him. My breasts hang, just barely brushing against his chest. "I never do this."

"Do what?" He lifts his hand and rubs his finger across my cheek.

"Casual sex."

"Seems I'm breaking a lot of your rules."

I struggle to keep my voice steady. "I would say so."

"Do you want to stop?" His fingers slide down my neck and over my breast before he rubs tiny circles around my nipple.

"No."

He smiles. "Do you like the way I touch you? The way my fingers feel against your skin?"

"Yes," I admit.

"How bad do you want this?" Eli asks as he takes my nipple between his thumb and forefinger.

There are no words. I've been tasered, and this is more electric. Every inch of me is humming. I want this to never end. One-night stands aren't all that bad, I've been missing out.

I drop down and kiss his lips.

"Heather?" He pulls my attention back. "Answer me."

"What was the question?"

He chuckles. "Do you want me to fuck you?"

"Yes," I moan.

As soon as I say the word, he rolls me onto my back. His hands grip my breasts as he massages and kneads. I close my eyes and lose myself in his touch. Then I feel his tongue against my skin. The heat from his mouth and the cool air in the room sends shivers down my spine.

I need more. I rock my chest up, silently begging. He sucks and licks the right side and then pays attention to the left. Eli starts to move lower, and I lift my head. No way is he going down on me. I can't. I've only ever let Matt do that, and it was not a good experience.

He unbuttons my jeans that took me five minutes to get into, and I grab his hand. "You don't have to," I say quickly.

"I want to."

Want to? Matt said no man wants to do this, they do it because they have to.

"I'm serious." I give him another out.

Eli rises onto his knees then hooks his fingers in my jeans. "I'm serious, too. I want to taste you. I want to make you scream my fucking name so loud that everyone here knows what I'm doing to you." The heat in his eyes melts me.

"I know that most guys don't like it . . ." He stops, giving me a confused look, which makes me feel naïve and a bit stupid. "I mean, I've been told by . . . that . . ."

Eli pulls my pants lower. "Did you ever come on a man's tongue?"

"No."

"You're going to come on mine." He leaves no room for question. "A real man eats pussy. Only selfish pricks refuse to give their girl what they need."

I lie completely speechless. But I don't have time to think about what he said, because he's ripping my pants and underwear off. Eli lifts my legs, throwing them over his shoulder, and his gaze melts me. He watches me as he moves closer, taking his time, causing my heart to race.

At the first swipe of his tongue, I'm done.

But it only gets better. Eli knows what he's doing. His tongue presses against my clit, moving in circles, then up and down. It's like nothing I've ever felt. Sweat starts to bead on my forehead as my climax builds. He wasn't kidding about making me come.

My fingers grip the blanket as I try to hold back, try to stay on the ground. He forces me to climb higher and higher as he continues to drive me toward ecstasy. "Holy shit. Oh, my God," I mumble.

He stops for a second, slips his finger inside, and sucks even harder. I twist and start to tremble as he continues to drive me forward. Another finger joins the first, and he pushes deeper, crooking them just right and hitting the blessed spot that no man has ever found before. I burst apart.

Everything inside of me clenches as I fall over the cliff. I scream his name, exactly like he promised I would, and then become mush.

Holy shit. I'm dead. Died. Gone to heaven. I've met my maker because this man is a God.

My breathing is erratic, and my heart is thumping so loud that I swear he can hear it. "Wow."

"I told you." Eli crawls his way toward my face.

"You made good on your promise." My voice is low and full of appreciation. "I think you're a little overdressed, Eli."

"What are you going to do about it?" he taunts.

Making the most of the space between us, I slip my hand down and slide the zipper the rest of the way open. Then I remove his pants and boxers, allowing his impressive length to spring free. "This," I say as I wrap my fingers around him.

He lets out a low hiss as I slide my hand from base to tip. I watch his face, learning what makes his jaw tick or his eyes close. My thumb grazes the tip, and he pushes me back. "I want to fuck you."

Our mouths connect, tongues swirl, and our hands roam over each other. "I need you," I beg almost desperately. "I need you right now." I've never begged or been vocal during sex before. Ever.

Eli grabs a condom from the nightstand and rolls it on before getting back to where we were.

"You're making me break my rules, too," he confesses. I don't have a chance to ask what the hell he's talking about before he enters me.

My eyes slam shut as I stretch to accommodate him. He's big. Bigger than I've ever had before. He doesn't move like I expect him to, and I open my eyes.

"You okay?" Eli asks.

I nod quickly.

Eli drops on his forearm and kisses me with care. This kiss isn't the same as the ones before. It's slow, sensual, almost sweet. My fingers tangle in his hair as he begins to rock back slowly. He moans in my mouth as he continues to be gentle.

"Eli," I groan. It's too much. Everything about him is incredible. His thumb rubs back and forth on my cheek as he slides in and out. "You feel so good."

"So do you. What are you doing to me?" I glance up at him to find him watching me. "I want to make you come again."

Well, that would be nice.

He rolls over, forcing me to be on top. I never got to be on top much in the past. When I did, it was the only time I got off. Considering how good this feels, I doubt I won't climax again.

"Ride me, baby."

And I do. I glide up and down, allowing him to fill me to

the brink. I rake my fingers across his chest, enjoying the way he groans. Eli is just as lost as I am. I move faster as my orgasm builds again. "I'm gonna come."

"Good. Hurry, baby. You're going to make me come the way you're gripping my cock." Eli grits his teeth as his fingers dig into the flesh of my hips, pulling me down harder as he thrusts up to meet me. I'm undone.

"Eli!" I cry out as my climax hits me hard. He continues to move me as he follows me to the end.

I fall next to him and try to catch my breath. Neither of us speaks as we come down from the high.

As I lie there naked, it hits me that this really happened. It isn't just some dream. This is real. I had sex with a member of Four Blocks Down on his tour bus. Where he's done this with I don't know how many girls. I've never had sex with a random stranger before and now I'm lying here with a man that probably only does that. I'm not special, he probably doesn't even remember my name since all he did was call me "baby".

The bed shifts as Eli rises. "You need anything?"

A shower and a lobotomy. "No," I reply quickly.

"I'll be right back."

He heads into what I assume is the bathroom, and I jump up. I can't believe this. What the hell is wrong with me? What was I thinking? Clearly, I wasn't. I blame Nicole.

"What's your last name?" he asks from the other side of the door.

I quickly throw my clothes on. I need to get out of here. "Covey," I reply while pulling on my jeans. Where the hell did my underwear go? I look around and under the bed but don't see them. Damn it.

He flushes the toilet, and I'm out of time. I can't look at him. I need to go before he returns.

I grab my heels and phone and rush off the bus. I need Nicole, and then we need to leave. Now.

I spot her as soon as I walk through the door. Thank God. Nicole is making out with some guy in the hallway. Typical. I grab her arm and pull.

"We have to go," I explain.

She looks back at the guy, "I'm—"

"No. We have to go right *now*."

"Heather," she protests.

"Now!" I yell at her, and her eyes widen.

I'm not known for yelling, but when I do . . . I mean business.

"Bye." She says to the guy, and I drag her along. "Slow down."

I don't even acknowledge her. My mind runs in circles as I think about what just happened.

"We have to go." There's no way I can look at his face.

"You said that," she grumbles as we move. "What happened?"

I shake my head, pulling her into almost a sprint. I'm going to be sick. It was amazing, and so ridiculously good, but so wrong. I'm not a one-night stand girl. I'm a commitment and get-to-know-you girl. The guys at least know my last name. I'm a slut. I'm worse than a slut . . . I'm a *groupie* slut.

"Don't make me stop walking," Nicole threatens. "You know I will."

"Fine," I stop as we get to the exit door. "We had sex. Really good sex. You happy?"

The size of the smile on her face is all the answer I need. She looks like a proud mother at a talent show.

"Fuck yeah, I'm happy. Why are we running away?"

"Because . . ." I huff. "We had sex! I had sex with him! We have to go."

I push through the door, still dragging Nicole behind me.

"That doesn't explain why you're running barefoot through the arena."

I'm not explaining this to her. "Just keep moving."

We finally exit, and I could literally cry. They closed the gates to the parking lot.

"Now what?" she asks, looking at the tall metal gate with big ass locks on it.

We could go to the south entrance, but that would take too long. There's only one option. "We climb."

"The hell we do!"

I let out a heavy breath and glare at her. "Nicole, I just did something so unlike me that I'm not even sure it was me. So, we're climbing the fence because you're my best friend and I need to get the fuck out of here."

"Babe." Nicole's eyes fill with sadness. "You didn't do anything wrong."

"I'm a groupie slut."

"You're so not a groupie. You're the furthest thing from a slut."

I don't respond. Instead, I chuck my shoes over the fence and start to climb.

When I was twelve, I could climb fences pretty quick. Especially growing up in Tampa where we would hop fences to get to each other's yards. But I'm not even halfway up and I'm winded, my foot has slipped more than once, and I can only imagine what I look like from below.

"Shit!" I yell as my toe misses the next opening. Nicole's laughter fills the air. "Stop laughing and start climbing!"

"This is priceless." she laughs harder. "Wait. Let me get my camera!"

"Nicole! We need to get out of here in case he comes looking for me."

"Fine. Fine. Chicken shit." Her shoes fly over my head, and the entire fence shakes. "You owe me."

"Stop moving!" I try not to laugh, but it's futile. This is hysterical. "I'm going to pee," tears fall from my eyes as I hold on.

"I need a Go-Pro for the next time we go out."

"I hate you," I say between giggles.

She purposely rocks back, causing me to almost fall. "You only wish you did."

"If I fall . . ." I warn as I sway and try to climb higher.

"It'll be what you deserve for making me climb a freaking fence at one in the morning!"

The amount of ways that I'm going to pay for this is unimaginable. My co-workers saw me being sung to on stage, I'm sure one of the guys from my squad caught me going backstage, I'm going to have scrapes from climbing a fence, and Nicole will never let me live this down.

I reach the top, one leg swung over on one side and one still in Eli-land. And that's when I hear him. "You're going to just run out?" Eli's voice is filled with disbelief. "Just like that?"

I get myself over the other side and climb to the ground so I have the fence between us. Nicole is near the top, watching this unfold. "This was a mistake. It should've never happened."

"So, you run?" He takes a step closer, and I thank God for the metal between us.

"Nic," I whisper-shout, urging her to come down, and she starts to descend. I glance back at Eli, who stands before me with no shirt or shoes. His chest heaves as if he ran here to find me. I stare at him. "It's better this way," I say, wishing Nicole would hurry the hell up.

"Why? Says who? You didn't even give me a chance!" Eli grips the back of his neck.

"This would never work. Seriously. You don't have to try."

Even if my life were completely peachy, which it isn't, Eli

and I would never work. We had sex, it doesn't mean I want more, but there isn't even a chance I could. I've already seen that men are selfish, and I can't even provide enough attention for a local police lieutenant, there's no way I can do it for a world renowned actor and singer.

Eli takes another step, his hand gripping the steel separating us. "You said you don't do this before, well, I don't chase after girls who run out, so we're both doing something different. I wanted to talk . . . I wasn't asking for anything, Heather."

So, he does know my name, that makes me feel marginally better.

Nicole finally drops down beside me, and tears fill my eyes. I know she sees it. I'm not upset because of him. I'm upset because of me.

"Let's go."

She knows me well enough to know I'm in over my head. The reason I've never done casual is because I feel too much. I've had life-long friendships, one boyfriend who I married, and a sister who needs me—casual doesn't fit into my life. Now that I've come down from the buzz and adrenaline, I feel empty.

I release a heavy breath and shove down my emotions.

"Look. I'm sorry I ran out, but I have to go. I don't belong here anyway." I'm not sure what the proper etiquette is for running away from a man you've spent your entire adolescent and part of your adult life dreaming of and then slept with, but this seems appropriate. I grab my shoes and start to walk away.

"Heather, wait." I glance back at him over my shoulder. "I just—"

"Goodbye, Eli."

There's no way I'm looking back, because if I do, I might not keep walking.

As we start to sprint, my phone dings with a voice mail. It's Stephanie's facility.

With my fingers trembling, I press play. "Hi, Ms. Covey, this is Becca from Breezy Beaches Assisted Living. Stephanie had a . . ." She pauses as if she can't find the right words. "She's been transferred via ambulance to Tampa General Hospital. Please call me as soon as you can."

The tears I fought back fall without a thought. "It's Steph. We have to run."

"I'm fine," Stephanie says while swatting my hand away as she lies in the hospital bed.

"If you'd stop fidgeting."

Her seizure was the worst one yet. Thankfully, there hasn't been any damage that has manifested, but I've refused to leave her side, not even for a second. I hate myself for being at that stupid concert instead of here with her. She's my entire world.

"Go to work, Heather. I can't handle you being around me. You're like a fucking helicopter, always hovering over me. You annoy me."

One of the worst parts of Huntington's is the mood swings. Stephanie was a sweet, kind, and happy-go-lucky kid. When she was nineteen, she had her first onset of tremors. Her body would go stiff and she couldn't move. Immediately, Matt and I took her to the doctor, but they couldn't find anything.

Then her mood did a complete one-eighty. It was as if someone stole my sister's identity and replaced it with the angriest person I'd ever met.

"I am going to work today, thank you."

"Good. Do I go back to Breezy tonight then?"

"Depends what the doctor says."

According to the neurologist, we can expect her to continue to deteriorate, and she's at high risk of another seizure that could leave lasting effects. The younger you are when you become symptomatic with Huntington's the faster things get worse.

"Yet again, I have no say in anything. It's always you and the doctors. I'm a fucking adult!" She rolls her eyes and turns onto her side.

"I know you are, but yelling at me isn't going to help."

My patience with Stephanie is unending, but at times, I lose my cool. Being told how awful, worthless, and depressing I am eventually wears me down. I know it isn't her. She acts this way because she's frustrated and in pain, but I still hate it.

However, it was Stephanie who made the decision to move into Breezy Beaches. She knew I couldn't quit my job to take care of her. I needed to make whatever I could, and a live-in nurse was way over our budget since insurance wouldn't cover it. She needed around-the-clock care that I could no longer provide.

It was the single most devastating day of my life. I cried harder after dropping her off than I did the night our parents died.

"I hate you. I hate this disease." She flips back over and throws the cover back, staring up at the ceiling. "I hate it all."

I touch her shoulder, and her hands start to move. They took her off the medication for the tremors when she was admitted, and it took less than forty-eight hours for them to come back.

"Steph," I say carefully. "Please don't shut me out."

"I c-ca-can't." Her eyes well with frustration and tears. "I h-hat-t-e th-this."

I move to the side of the bed and lace her fingers with

mine, trying not to cry as well. Our hands move together as her body takes control. I do my best to comfort her. "I know, love. I hate it, too. Right now, we're just dancing. That's all."

In the beginning of the disease, this was what I used to say when her hands and feet would go. It was our dance break. I muster a smile and start singing as we move with no rhythm or purpose.

My heart breaks as I watch this disease rob my sister of a life she deserves. It isn't fair that she got the gene and I didn't. I would gladly take it for her if I could. So many times I've watched her and tried to stay strong, but sometimes there is no strength. Sometimes I can't help myself from losing it. My lack of strength sometimes won't be my demise—love will be. Love is what breaks me down. Love is what makes it so hard to forgive God for doing this to us. Stephanie should be hanging out with her friends, working, *living* life. Instead, she's stuck in a facility because we have no idea when the next symptom will arise.

The tear I was fighting so hard to push back, falls.

Stephanie's eyes lock on mine, and we both cry together.

"IS YOUR SISTER BETTER?" Matt asks as we finish roll call.

"Yeah." I nod. "She should be going back . . ." I stop myself from saying the word "home" because it isn't home. It's a fucking group home, and I hate that she's there. "to the place soon. Thanks for covering for me."

"I know this is hard for you," he says, trying to comfort me. "I hate seeing you like this."

Right. I'm so sure that's the case.

"Wouldn't have been if I had my husband's support." I toss back at him.

I watch his face shift to hurt. "Heather," Matt whispers. "It wasn't like that."

I roll my eyes and huff. While Stephanie takes her hurt out on me, I channel my anger toward Matt. "It was exactly like that. You left me. You moved out because I wasn't willing to put my sister in that home. You made it so that I had no other choice in the end. We were supposed to be a team, but you . . ." I pause and try to get myself back under control. "You left."

"You didn't give me any choice!" Matt's voice rises. "I was watching my wife drift away. I couldn't do anything. I couldn't make you happy. You act like I'm the villain here, but I had to sit around watching you lose yourself."

I can't believe him. "It was not about me or you, it was about her."

"Take a minute to think about who left who, Heather. You were gone a long time before I walked out that door."

Matt turns around and walks out. How fitting. It's a different time, but the same result—he walks away first. We've had this fight before, several times, and each time, it reminds me of what a selfish dick he is.

"You ready to hit the road?" My partner Brody asks as he slaps me on the shoulder, breaking me from staring daggers at the door Matt walked through.

I sigh and relax. Thank God for Brody. He's funny, gets my sarcasm, and is completely dependable. I know he has my back in the same way I have his. It's a relationship that is essential between partners. Aside from Nicole, Kristin, and Danielle, Brody is my best friend. We've been riding together for the last seven years, and there's no one in this world I trust more.

"Yup. I need lots of coffee today."

"Do you need me to sing to you?" he asks with a smirk.

"Heard that does it for you. Or do I have to be rich and famous?"

My heart freezes, and I squeeze my eyes closed, mortified. I completely forgot about the concert. It all comes back like a freight train. The singing, the dancing, the sex with Eli Walsh. How the hell could I forget that there are probably videos and . . . oh God.

I look around the break room and there, on the bulletin board, is a photo of me sitting on the stage with Eli singing to me.

Damn it.

Shit. Shit. Shit.

I walk over and rip it down, trying to pretend as if I don't care. "Real funny guys."

"But," Whitman, one of the idiots on my squad jumps in, "you're my once in a lifetime girl."

"Shut up," I crumple the paper and toss it in the garbage. "You're all tools."

"We all know what you like, Covey. Maybe we should just pretend to be cops on television, then you'll think we're sexy."

"You need to lay off the greasy food and lose some weight. Then maybe the half blind lady down the street will think you're sexy."

A few guys laugh, and jab his side.

"Yeah? Tell your boyfriend that we don't all eat donuts! I work hard for this physique. Besides, we need to be in a boy band to get you tossing your panties at us."

This is never going to end. The more I feed into them, the worse this will be. I grab the keys from Brody's hand and walk off. They start to sing and yell at me, but I keep moving. Idiots. I work with idiots.

Brody climbs in the passenger seat and chuckles. "Oh, come on, Heather. We're just having fun."

"Clearly. It's not that, though." I toss my hat on the dash.

"Stephanie had an episode, which is why I didn't come in yesterday."

Brody's eyes soften, and he sighs. "I'm sorry. I figured you were recovering from your night of singing and drinking. Is she better?"

"She's okay now, well, as okay as it gets for her."

Brody was the one who helped me move Stephanie in to Breezy Beaches. He's been more of a husband than Matt ever was. His wife Rachel has been great. I'm glad she and I have become as close as we are. There's a very strange bond between partners, which can lead to a lot of questions, and I've seen more than one wife accuse her husband of cheating. I've also seen more than one occasion where she wasn't wrong.

As much as I love Brody, it's a brother-sister kind of love. I would take a bullet for him, but his "gun" isn't going anywhere but in his holster.

"You should've called me, Rachel and I would've come to the hospital."

"No." I shake my head. "That would've been totally unnecessary."

"Let me guess, you had it?" His tone is laced with sarcasm.

I turn the key in the ignition and start to drive. I'm not going to let him goad me. He's way too good at it.

We drive toward the section we're patrolling. Even with Matt being the asshole he is, he always puts me in the section near Tampa General Hospital, which is something that I should probably thank him for. At least I'm close if something changes with her condition.

Brody tells me about Rachel's new kick with some crazy diet. She's so pretty and already skinny, I don't know what she's thinking.

"Well, when you finally have kids, she won't care."

He gives me side eyes and grunts. "I'm not sure we'll have kids."

"Brody," I touch his arm. "You need to let go of the past."

Two years ago, Brody was in a horrific wreck. He was doing code and a driver plowed through the red light, T-boning his cruiser. It was a miracle he survived. It was one of the nights we were shorthanded and weren't riding doubles. I've never been so scared in my life, and neither had Rachel. She was so terrified that the stress caused her to miscarry. Brody never recovered from that.

"Says the girl who refuses to date because she married an idiot. Hell, when's the last time you even had sex?"

My cheeks burn, and I hope he isn't looking at me.

"I know that look, Heather." Brody shifts in his seat and laughs. "Who did you have sex with?"

"None of your business."

Shit. He's going to keep prying until I have to tell him just so he'll shut up.

I focus on the road and want to throw my hands up hallelujah style when the radio cuts in.

"We have a report of a domestic in Hyde Park."

Brody's grin is gone, and he grabs the radio. "Car 186 is on it."

"Central copies, dispatching the address now." The dispatcher cuts out, and I flick the lights on.

I focus on the road as Brody gives directions. We head into the small upper-class suburb and pull in front of the house.

Both of us cautiously approach the door, we knock twice, and a woman opens the door with a smile.

"Hello, officers."

"Good morning, ma'am. We got a call about a disturbance. Is everything all right here?" I ask.

She smiles warmly and opens the door. "Yes, my son is

autistic, and well, sometimes he gets really loud. My neighbor behind us keeps calling. No matter how many times we explain that there's nothing we can do but let him work it out, she continues to call the cops."

"Do you mind if we come in?" Brody asks.

We've seen too many instances of a wife covering for her husband because she's terrified of him.

"Of course," she steps back, giving us room to pass. "Please, come in."

"Thank you, Mrs. . . . " I leave it open.

"Harmon. I'm Delia Harmon"

We step forward, and a boy around fourteen comes to the door, and I smile. "Hi."

He stares off to the side and grunts.

"Sloane doesn't speak, but he loves lights," Mrs. Harmon explains. "It's been a rough few months. His father took off a while ago, so it's just us, but we're doing fine. Aren't we Sloane?" She looks adoringly at her son.

I smile, thinking of how lucky this boy is to have a mother like her. The way she stares at him reminds me of how my mother looked at me, and my mother was always brimming with love. Stephanie and I were her life.

"Hi, Sloane," I kneel in front of him and his eyes dart outside.

"Can you say hello to the police officers?" Delia encourages.

Sloane doesn't say anything. Instead, he points to the cruiser outside. The look of wonder in his eyes is shining bright. He starts to pull on her arm while she tries to pull him back.

"Would he like to see the police lights?" Brody asks, breaking his silence.

"Oh, he'd love that."

Brody and I spend the next few minutes with Mrs.

Harmon and Sloane. We show him the lights and watch as the joy spreads across his face. He seems much calmer, and I wish there were more we could do for him. Inevitably, another call comes in and we have to leave. Sloane starts fussing, and I know it's only going to get worse. He wants us to stay, and I hate that we are leaving Mrs. Harmon to calm him down.

We head back on the road, and our day is filled with bull-shit calls. Two traffic accidents, a possible shoplifter who ended up being the owner's daughter, and a police report for a stolen car. Paperwork sucks.

"Do you mind if we stop in and check on Steph?"

"You know I don't."

Brody calls in that we're on break, and we head over.

When we get to the turn in by Tampa General, a sleek, black Bentley comes peeling out of the side street, almost hitting two cars in the process.

"Oh, hell no," I say and flip the lights and sirens on. "I hate these assholes on this side of the island. They all think they can do whatever they want."

Having money doesn't mean you're above the law.

Brody and I approach the car and the tinted windows lower.

"License, registration, and insurance," I say without looking at the driver.

"Sorry, officer," a familiar voice causes my eyes to lift. I stare into the green irises I doubt I'll ever forget. A five o'clock shadow paints his face, and the sun only makes every-thing seem brighter. His mouth turns into a radiant smile, and my heart begins to race. "I was on my way to see someone. But it turns out she came to me."

My life . . . is . . . a freaking comedy show.

There's nothing I've done to deserve this amount of bad karma. I've been a good friend, sister, daughter, I uphold the law, and I'm a good person by most people's standards.

What the hell have I done to have this happen to me?

I release a deep breath and go back into work mode. "Do you know why I pulled you over, sir?"

"Are you going to pretend you don't know me?" Eli asks with his brow raised.

"Mr. Walsh, we all know who you are. However, that doesn't mean that nearly colliding with two vehicles is acceptable."

Eli looks over at Brody. "What's up, man? Is she always this way?"

"You two old friends?" Brody asks.

I clear my throat. "License, registration, and insurance . . . please."

I somehow get the words out without squeaking or sounding unstable. Brody laughs, and it takes everything I have not to look at him. I hate him right now.

"Sure thing, Officer Covey."

"Don't go anywhere," I warn as I take the paperwork from him.

"Don't worry, I'll be right here, Heather. I don't run away."

Bristling at his words, I walk away, feeling Brody's gaze on me. There's no doubt that as soon as we get back in the car, I'm going to get it—good.

Instead, Brody stays quiet while I assemble the paperwork. He may not be speaking, but he's saying a whole lot in the silence.

"Just say it," I mumble and finally look over.

"I'm not saying a word." He raises his hands. "Clearly, you two know each other, and it ain't from growing up here. You tell me everything, so there is no way you wouldn't have told me you know him," Brody pauses and leans back. "I'm not saying a word about who you may or may not have slept with recently. Even though, it's pretty obvious."

"You know, you not saying a word took you a long time."

"It's not like you've had a five-year drought since your divorce. Or that you slept with a singer/actor. Nope. I have nothing to say about that. Not a thing."

I groan. "Could you not say anything for real this time?"

"Sure thing, boss. I'll just be over here, watching Hell start to thaw."

This is not going to get any better. I'd almost rather hear the questions. This is Brody Webber. My partner, my friend, and the one person who I have enough dirt on to make his life hell if he repeats this.

"Okay, fine. Yes, I slept with Eli Walsh. I was crazy and dumb. I also had about six beers, which is two over my threshold, and I was trying to be in the moment for once. Fucking Nicole and her pep talks."

Brody coughs a laugh and then recovers. "Sorry, go on."

"I swear, you better keep this to yourself. If you tell anyone . . ." I give him my best threatening face. "I mean *anyone*, I'll make your life a living nightmare."

He shakes his head and laughs again. "I won't say a word, but you had a one-night stand with one of the most famous men in the boy band atmosphere. You're too cool for me, Heather. I don't think we can be friends. I'm sure you and the band will be happy without me."

I huff and grab the papers. "I'm getting a new partner."

I walk back over to the car, praying this will be painless. "I'm not going to ticket you this time," I explain.

"Because that would be awkward since I've seen you naked?"

Oh Jesus.

I ignore the comment and proceed as if he didn't say that. "Just slow down, Mr. Walsh."

"It's Ellington." He takes my hand in his as I hand the papers back. "I figure since we've you know . . . had sex and all . . ." He pauses and gives me a blinding smile before continuing, "You should at least call me Ellington."

Thanks to my obsession, I know most things about him, but I truly didn't know his full name. I guess back when I was searching for info, Google wasn't what it currently is. Now, though, I feel like he let me in on some secret.

"Fine, Ellington, please drive safe."

"We should talk about what happened the other night."

"That's not necessary."

Eli grips my hand as I start to pull back. "Dinner."

"What?" I ask with shock.

"Have dinner with me."

Is he for real? He wants to have dinner with me after I ran out? Either he's crazy or I'm still dreaming. "I appreciate the offer, but I'm really busy." I tug my hand back and smooth my uniform shirt. "Make sure you don't run anyone off the road."

"For you, Heather, I'll drive with both hands on the wheel and follow the speed limit."

"Oh, so you'll actually obey the law?" I smile without permission. Damn him.

He leans so his head is out the window. "I have a feeling you and I will be seeing each other again."

"I don't think so."

In fact, I know we won't. I know that I'll never pull over his car again, and he doesn't know anything about me other than my name and that I'm a cop. Okay, so maybe he knows a lot more than I'd like. Still, there's no reason for him to talk to me again. Ever.

"You and your partner be safe on the job. I hate seeing fellow officers in the line of fire."

My body twists, and I scoff. "You're not a cop. You play a cop on television."

"I have a badge."

"It's fake."

Eli reaches across the seat and puts his "badge" on his lap. "Doesn't look fake to me."

I roll my eyes. "We both know that's not real. Also, impersonating a police officer is a crime."

"Are you going to arrest me?" Eli asks with a coy smile.

"You're not worth the paperwork."

With that, I turn and start to walk away. I don't get too far when I hear him yell, "I'll see you soon, Heather."

Brody leans against the car with a huge grin on his face. I point at his chest and warn him again. "Not a word."

He chuckles and climbs in the car. "You better pray no one at the station hears about this."

I groan and rest my head on the seat. "I sure know how to complicate things."

"Yeah, you sure do."

With that, we both fall silent as I drive to the hospital. Brody and I walk to Stephanie's room without commenting further on my life choices. It's the one saving grace in my job, guys don't want to talk about it all. Brody lets me say what I need to say, and then once he's had his input, he's done. I don't have three-hour-long discussions to analyze the "why" of things with him. Nicole, who I'm sure is dying to grill me for details, is the exact opposite.

I make a mental note to avoid her as well.

As soon as I see Steph, I can tell she's doing better. The shades are open, and she's sitting on the guest chair and looking out at the water. Her hands are steady, and the overall mood in the room is lighter. But I know my instincts are correct when I see Stephanie's big smile as we enter. "Brody!" she practically squeals.

Stephanie has had a crush on him for as long as I can remember. If I didn't see him as an annoying guy who has gas issues, I probably would think he's hot, too. He's tall, has dark blue eyes, a chiseled jaw, and he oozes confidence.

"Steph!" He grins and pulls her into his arms. "You're looking hot."

I fight back slapping him, but I know he's trying to make her happy. He is all too aware of her affections, and I'm grateful he doesn't ever make her feel silly.

Rachel thinks it's cute as well.

I think it's ridiculous.

"Stop," she says as the blush paints her cheeks. "How's work?"

Brody fills her in on the call we just came from, and she clutches her chest. I could leave the room, do handstands, or juggle and she wouldn't notice. When he's around, he's all she sees. He's the only man in her life that doesn't treat her like she's dying.

"But the best part," Brody leans in and my eyes widen, "was when your sister pulled over a famous actor!"

"Brody—" I try to stop him, but Stephanie waves her hand at me.

"Yup. Eli Walsh."

"Oh my god!" Stephanie yells. "Eli! Like, the same guy you went to the concert to see?" she asks, looking at me and then Brody.

"The same one." Brody grins. "Did Heather tell you they know each other?"

"Dead. You're dead," I state.

My hands start to sweat and regret washes through me. I didn't want to tell anyone this. And my big mouth told Brody. Yes, he sort of figured it out on his own, but still. Now, the last person I want to tell is my sister.

I don't know why, but I feel like an irresponsible adult who did something completely out of character. Letting her see that makes me want to crawl in a hole.

"Heather!" Stephanie shifts quickly. "Why the hell didn't you tell me?"

"There's nothing to tell. You need to focus on you and not me."

"What?" She looks affronted. "What does that mean?"

I walk toward her. "It's nothing that I want to talk about."

"But you'll tell Brody?"

I *was* enjoying her good mood.

"Because Brody is nosey and figured it out. You don't need to know about these things."

Her face morphs from annoyed to pissed off. "You're not my mom, Heather. You're my sister. You act like I'm some kid. I'm twenty-six, and I'm so tired of you treating me like this."

This the part of our relationship I absolutely hate. Stephanie doesn't get that, while she's technically an adult, she's still a kid to me. I'm twelve years older than she is and practically raised her because she was a minor when our parents died. I wasn't.

After that, we no longer had the relationship where she would try on my clothes and we'd spend hours watching movies. It became about homework, bills, laundry, and making sure she wasn't cutting class. I don't resent it. I would do it all over again. But it didn't mean I liked the way it changed the dichotomy of our relationship.

"I know I'm not Mom. Believe me, I know."

She's used every opportunity to wield that sword at me, and it cuts deep each time, leaving wounds that aren't superficial.

"Then stop treating me like your kid and treat me like your sister. I don't know how much time I have left, and I would like to have our relationship be different."

Tears fill my vision as she brings forth the truth of what time we have. Brody clears his throat and touches Steph's arm. "I'm going to grab some coffee. See you later, Squirt."

She fumes at his nickname and turns her head away.

I take Stephanie's hand in mine. "I'm sorry you feel that way."

"I ruin everything!" She bursts out and pulls her hand free from my grasp so she can cover her face.

"Why would you say that?"

"Because! I do!" Steph turns a little and a tear falls. "I know I'm the reason Matt left."

"Steph—"

"No, I know." She wipes the tear away and draws a long breath. "I hate that my illness brought you pain. You didn't need that."

My heart pounds in my chest, and I'm doing my best to stay strong. The fact that she thinks she's responsible for

Matt's crappy decision is unreal. It isn't her fault he wasn't man enough—it's his.

I open my mouth to dispute her, but she puts her hand to my lips.

"I'm not done. It's been hard watching you scrimp and save because I can't work. There's nothing you wouldn't and don't do for me, and I love you so much. However, it doesn't mean you can't live, Heather. Jesus, live because I can't." Stephanie's voice is strangled on her last word. The tears I was trying to keep at bay fall. I pull my baby sister into my arms and hold her to my chest. "I can't live, but you can . . . and you should," she says as both of us fall apart a little.

I grasp her face and pull her so we're eye to eye. "You're living now, Steph."

"This isn't living. This is waiting to die."

The words I want to say all feel wrong. She has every right to be angry, sad, and anything else she grapples with. Her life was stripped from her in a way that took our world and knocked it over. There was no warning or planning for this disease.

Instead of demeaning her feelings, I hug her tighter and let her cry.

After a few minutes, she calms and leans back. "You okay?" I ask.

"No, but I feel a little better."

"You don't have to hide your hurt from me," I remind her. "I'm always here for you."

Stephanie nods. "I know, but I miss my *sister*. I want to know when you do dumb things, and I sure as hell want to know when you meet some famous person."

I groan, and my head falls back. "Fine. I'll tell you all about it, but it's so much more than meeting him."

"Oh. My. God. Tell me you actually hooked up with him!"

There's no way I'm getting out of this, and the joy that she has right now will be worth all my embarrassment.

I shift a little, trying to relax for this awkward confession. "I did. Get comfortable because I spent the other night being completely irresponsible."

"Finally!"

CHAPTER SEVEN
ELI

"Let me get this straight, you slept with her, she ran off, you see her again, and she walks away — again?" Randy asks with a shit-eating grin. "Man, you really have the touch."

I regret coming here. After my run-in with Heather, I took a drive to Sanibel Island where Randy lives. I don't know why I thought it was going to help me in some way. I should've known my brother and sister-in-law would be all too happy about this story.

I'll get her, though.

It's just going to take some finesse and a lot of patience. Plus, I still have the ace up my sleeve.

"Yup. It was fucking unbelievable."

"You got out of the bathroom, and she was . . . gone?" Randy keeps pushing as he laughs.

"It was ridiculous. I couldn't find her, and then realized she took off. Who the fuck does that?"

Savannah giggles. "Umm, you!"

Exactly. That's my deal. I'm the one who runs out or finds someone to escort the stage-five clinger off the bus. I don't go searching for the girl, and I definitely don't go back for more when a girl brushes me off—twice.

"I never thought I'd see it happen." Vannah leans back in her chair.

"See what happen?"

"A girl has you all twisted in knots. For once, you're the one seeing what it feels like."

I shake my head. She has no idea what she's talking about. My sister-in-law is oblivious to the issue. It isn't about her, it's about how she seems not to care about me. I have feelings, too. I was in love before, but they forget that. "I'm not in knots. I'm goddamn confused. Why the hell would she push *me* away?"

"Oh, don't even, Eli. You're not some God. You're a spoiled shit who has had everything handed to you on a silver platter."

"The fuck I have."

It's her turn to give me a stare that would make any grown man cry. She looks around to make sure the kids aren't near and then her face softens. "Watch your mouth. It's bad enough Adriel told the teacher to kiss his ass the other day, we don't need the F-word thrown around."

Savannah is a great woman. She deals with a lot, but my seven-year-old nephew is a little shit. Adriel is the oldest, and he's beyond overindulged. Randy was gone a lot when he was a baby and then overcompensated when he was home. I feel bad for her since she's the one dealing with the fallout.

I put my hands up and flash her a smile. "Sorry. I'll be more careful."

"Good."

"I'm just saying that we didn't have it all that easy. There were no silver platters."

Randy laughs. "You were eighteen when we were signed. Since then, have you had any issues?"

"Have you?" I gesture toward the walls around us. They act like they're struggling. This nine million dollar mansion they're living in doesn't seem to be roughing it if you ask me.

"I remember Mom having to work an extra job for us to eat and take music lessons, do you?"

It always comes back to this. Of course, I remember. When our father passed away, everything changed. Yes, I was young, but that doesn't mean I have no memory of it. My mother was great at hiding things, but no matter how hard you try, some things show through. When his child support stopped coming, we stopped doing a lot.

"Why do you think I took care of her when we got money?"

"Because you wanted to be her favorite," he tosses back and chugs his beer.

"I already was, I didn't need to buy her that house to solidify it."

"Keep telling yourself that." Randy laughs and shakes his head at me.

"Okay, boys. Back to my point. You've had a pretty easy *adulthood*, Eli. Girls flock to you, the band succeeded beyond anyone's expectations, and then you landed the role on *A Thin Blue Line* without having any acting experience. Things fall in your lap, but this time . . . not so much."

She has a point, but it doesn't mean I don't bust my ass. Sure, I was scouted and asked to join *A Thin Blue Line*, but I immediately started taking acting lessons. I hired the best coaches to make sure I earned my money. I can't say anything about Four Blocks Down, that was a guy who promised us we'd be huge if we signed with him and a shit ton of luck.

Heather, though. She's something completely different. For the first time, I don't have someone chasing me because of who I am. Hell, she fucking ran.

I want to know why. I want to know what she's hiding

behind her tough-girl exterior. I've never spotted a girl in a concert like that. It took every ounce of self-control not to stare at her all night. There's a pull between us, and I know she felt it.

I mentally scoff. It's absolutely ridiculous that some girl is having this effect on me. But yet I keep wanting to go back which only proves that there's something different. Why is this girl the only thing I can think about? The truth is, I wasn't going to kick Heather out of my bed that night. I wanted to hold her in my arms, breathe her perfume through the night, and feel her skin against mine. Instead of getting any of that, she bolted. The worst part is then, I fucking chased after her, and I'm debating doing it again.

Savannah waves her hand in my face. "Well?"

"I think you're wrong, Vannah. It has nothing to do with the thrill of the chase." And it's not, it's *her*.

"Oh?" she asks with surprise. Shit, I said that aloud. "What is it then?" Vannah pushes.

"I don't know," I admit and take a drink. "It was something in her eyes. I'm sounding like a pussy, but I'm serious. It was like there was this . . . thing . . . and I just want to figure out what it was."

Savannah does her best to hide her smile, but I see it. The eternal believer. She laid eyes on Randy and knew they'd be married. I've heard the story a million times, and each time, I fight back the need to puke. She swears that when it happens, you can't go back.

"I'm not in love with her," I quickly defend.

Randy elbows me. "Sounds like the first time I laid eyes on Savannah."

"You were an idiot. Hell, you still are."

"As is every man when he falls in love."

"For fuck's sake!" I throw my hands up and stand.

"Mouth!" Savannah yells.

"Sorry! But I'm not in love with anyone."

I can't believe these two. How does thinking about some girl equate to falling in love? It doesn't.

It means I need one more time with her to prove that it's all in my head.

That's it.

I grab my wallet and keys, grumbling as I walk off. They're wrong, and I'm not going to sit around with them as they try to convince me otherwise. All I know is her name, that she's a cop, and her address, that's it. How do you fall in love with a name? It isn't realistic, and I have no intentions of ever loving another woman.

Been there, and I'd rather be broke than give anyone that kind of power over me again.

The last bitch wrecked me and almost destroyed everything I worked for.

"Hey," Randy gets to his feet, "don't be like this."

"I'm going to prove you all wrong."

His brow raises, and he grins. "Eli, stop being an idiot."

"Untle Eli!" My niece runs over and leaps into my arms. "I missed you!"

"Hey, beautiful!" Daria is the only girl I'll ever love. She's three and owns my heart. I pity any asshole who ever tries to come near her. I don't give a fuck if I'm in a wheelchair, I'll kick his ass. "I missed you more."

"You and Daddy sing me a song!"

I look over at my brother and see the same adoration in his eyes. Adriel may be spoiled, but Daria . . . she had him wrapped around her little finger. There's nothing Randy won't do for Daria.

"I need to get home, pretty girl." I try to explain, but she crosses her arms and pushes her lips into a pout.

"Untle Eli, you don't love me."

"You know that's not true."

"Puuuuuleeeeeease," she begs and grabs my cheeks. "I lub you."

I'm just as screwed as Randy. "I love you, too. One song."

"Yay!" She claps her hands and wiggles for me to put her down. Three years old and has this whole world domination slash manipulation thing perfected already.

Eleven songs later, I'm finally standing at my car with my brother. "Listen, I know we gave you a load of shit in there, but you're not the guy who has ever been hung up on a piece of ass."

My blood pressure spikes a bit higher with each word, and I clench my fists. Heather isn't a piece of ass.

Fuck.

What the hell am I even thinking?

That's exactly what she is.

Randy smirks as if he expected this exact response and knows what I'm thinking.

He claps his hand on my shoulder and chuckles. "Go talk to her. If it's nothing, then come here and we'll tell Savannah how wrong she is. If nothing else, you'll know for yourself."

"You know that I refuse to do this again."

"Because of Penelope?"

Just her name makes me want to punch something. "Yes."

"That's sad, man. You and her were a lifetime ago, and you're older and wiser. No way you fall for another gold-digging whore like her."

"This is a moot point anyway. I'm not in love with anyone."

"Good." Randy nods in agreement. "It should be no problem seeing her then."

With that, my brother walks back up his drive, and I flip

him off. I should've been an only child. It would've made life so much easier.

I start the car and turn all my focus to this Heather situation.

My eyes catch on the plastic card sitting in my cup holder, and I know exactly what I'm going to do.

After Brody and I left Stephanie, we had back-to-back calls. We were nonstop all day, and I'm exhausted. Thanks to shift work, I have the next three days off, and I couldn't be happier. Which is good since I need all those good vibes for the phone call I'm about to make.

I have to call Nicole back.

"Hey," I say as I flop on my couch.

"Hey yourself. Where the hell have you been? I called you four times."

I give her a rundown of the calls we had, purposely leave out the encounter with Eli, and lay my head back. "I'm beyond beat."

"Is Stephanie okay?"

"She seems to be. We had a really good talk." I fill her in on my hospital trip. It feels good that we got everything out in the open. I know both of us dance around each other sometimes. Stephanie a lot less than me. When her mind isn't in the right place, she lets it all fly.

"I'm glad. So, since that's out of the way, let's talk about the other night."

"Nic," I grumble.

"No. You made me scale a freaking fence. You're not getting out of this. I've given you space, but that's not happening tonight."

I can only imagine how much this has been eating at her, but I don't want to get into this right now. Maybe not ever.

Thankfully the doorbell rings.

"Shit, my pizza's here. Hold on, Nic."

I put the phone on the coffee table and grab my wallet before opening the door.

"Good to see you again, Heather." Ian the pizza delivery guy smiles. I try not to let the fact that the pizza guy knows me by name depress me too much. It's my go-to food after a twelve-hour shift.

"You, too." I return his smile, and he looks me up and down. He's a nice kid, but his roaming eyes are a bit much.

Ian hands me the pizza, and I head inside for a night of Nicole's interrogation.

"Okay," I put the phone to my ear. "I'm back."

"And you were about to tell me about your sex with Eli."

I take a massive bite of pizza and moan. All the gooey cheesy goodness is like a party in my mouth.

"Heather!" Nicole yells as I take another bite.

"I'm eating," I say as I chew.

"Pizza is not more important than my need for information."

The doorbell rings again, and I thank God for small miracles. "Hold again," I say as I hold the phone against my shoulder.

I walk over, smiling because I know that Nicole must be going out of her mind. "Did you for—"

"Hello, Officer Covey." Eli grins as he leans against the doorframe. "I was hoping you were home. We didn't get a chance to finish our conversation."

Not even thinking, I close the door and stand there. Holy shit. What the hell?

"Heather?" Nicole's voice is a buzzing in my ear. Or is that my suddenly frantic pulse?

"Hmm?" I can't speak. Eli Walsh is at my freaking house.

"Is that who I think it is?"

I rise onto my tiptoes and peek out the peephole. Sure enough, he's right there, smiling as if he has not a care in the world. "Yup."

"Are you fucking kidding?" Nicole screams.

"Holy shit, Nic. What the hell do I do?" My heart continues to race, and I'm completely freaking out.

Nicole chuckles and then proceeds to yell again. "Open the goddamn door!"

I look in the mirror and groan. I have on shorts and an oversized sweatshirt, which now has a beautiful pizza stain on the front. My hair is in a messy bun, I'm not wearing any makeup, and I have my glasses on instead of my contacts. I can't believe this.

Eli knocks again. "Heather, I can hear you on the other side."

My hand presses against the wood, and I close my eyes. "What do you want, Eli?"

"Heather! Open the fucking door right now!" Nicole's voice raises in my ear.

"Shut up!" I yell at my jackass best friend.

"I didn't say anything," Eli answers.

I sigh and drop my head against the door again, making a *thump* noise. "I know. I . . . I . . . just."

Nicole growls at me, "I swear that if you don't open it right now, I'm coming over and giving him your spare key."

There isn't a single doubt that she'll do exactly that. "Fine. Goodbye," I say and disconnect the phone.

With no other options, I fix my hair the best I can and pull the door open. Eli is still standing with his arm resting on the frame and a huge smile on his face. "Hi." His deep voice washes over me, making my toes curl a bit.

"Why are you here, and how did you know where I live?" I ask, trying to keep my heart from flying out of my throat.

He's ridiculously sexy. Even more so than earlier today. Everything about him screams heartbreak, but every muscle in my body wants to be close to him.

Eli doesn't say anything, he just stares into my eyes. "You going to let me in?"

"Are you going to answer my questions?" I counter.

"If you let me come in."

There's no way this is going to lead to anything good. Letting Eli any deeper into my life is not part of my plan. I can't get mixed up with some playboy singer slash actor and his overly problematic existence. I have enough complications, I don't need another.

I also don't think he's the kind of man to give up. If I send him away, he'll be back tomorrow. Saying no to a man who probably has never heard the word will only be a challenge. It's better to get this all out and over with now so I can move on.

"Fine, but you have five minutes." I push the door open more, and he stands in my doorway so we're chest to chest.

Eli's eyes don't stray from mine as his hand gently touches the side of my face. "We'll see about that."

I fight the impulse to crush my lips to his. To taste his kiss and feel his rough hands on my skin again. There's nothing I've wanted more than to stop replaying it in my head, but I can't.

It's been so long since a man has made me crazy, driven me to the point of complete madness, but Eli pulled it off with ease.

I shake my head and pull his hand down. "Start talking before I get my Taser."

"I'd rather you get the cuffs." He winks and walks deeper into my living room.

For the first time since I can remember, I look around and feel a wave of embarrassment. I live a modest life, I can't afford the repairs needed on my house, and I haven't bought new furniture since my engagement to Matt nine years ago. Here's a man who could buy the entire Pottery Barn catalogue, and I can't even afford a blanket.

"Eli?" I ask, trying to get him to stop looking around. "You found out where I live, how?"

"Relax." His smile is easy and warm. "I found something of yours. I figured you probably needed it."

"What? Something of mine?"

He pulls out a card, and my jaw falls. "Need this?"

"Holy shit! I didn't even know it was missing!" I walk over and take my license from his hand. "Thank you. I would be in deep shit if they did a paperwork check and I didn't have it before shift."

"I thought being the law-abiding citizen you are, it was important."

Relief floods me which is quickly followed by confusion. "But wait . . . you saw me earlier today."

"Yes, but I was in a rather precarious situation with a police officer who wanted to bust my balls, so I didn't have a chance to give it back."

My arms fold across my chest as I stare at him. "You had more than enough time."

He shrugs and plops himself on my couch. "I thought it would be better now. Plus, I wouldn't want to play all my cards on the first hand."

"So, this is what?"

"This is us becoming friends."

"Friends?" I ask.

His lazy smile grows, and he leans back. "Yup. I decided today we're going to be friends."

"Why is that?"

I'm not sure why I'm asking, but I can't help but want to know why he feels this is going to happen. Since it's totally not. I don't need any more friends, especially not rich sex Gods who out of nowhere want to make my life even more of a mess.

"Because that's what people do after they've slept together. Plus, I'm a good friend."

I huff and move closer, "I don't need any more—" Eli opens the pizza box and pulls a slice out. "Hey! That's my pizza."

"I'm starving." He grins and then takes a bite. "Mmm." Eli moans as he chews, and I would give anything to be what he's eating.

My eyes widen, and my cheeks burn as I chastise myself for even thinking that. What is wrong with me? Why do I become some addled teenager when I'm around him? I'm definitely not some sex-crazed woman. Since Matt, I've had one guy in my bed.

One.

And he sucked.

Now, I'm standing here thinking about Eli and all he did to me.

"Listen, new friend that I didn't particularly ask for, I appreciate you bringing my license back." I motion toward the door, but he leans back and throws his leg over his knee. "Really, I do, but—"

Eli cuts me off. "You're not going to eat?"

"No, I'm definitely going to eat, but you're definitely not staying."

"You can't share some pizza with me? I mean, isn't that

what friends do and all? They break bread, have some fun, talk, hook up a little?" He wags his eyebrows with a grin.

I shake my head and sigh. "No hooking up, and while I love the idea of our newfound friendship, it's been a really long day. I was planning to head to bed."

"We can do that, too." He takes another bite as if he didn't offer to sleep with me again.

"What? No! I wasn't offering that!"

He laughs and tosses the pizza down before brushing some crumbs off his hands. "Jesus, relax, Heather. I was joking. I'm here because I wanted to talk about what happened. You ran off without a word, and when I found your license on the ground, I figured it was a sign."

"A sign?"

"Yes." He stands and then walks closer to me. "A sign that we have unfinished business. You know, most girls like to leave something behind so I have to come return it. Is that what this was? A game so you could see me again?"

Each step that Eli takes makes my pulse quicken a bit more. I'm not sure what unfinished business he thinks we have and what girls he's used to dealing with. I was pretty clear when I ran out that there was nothing more. I was half drunk, stupid, and pressured by my idiot best friend to do something outside my comfort zone.

"I don't have time for games. I never planned on seeing you again. The only sign was that I dropped something and you happened to find it."

Eli stands in front of me, and I have to tilt my head back to see his face. His gorgeous eyes hold me hostage, and his arm wraps around my waist. "I think we both know that's not the truth. You can feel it right now. I can see your breathing accelerating, your eyes keep moving to my lips, and while you can keep fighting it, I know you want me."

I shake my head, trying to make him wrong, but when his

tongue slides against his lips, I know he hears the intake of breath. I know because it's loud, and in the silence, it might as well have been a sonic boom.

"Eli . . ." I try to move back, but his arm holds me in place.

"I'm not going to do anything, I just want to talk."

"This is crazy," I say, wishing I didn't want crazy with every cell in my body.

Eli's other hand slides up my back and holds me tighter. "What would be crazy is walking out the door without seeing if this is in our heads."

"If what's in our heads?"

"Whatever has us both so twisted that I'm here in your house, and you're running out in the middle of the night without a goodbye. There's something going on, and I want to see what the hell it is. Don't you?"

My gaze doesn't leave his, and the sincerity and conviction in his words stun me. If I tell him to walk out this door, I'll regret it. I'll think about this one moment for the rest of my life. Plus, Nicole knows he's here, so if I ask him to leave, she'll never let me live it down.

Before I can stop the words from falling from my lips, I agree. "Okay, pizza and talking only, though."

Eli's smile widens, and he squeezes me a little. "Pizza, talking, and who knows what else," he counters.

There will be nothing else, but I keep that to myself. Arguing with him seems to only lead to him staying, eating pizza, and thinking we're going to be besties.

We make our way back over to the couch and sit. He grabs a slice and hands it to me before going back for the piece he had. I curl my legs under me and try not to gawk. But Eli Walsh is sitting in the living room of my crumbling house. It isn't that I live in a shithole, but I'm sure it's nothing like his home.

My dad was a man of many projects. He started them and

then quit before ever finishing. Matt helped a little, but he was in no way Bob Vila, if anything, he was Tim Allen from *Home Improvement* and broke more than he fixed.

After he left, I did my best to patch the holes of my home and my heart.

"So, a cop?" Eli asks after a few minutes of silent eating.

I wipe the sauce from my lips and then smile. "It was what I always wanted to be. My parents were killed by a drunk driver when I was twenty-one. After that, I knew I wanted to help even just one person be saved from that tragedy."

"I'm really sorry," Eli says and touches my arm.

"It was a long time ago."

"Still, that must've been tough."

I sigh and shrug a little. "It sucked, but I think it made me who I am today."

"I get it. My dad died when I was young, too."

"I'm sorry."

Losing your parents is never easy, but when you're young, it's impossible to navigate the emotions of it. So many times I wished I had my parents there to guide me. It would've been so much easier.

"Don't be, he wasn't a role model anyway." He waves away my condolences and says, "So, tell me, Heather . . . who are you?"

"I'm just me."

There's no way I'm going to divulge my deepest secrets. Eli will walk out this door tonight and never be back, which is exactly what I should want. Right? So, why don't I spill all the dirt? For all I know, I'm just some conquest to him. The girl who walked away from a man that girls flock to. It's what Nicole refers to as the rejection reaction. If I had stayed and pined for him, he would've brushed me off into the pile of other nameless, faceless girls he's slept with.

Eli removes his keys and wallet from his back pocket, tossing them on the table.

Sure, make yourself comfortable. I guess he plans on staying.

"I'm serious. I want to know more about you," he pushes for more.

"Why?" I ask with frustration. "You and I both know how this goes."

He grips the back of his neck and lets out a heavy sigh. "How is that?"

"You're going to go back to your lavish life, and I'll be here . . ." I gesture around the room.

"Maybe that's exactly what will happen, but only because you're so hell bent on pushing me out that door."

He isn't wrong, but that still stings a little. "I'm protecting myself."

Eli seems to recover and grabs another slice of pizza. "It's fine, you're going to have to try a lot harder. I'm basically a cop, too."

I laugh and roll my eyes. "We've already established that you're just a cop on television. Real police work isn't anything like that."

"So, you watch my show?" He says it so casually, so coolly, that if I weren't an actual cop, I would have missed his real reaction. He's practically preening inside over that little tidbit.

"I've seen it once because nothing else was on." I'm so full of shit. I watch his stupid show every week. At first, it was because I wanted to see how much they butchered the real way police are, but then I was hooked. Watching him is my guilty pleasure. After five seasons, I can admit that I'm officially addicted.

He'll never know that, though.

No way will I give him one more thing to try to use against me.

"Well, my partner, Tina, is a lot like you."

"Is she?"

She is so not like me. Tina is a hard ass who wants nothing to do with men, and her husband left her for another woman.

I want a man, I don't want another guy who will cut tail and run because life isn't perfect. And Matt left because he's a dick.

"Yeah, she lives alone and pushes any guy away."

Screw him. He doesn't *know* me. So what if I'm alone and I don't want to get involved with a guy whose life is the polar opposite of mine? I'm thirty-eight years old; I don't have to play by his rules or beliefs.

"I'm not pushing you away; I'm just living in reality."

Eli leans forward, and I force myself not to retreat. "The only reality is the one we make."

My reality isn't movie stars and playing a cop on television. I'm an actual cop. I deal with all kinds of shit, and there's no one to yell cut when it gets too intense. There are real bullets flying, people dying in car wrecks, immense amounts of paperwork, and shit pay. Keeping myself guarded isn't a choice, it's a necessity.

"Maybe in your world, but in the real world, we have crap to deal with."

Eli drops the slice and huffs. "I live in the real world too you know."

"Well, since we're friends and all, tell me about it." I toss the ball back in his proverbial corner.

I'm fully aware I'm coming off like a bitch. However, there's a reason I ran away after we had sex. I'm terrified of anything new. Things in my life disappear or fall apart, trying to start anything with someone else, isn't in my plans. I can't lose anything else.

Looking at Eli, though, makes me wish for another life.

One where we could be friends. One where we could maybe be more than friends, but that isn't the life I'm living.

Still, a girl can hope.

Eli shifts a little and clears his throat. "My full name is Ellington Walsh, I'm forty-two years old, never married, and grew up here in Tampa. I have one brother, Randy, who's two years older than I am. We've been in Four Blocks Down since I was eighteen, and now I'm an actor. I plan to go into movies soon, but I'm waiting for the right part. Oh, most importantly, I like blonde girls who tell me they love me."

I laugh. "Tell me something I wouldn't find on Wikipedia."

That look of silent preening is back in his eyes, and I want to smack myself. "You looked me up, huh?"

"Sure." I snort, trying to play it cool. "No, I've grown up watching you in a non-creepy way. It isn't like I don't know all your bullet points. How about you tell me something about your life that your *friends* would know."

Let's see how much Eli wants to tell me. I'm not sure he actually wants this friendship like he thinks. I'm not even sure what a friendship with a famous person even looks like. Will there be people following him around? Is there some crazy security team he has? Does he have people? Do I even know what that means? Nope. The only people I have are my best friends and sister.

"Okay, I would've been here an hour earlier tonight, but a girl kept me held hostage."

My eyes widen. Is he seriously telling me about another girl? "Wow."

"Not like that!" he quickly says with his hands raised. "Shit. I'm not good at this. I'm talking about Daria, my niece."

"You have a niece?"

I haven't followed Randy's personal life since he's married. That crosses the line into creepy. I do know that he and his wife were together when the band formed, so he's always kind of been off limits. It was always Eli that was the heartthrob.

"Yeah, she's a man-manipulator already. My sister-in-law has trained her to terrorize my brother and me. She has this whole big eyes and squishy face thing down pat."

I smile, understanding how kids can get you to do what they want pretty easily. "Basically, she rules your world?"

Eli nods. "I promised her one song. One. And eleven songs and fifty minutes later, I was in the car. If that doesn't show you what one little 'I love you' from her does, I don't know what will. Basically, if she wills it, she gets it. She even got me to play with dolls." He shudders.

I can't imagine him playing with a little girl, but a part of me swoons at the thought. It's hard to picture him as anything but the elusive manwhore that the tabloids make him out to be.

"That's actually kind of sweet."

"You think I'm sweet?" he asks with hope filling his voice.

"I think *that* is sweet."

My clarification goes unnoticed.

"I'm taking that as you like me. I don't blame you, I'm quite charming."

I groan while grinning. "Wikipedia didn't mention that."

His finger grazes my bare leg before falling flat. The skin under where his hand rests tingles. "I'm saving the good stuff for you."

"Lucky me."

He laughs. "Well, most girls would think so."

"I guess it's a good thing I'm not most girls then," I throw back.

"Why is that?" Eli asks.

"Because you aren't trying to be friends with them."

Eli's deep, rich laughter fills the room. "Touché."

Eli and I finish the rest of the pizza as he tells me more

about his niece and nephew. I love that he speaks about them with such affection. It's great seeing him as—normal. He isn't special sitting here in my rundown house. He's just a regular guy. A guy who eats pizza and talks about how much he loves annoying his sister-in-law.

We cover more about my job, his show, and about how happy he is to get to spend some time in Tampa.

I yawn and then look at the clock. Holy shit! He's been here for almost three hours.

Wow.

It's been easy, fun, and filled with smiles.

"It's really late." He gets to his feet and shrugs on his coat.

"Thanks for bringing my license."

I walk him to the door, and when we get there, he turns to me. "Can I see you again?"

"Eli . . ." I hold the door in my hand, trying to find the right words. This was fun, but this is complicated. "I don't know if that's such a good idea."

He moves closer, keeping his eyes on mine. "I was hoping you'd see that I'm not just some dick who doesn't care. I thought we were getting somewhere, maybe even becoming friends. Seems I was mistaken."

"You're not!" I say quickly and grip his arm. "I'm being crazy, and I'm sorry. The truth is—" I sigh and decide to give him the truth. "You scare me. I'm not a one-night stand kind of girl. I have a lot, and I mean a lot, of shit going on in my life. Things that take up all my headspace, and I just don't have room for more." I take a deep breath, willing myself to continue. "I've had a lot of fun tonight with you, though. Honestly, it's been great talking, and yes, there's something . . ."

His smile is effortless as he leans in. "Listen, I head back to New York in a few weeks, but I'm staying around Tampa until then. I want to see you again."

"Why?" I ask with complete bewilderment.

"Because regardless of how hard you're pushing me away, I can't help but want to see you more. I liked hanging out, I don't get this with anyone but my brother. You don't treat me like I'm different." Eli winks. "Think about it."

He leans in and kisses my cheek before turning and walking down the porch steps. I stand like a statue, unsure of whether I could find my voice if I wanted to. I watch Eli walk to his car, not expecting him to turn around. When he does, he grins again and adds, "Besides, I know where you live and work, I'm sure we'll run into each other again anyway. Wikipedia should mention I'm relentless in pursuing what I want."

My lips part, but he's in his car before I can speak.

Damn it. This was not how that was supposed to go.

CHAPTER NINE

"You're shitting me!" Nicole yells as she almost drops her glass of wine. "I'm going to rub myself all over your couch."

"You would."

We're at her lush apartment in downtown Tampa working on killing off our second bottle of wine. I spent all day at the hospital with Stephanie and then refused to go home. So, instead of answering any of her twenty texts, I came here.

"What is wrong with you?" Nicole has probably asked me that ten times since I got here.

"Nothing is wrong with me! I'm being realistic. If Matt, who was a local cop that I've known for almost my whole life left because of Steph, what do you think an international superstar is going to do? Huh? Have you thought about that?"

"You're so dumb."

"You've been telling me that for a long time." I huff and take another gulp of wine. I get that she thinks I'm foolish, but I can't open myself up like that again. I'd be asking for my heart to be broken. I'd rather not. "There's no way that Eli is going to stick around Tampa, and I'm never going to move away from Steph."

Nicole takes the glass from my hand and places it on the table. Her eyes are soft, but I know what's coming. She's going to lay into me something fierce. "I've watched you make mistakes before, and I haven't said shit. Not this time. I'm telling you right now that if you don't do this, you'll regret it for the rest of your life. You can't tell me that you don't feel something for him."

"I don't know what I feel."

"Yes, you do. You had a crazy night with him, and it threw you for a loop. I get it. You're the straight-laced one of us. You don't do wild, and you don't take risks. Life has been a series of heartbreaks for you. I know this. We all do, but fuck, Heather, you have to live! There's no reason that you can't actually *live* the life you've been given."

Tears form, and my heart aches. I know she loves me and what she said is all true, but damn it, I hate her for it. I do the best I can, and I don't know how many times I can be hurt before I finally have enough.

When my sister dies, it's going to kill me. I'll have no family left, and I can't waste any of the little time I have with her. It's the truth I can't bring myself to say.

I sure as hell can't chase the idea of a guy who can essentially wreck my world. It's stupid, and I won't make mistakes like that. Not when my sister needs me. Eli is always photographed traveling, partying, and eating at all these expensive restaurants where I couldn't even afford a salad.

"Jesus, have you and Steph been swapping notes?"

"No, but if she's saying anything like I am, she's freaking right."

"You know why I'm this way." I wipe the bead that trickles down my cheek.

"I do." Nicole takes my hand in hers. "I'm not trying to

hurt you, but I can't watch you like this anymore. Your sister doesn't want you to keep going this way and neither would your parents. It's okay to take chances and get hurt. It's okay to have regrets and triumphs, but it isn't okay to just . . . be."

"And what if he's like Matt?"

She smiles. "Then you dump his stupid ass and I'll feed you ice cream and wine."

I groan and drop my head against the back of the couch. "I hate when you make sense."

Nicole laughs. "I bet. It doesn't happen too often, so don't worry."

"I miss when all we worried about was if we'd go to prom with our boyfriends."

"I always knew that I wouldn't. Boys are dumb. I was much happier going stag and hanging out with you, Kristin, and Danni."

Crap. We're going to have to tell them about this. I've avoided their calls because I'm the world's worst liar. They will see right through whatever crap I try to sell them. "I have to tell them, don't I?"

"Nah, I'll tell them we couldn't meet him." I let my head fall to the side so I can look at her, and then I pull her against me for a hug. "Keep this to yourself for a while. You need to decide without anyone's influence."

"So, what you're saying is that I should just listen to you?"

"Precisely."

I laugh silently and let that go. My mind wanders to last night. I can't help thinking about how normal Eli seemed. He wasn't pretentious, he ate pizza from the box while we lounged on my ratty, old couch. There were no demands. It was only the two of us. It was comfortable even.

Just like the first time we were around each other.

Maybe I am being crazy and overthinking this. There's something about him that I can't stop thinking about. His smile causes butterflies in my stomach. His laugh is music that speaks to my heart. And even though I've spent all day trying to convince myself that he's the last thing I even want to think about, he's what I've spent all day talking about.

I'm screwed.

"What if he never comes back?" I ask Nicole.

"Then he's a complete idiot. You're worth chasing."

People can say what they want about Nicole, but she's the best person I know. Sure, she drives me nuts, but I love her. She's been there for me every step of the way, and I couldn't imagine my life without her.

I PASS through the metal gates of the only place I feel close to my parents. Once I park, I grab the bouquet of flowers and head to their graves. It's been a long time since I've been here, but I haven't really had a reason to come talk to them.

If I'm completely honest, I've been angry for a long time.

Navigating the paths isn't difficult, and soon, I crouch in front of my parents' final resting places. "Hi, Mom and Dad." I start to pull overgrown weeds and wipe away some of the dirt. My fingers trace the cool stone, and I close my eyes, allowing sadness and the smell of fresh cut grass to fill my body.

"I know I haven't been here in a while, I'm sorry." I tuck my hair behind my ear. "It's sometimes hard to get here, especially lately."

After passing out on Nicole's couch, I woke this morning and drove here. There's a lot I need to say, and sometimes a girl just needs her mother.

This is one of those times.

"There's so much that's happened since I last visited. Matt and I are divorced now, but that's kind of old news. Let's see,

I'm still partnered with Brody, he's annoying as all hell, but I can't imagine working beside anyone else. Stephanie is living in Breezy Beaches full time. It's hard not having her with me, but it got to be too much. Everything is a mess, Mom. I did something stupid, and now I don't know what to do."

I place the flowers on the ground and start to arrange them. "I met this guy, you probably remember my obsession with Four Blocks Down—Eli specifically. Well, we met at his concert the other night, and I . . ." I feel weird telling my mom about our one-night stand. Not that she can respond and tell me about her disappointment, but still. "Anyway, he showed up at the house the other night, and we talked for hours. I like him, but it's so complicated. I'm not special or anything. I'm worried that he'll break my heart, and I really don't have much left of it as it is."

As much I want to talk to her about this, there's something else that forced me to finally drive here. The confliction I feel isn't just about Eli, it's about my whole life. All the things that I can't control, and I'm tired of spinning.

My fingers trace her name on the cool headstone, reminding me that everything here is dead. "I hope you under-stand why I've stayed away. Seeing your names like this hurts so much sometimes. Hell, pretty much all the time. And soon, Steph will be here with you." I drop my hand and fight the surge of tears that threaten to fall. "I don't know how I'll go on when that happens. I've tried so hard to accept this, but I can't. I've done everything I can for her, but she keeps getting sicker, and it's killing me. I love her so much." There's no stop-ping the tears now. They flow, and I know that I need this. I need my mother to hear me. "I know she isn't my daughter, but she's been mine to raise, and she's going to die. Just like you and Daddy. Just like everyone I love. You all get taken from me."

My hand finds its way back to the top of the stone, and I

let my forehead rest against my knuckles as I fall apart. Fears that I've shoved deep for years all bubble to the surface. Losing my sister will be the nail in my own coffin. I will have lost each member of my family without any way of stopping it.

"I'm supposed to help people. I save people every day, but I can't save her, Mommy. I can't help her. I can't give her a life that she deserves. I'm so sorry. I know you trusted me to keep her safe." All the emotions I've been holding in pour out. The crying is loud and painful, but necessary. I've been strong for so long, I don't have it in me anymore. "How can you let God take her from me, too? I'll be alone and have failed you all. Please forgive me—" My words choke off and I fold in on myself, sobbing and trying desperately to draw air into my too-tight lungs.

Eventually, when my eyes are red and puffy and my emotions have run dry, I stand and touch my hand to my lips before pressing the kiss on the headstone. "I love you both. I miss you more than you'll ever know, and I hope it's a while before I'm back here again."

Because the next time will be Stephanie's funeral.

I walk back to my car, draw a few calming breaths, and then flip the visor down. I'm a mess. I wipe away the makeup that was ruined by crying.

There's a reason I don't come here often: it's too damn hard.

My phone pings with a text.

STEPHANIE
Are you coming to visit today?

Of course.

STEPHANIE
See you soon?

> I'm on my way now. Just leaving the cemetery.

STEPHANIE

Tell Mom and Dad I miss them.

I close my eyes and try not to think about the fact that I lost it over her impending death.

> I did. They love you and miss you.

STEPHANIE

Glad they told you that . . . LOL.

My lips turn into a smile and a giggle slips from me. I can picture her rolling her eyes at me.

The drive to the hospital takes about ten minutes, all of which I use to collect myself and put my mask firmly back in place. If she sees that I've been crying, she'll do what she can to tell me about her acceptance of her fate. That isn't what I need to hear . . . ever.

Sometimes, I wonder if she would rather it happen already so she can stop suffering. I'm too selfish for that. I want every minute I can get with her. I'll take a hundred bad days as long as I can touch her, talk to her, and keep her close.

I enter the room and completely freeze. Stephanie is flirting with a male nurse. He's sitting on her bed, and her eyes move down as she smiles. I watch as she bats her eyelashes and tucks her brown hair behind her ears like I do when I'm nervous.

Then Stephanie's gaze shifts, and she spots me. "Heather!" She jumps, and the man leaps to his feet. "Hey! I didn't see you there."

I grin. "I see that."

"This is Anthony," Steph says with a sigh. "He's my daytime nurse and friend."

Oh, boy. I've seen this look before. This must be why she isn't fighting her doctor to be discharged anymore.

"Hi, Anthony," I say as I walk forward. "It's nice to meet you."

"I just finished my shift and was checking on her," he explains, as if I haven't already gotten his number.

"That's awfully nice of you." I look over at Steph, still grinning.

She gives me a look that clearly tells me to stop it. I haven't seen her even look at a man since she was diagnosed with Huntington's all those years ago.

"Well, she's a huge comic book fan, and I promised to show her my latest collector edition *Superman* I bought yesterday."

"Yes," Steph interjects and touches his arm. "He got the one I was looking for online."

"Really?" I bury my skepticism deep. Stephanie has never touched a comic book.

"Yes, *Heather*." Her eyes narrow, and she purses her lips. "Anthony is going to let me see it tomorrow."

Oh, I get it.

"I'll let you visit with your sister, Stephy, I'll see you tomorrow." Anthony squeezes her hand and moves toward me. "It was great to meet you. She talks about you a lot."

"It was nice to meet you also," I reply as he walks away.

As soon as he's down the hall, I rush over to her side, and we both laugh. "Comic books? Stephy? You hate that nick-name! You are in *so* deep if you're already being all dorky."

"Shut up!" She slaps my arm. "I'm not dorky. I'm doing what *normal* girls do when they like a guy. He's cute. He kept coming to check my vitals way more than necessary, and I don't know . . . I wanted someone to talk to."

"I think it's great," I say to assure her. "And I am too normal."

"Yeah, you're normal my ass," Steph retorts.

She's right, I'm totally not normal.

"Anyway, I'm glad you're putting yourself out there a little."

I love that she's getting some human interaction other than with Brody and me. Nicole checks in on her once in a while, but usually it's just the people in the home and me. She has no friends that are around anymore, which is sad but unsurprising. Most people don't stick around long when something this serious happens. Not because they are cruel or uncaring. They just didn't know what to say or how to handle themselves. I understand to some extent, but I hate it for her.

Unfortunately, it's made it so there's a great amount of loneliness that my sister struggles with. I can take her anger, knowing it isn't really her, it's her illness. What I can't stomach is the thought of her feeling lonely. It breaks me in ways that I would sell my soul to prevent.

"I know there's no future," Her face falls, and her tone becomes sullen.

"Stop." I shake her hand. "You're allowed to have friends, and if you both like comic books, then let it happen."

She laughs. "Can you go buy me a comic book so I know what they look like?"

I burst into laughter. "Sure thing."

Stephanie looks away as her exhilaration fades. "I don't want to get attached."

"Babe, he's a nurse, he knows what he's getting into."

Of all the possible people she could have met, I'm happy it's him. He probably understands better than anyone what her future looks like.

"May—" she starts to say and begins to cough, which is deep and wet and sends me straight into panic mode.

I rub her back as she gets control. "I'll get the doctor," I say, but she grips my arm.

"No, it's fine. It's just from the air conditioner. I had them fix it."

"Are you sure?" I ask.

"Yes, it's fine. See? I'm fine."

She crosses her arms across her chest and waits for me to relax. I hate that I fuss over her so much, but I can't help it. I feel like my vigilance is the only thing keeping her alive. I'm not going to quit now.

"Fine, but if you cough like that again . . ." She doesn't need to hear the rest to know what I mean.

"You're so not normal." She rolls her eyes while shaking her head. "So, you went to the cemetery?"

"I did." I pause, thinking about what led me there. "I had an interesting night and needed Mom."

"Interesting how?" The curiosity seeps through her words.

I sigh, lie back on the bed with her, and tell my sister about my night with Eli Walsh.

"There's no need to fight us on this, Eli. We feel this is a generous offer," Paula says.

If it were so generous, I wouldn't have had to fly here to make sure my agent wasn't letting the studio try to give it to me up the ass. I could be in Tampa, working on getting Heather to stop fighting me.

I don't know what the hell it is about her. She's frustrating as all hell, but I like the challenge.

I'm not some young musician anymore. I'm older, wiser, and I know there's something with Heather that I shouldn't walk away from. I want to know her. I need to see her and touch her, which has to mean something.

"I'm not signing that, and you know why."

It isn't an ego thing. It's a value thing. If they don't pay me what I'm worth, then there's no reason they'll fight for the show. I'm not stupid. If they get this new contract to pay me less, there's no incentive for them to keep pushing it.

I don't work on dead ends. That's my only motto in this industry. Since landing the job on *A Thin Blue Line*, I've done a few movies. They were small parts, but I felt passionate about them. While I love my character and the storyline, I'm not working for less than what they've paid me the last five years.

"The show is lucrative, but they want to bring on some new blood," Paula tries to explain. I can see how frustrated she is, but that isn't my damn problem. "They need to free up money somewhere, and you're by far the highest paid actor on the show."

"Don't care." I lean back in the chair and scratch the back of my head. "It's not my problem."

Paula crosses her arms and goes silent. This is the thing about my agent I love. She's a shark. She smells blood in the water and circles until it's the right time to make her move. I see her predatory gaze as she studies me. She's on my team, but I'm also the only way she makes money.

Agents are awesome when you're making them money. When you're not . . . you're chum. I'm not about to be her afternoon snack.

"You know I heard they want a new love interest for your character. I heard that Penelope Ashcroft is back in town and looking for work. Isn't she a friend of yours?"

There's nothing friendly between us. Paula is definitely throwing out the bait.

I don't take it, though. The last fucking person I want to think about is *her*. I go years without a mention of her name and now twice in a week? "Another thing I don't care about." Which is total bullshit, but if I let Paula think this is a scab to pick at, she won't hesitate.

"She's auditioning for a few shows." Paula picks at her nails, letting the silence stretch. I know this game, so I stay quiet right along with her. "I didn't think much of it until Michael mentioned the casting director has her file."

"Michael? As in my director, Michael?"

So much for keeping my cool.

She shrugs. "It was just in passing."

Nothing this woman says is in passing. I have no doubt that Michael, if he did mention it, said it to push me. He knew I'd be reluctant to sign. I was lucky twenty years ago, I had a mentor. He told me that our careers start dying the day we sign our deals, and that if we want to make it in this world, we need to make as much money as we can, as fast as we can. I'm not about to take shit pay with them because they threw out that bitch's name.

I stand, place my hands on the desk, and stare in her eyes. "I'm not signing that contract until you get me the money I want. The way I see it, they—and you—need me. I'm not some small part on that show, and if you don't get ink on that paper, you don't get a check from me. So, push them harder. If they want to even entertain Penelope on the show, I'm done."

"What did that girl do to you?" Paula asks as if I didn't just say more than the part about her.

"She's a gold-digging, lying, slut. When I needed her most, she broke my fucking heart. I won't allow that bitch anywhere near me, got it?"

There are non-negotiables in life—this is one.

Paula gets to her feet and I straighten. "I'll do what I can, Eli. But I hope you're prepared to walk away from the show that you love so much. I don't know that I can get them to go much higher."

"And Penelope?"

She grins. "I wouldn't worry about that part. I'll handle her. She's a non-issue."

"Good, and don't bring her up to me again."

"YOU GOT BALLS, MAN," Noah laughs before throwing back a beer. "I just signed the damn contract."

I've been here three days working with Paula on renegotiations, and this is the first time I've allowed myself to relax. Normally, New York is where I feel settled. I know this isn't my native home, but I love it. The lights, people, smells, and food make me want to stay forever. I think it's also New Yorkers' ability not to see famous people. I'm at a bar without a single worry that some vapid fan will come bug Noah and me. However, tonight I would much rather be on the beach or sitting in a beautiful woman's living room eating pizza.

"It's not balls, it's negotiating."

"How was Tampa?"

My mind shifts to Heather. It's funny how after a few days, she's what I'm associating with my hometown. Not Ma, Randy, or the hundreds of things that I love about Florida. No, it's the beautiful blonde who has taken up residence in my goddamn mind.

"It's definitely more interesting."

Noah may play my brother on the show, but I still don't want to share her with him. As soon as people find out about her, she'll be swamped by publicity, which will send my shot with her up in smoke. My world comes with a whole new set of rules, right now, I want to play by hers.

I think back to the night we were together. We were laughing, talking, and hanging out. I can't remember the last time I did that with a girl. Usually, it's expensive restaurants, clubbing, and the talk about how great we'd be together if I give the random girl a shot.

With Heather, it's nothing like that.

I'm not even sure she actually likes me.

"Yeah?" he asks with a knowing grin. "What's her name?"

I lift my hand, motioning to the bartender to head our way. I need to get off the topic so that I don't outright lie to my closest friend.

It's clear she knows who we are but does her best to mask it. Another point for New Yorkers.

"What can I get you guys?" The bartender gives a seductive smile. I take a second to look her over. She's hot, but all I can think is that her eyes aren't brown and her smile is wrong. When Heather smiles, my heart pauses.

"Two beers, please."

"Not a problem." Her blue eyes travel to my mouth before coming back to my gaze. I know the look. It's her come fuck me eyes. I've seen them a lot, but once again, my mind isn't there, so I turn away.

Noah chuckles, and I glance back at him. "Smooth."

"I'm here for business this trip. I don't have time for a woman," I try to explain. It sounds plausible. I'm here to kick my agent and the network's asses. I'm not here to fuck some bartender. I have a goal, a mission, and that doesn't include detours.

I'll stick with that line of bullshit.

Noah shakes his head in disbelief. "Because you've never been known to mix pleasure when dealing with business?"

I'm not quite the playboy everyone has made me out to be. Sure, I'm not known for being a long-term relationship guy, which I blame on the bitch, but my public persona and the guy Noah, Randy, Shaun, and PJ are friends with are not the same. I'm different on stage or behind the camera. I look the part they've created—a bad boy with women in every town. It could be true, but it's not. I don't know what it's like not to always be putting on a show, but the other night with her, I felt . . . normal.

"Not since, Pe—" I almost said her vile name. "Her. I learned my lesson on the importance of keeping a clear head."

Noah's head snaps back. "Who? Penelope?"

Penelope is the reason I started acting. She pushed me to take something that would keep me around more, plus, the band was getting old and had lost a lot of its popularity. I loved her and wanted to make her happy. My heart was hers, and I thought she loved me, turns out she doesn't love anything except herself.

"Yup."

Noah eyes me carefully and pulls a long draw from the bottle. Then he proceeds to pick at the label as we both sit quietly. "I've known you a long time, and I like to think we're friends."

"We are."

"I know you've got secrets, I don't push because I've got them, too, but whatever happened between you and Penelope Ashcroft was years ago. She's married now, she's moved on, and you're still reliving the shit she did."

That has to be the deepest few sentences we've ever shared. I'm a private guy, you have to be in this world, but Noah is perceptive. Penelope married another actor—one more successful than I am—and lives her perfect life with her perfect bullshit. I refuse to let myself get close to anyone because I can't afford to.

"I'm working on it," I tell him.

"Yeah?"

I need a girl who will be there for me.

Stick out the hard times because life is chock-full of them.

Actresses are as fake as the characters they play, I want a real woman.

I smile knowing exactly what woman I want. The blonde who has invaded my mind. The girl who has no problem slamming the door in my face, telling me to leave, pushing me away, and making me want to stay.

I drain the remainder of my beer and slap Noah on the back. "There's someone who I have in mind."

He shakes his head. "She must be special to make you even pause."

She's more than special. Heather is the complete contrast

to every woman I've ever known. She's strong, sexy, deter-mined, and I don't care that she has some preconceived idea of how this is going to go. Too bad her idea is completely different from mine. She's about to see how persistence will always win out.

CHAPTER ELEVEN

A week passes, and I've finally stopped looking over my shoulder, waiting for Eli to magically appear on my doorstep. It's clear that whatever infatuation he thought he felt for me has passed. I'm not surprised. Eli doesn't seem like the patient kind of guy anyway. Friends my ass.

It's fine. I don't need friends. I've done fine on my own for this long, sans the complication named Ellington Walsh.

After telling Stephanie how I felt about the deteriorating state of the house, she pushed me to do a few projects. There are so many, but I decided to focus on the main living area. I'm spackling nail holes, painting the kitchen cabinets and the living room, and updating the light fixtures. Nicole said she had a few pieces of furniture from a staging she wanted to get rid of and was happy to donate them. Luckily, my best friends agreed to come help and bring their jackass husbands.

I may hate Scott and Peter, but they're good with tools, so I'll play nice for an afternoon.

I hear the doorbell, and I rush over, excited to see my girls.

"Hey!" I smile and we do a big group hug.

"Morning, Heather," Peter says and gives the customary kiss on the cheek.

"Thank you for doing this," I say to all of them. "I appreciate it."

Scott grunts and pushes through. "Let's get this going, I have a game to watch."

This is why I hate him. Peter is at least nice to us on the surface, but Kristin's husband is a prick all the time.

"Don't mind him, he's crabby because the Gators lost," Kristin says, gesturing in the direction where her husband just sulked off.

I touch her arm and shake my head. "It's fine. I appreciate any extra hands, and I'm good at ignoring him."

Nicole makes her way to us with her two guys on her arm. "I brought extra help!" I hope they're contractors she works with, but with her, we never know. "This is Jake and Declan, they worked with me on my last redesign and graciously offered to donate their time."

There's no way they willingly offered, they were incentivized, I'm sure. However, I'm not going to look a gift horse in the mouth. The number of things I'd like to do to this house is never-ending, it's my cash flow that has a limit.

"Great!" I smile.

"We have a few of the pieces I was telling you about in the truck. I think the new tables will help, and I found a rug."

"You're the best," I say as I kiss her cheek. "Thank you."

"You're welcome. You should've told me earlier, I would've given you anything you wanted." She walks into the living room and pushes the guys aside. "Hold please. I need a minute to absorb the aura of a God," Nicole says as she flops on the couch and starts to squirm.

"Nicole!" I yell and grab her arm.

"Whatever! I told you this was happening."

She's unhinged.

"What the hell is wrong with you? Why are you rubbing yourself all over Heather's couch?" Danielle asks.

Nicole rolls her eyes and laughs. "Umm, Eli Walsh's ass was here, and I can now say I touched it."

Danielle and Kristin's heads twist to me, and their eyes widen. "What?" Danni practically screams.

Fuck. I haven't told them anything. I'm going to kill Nicole. My friends are great, but I wanted to keep this quiet as long as possible. Now there's no way I can explain away him being in my damn house. Not without making up some crazy bullshit, which they wouldn't believe anyway because I suck at lying.

"It's a really long story," I start to explain and glare at Nicole. "One that I promise I'll tell you about, but not now."

Kristin steps closer, and her voice drops. "Are you okay? Why the hell would he be in your house? What's wrong? What happened? Did you sleep with him?"

Her questions go so fast I couldn't answer them if I wanted to. "I'm great. I promise. It was a crazy night after the concert and then Eli returned something I dropped."

I guess it wasn't that long of a story after all.

"There's something you're not telling us," Danni says as she tilts her head. "Because how would he know where you live?"

My eyes move to Nicole for saving. She owes me that much.

"So, how about that work we're all here for?" Nicole says loudly. "I have two men who promised me a very fun night as payment for working here. Let's get to it. I'm all for my three-some that's happening."

That's one way to change the topic.

Danielle groans and shivers. "Yuck."

"You only say that because you're jealous."

"Danielle!" Peter calls from the kitchen. "I need your help."

Thank God for the interruption, because I don't know that I could've kept this conversation going without having to spill everything.

We spend the next few hours working on various projects. The cabinets are painted thanks to Danielle and Kristin. Apparently, there was some water damage on one of the walls, so Nicole's two helpers ripped it out, replaced it with new drywall, and helped repaint the living room. It's amazing how much all of us accomplished, and the house feels completely different.

I didn't have any motivation to spend time fixing anything until I saw Eli sitting in my space.

Everyone heads out with promises to call, and the looks that I got from Danni and Kristin say we'll be doing a lot more than talking about the weather.

I walk out onto the porch with my iced tea and sit in the swing that my dad hung the week before he was killed. I always feel a sense of calm when I rock here, as if the wind that blows is his spirit here with me. My dad was a quiet man, but he was full of so much wisdom. He loved my mother more than anything in this world. As hard as it is to admit, if my mother had been alone in that car, my father would've found a way to follow her in death. He would never have been able to survive in a world without her. It's the kind of love I want in my life.

It's the kind I thought I found with Matt. Boy was I wrong.

I lean my head back and close my eyes, hoping to feel that calm again.

Instead, I hear someone clear their throat.

My eyes open, and I come face to face with the man I didn't think I'd see again.

"Eli," I say, almost dropping the glass.

"Hey," he says as he climbs the stairs. "I'm glad you're home."

"What are you doing here?"

"I told you I'd see you again," Eli explains as if it makes total sense.

This is crazy. I thought we were done with him showing up. He's been in the wind, and I had no way to get in touch with him, not that I would have called anyway. I've already decided this will never happen, so I don't know why my heart is racing at the sight of him.

It makes no sense that the tight blue jeans and gray T-shirt that cling to his muscles have my mouth watering.

I'm completely unaffected by him in general. Yup. Totally. It's because I'm tired that I'm reacting at all.

I shake off the thoughts of how much more I'd like to see of him and take a drink. "You did, but that was . . ." I pretend to have to think about it. "Like, ten days ago?" It was eight, but I'm not going to tell him I'm counting.

He grins and takes a seat next to me. "About that."

I shift over a little, hoping some distance between us will help my racing pulse. "Were you out and about and then figured you'd stop by?"

I did not just say that, did I? Oh, God, I did.

"Nope." He chuckles. "I just got back from New York. My agent needed me to finalize some things for our next season."

"Oh." I take another drink as he moves a little closer. My heart races as his side touches mine. "I've never been to New York," I admit. I haven't traveled anywhere since my parents died.

Eli starts to move the swing. "You'll have to come with me one time."

"Come with you?" I squeak.

"Yeah," Eli laughs.

"That's a little presumptuous."

"Why? We can go away together if you want."

"What makes you think I'm going to go on a trip with you? We barely know each other. Hell, we're not even friends."

"I thought we established we were definitely friends last time."

It's going to circle back to my groupie slut status with us. There's no true friendship, there's a one-night stand and pizza. It hardly constitutes as anything. Besides, I don't need any more friends. I have my girls, Brody, and Stephanie. I'm set.

"Look, you don't know me, and I definitely don't know you."

Eli throws his arm around the back of the swing, and his fingers find their way to my neck. "I think I know you pretty well."

"Really?" I challenge.

"I know you're beautiful, like pizza, have the world sitting on your shoulders, and try damn hard not to like me, which you are failing at."

I smile and play with the ring on my thumb. "Whatever. I don't think about you."

I'm a big, fat liar. I think about him all the time, and last night, he managed to star in my dreams—again. As much as I tell myself I'm glad he stopped showing up, I was sad. There's something about being around him that makes me crave more, which is the dumbest thing I could allow myself to want.

Eli's thumb grips my chin, and he forces me to look at him. "I'm serious. Since the minute I laid eyes on you, I think about you all the time."

"Eli," I say, hoping he'll stop. I don't want to think about this.

"Why do you think I called you on stage? Why do you think I wanted you to come to the meet and greet?"

"Because you wanted me to sleep with you!" I say and try to shift away from him.

He cups my face and holds my gaze hostage. "No, because for the first time in all the years I've been doing this, I've finally met someone who managed to knock me off kilter. I didn't understand it until I was in New York. I kept wanting to look at you. Then I couldn't get to you fast enough after the show. That has never happened."

I want to believe him, but it's hard for me to even fathom. "Please don't feed me lines."

"It's not a line. It's you. I can't explain it, but you're all I think about. The way you hide your face from me when you're unsure of yourself. How your smile makes my heart stop, and how even now, with speckles of paint on your face, you take my breath away. Don't you see? I tried to stay away, but I keep finding myself back here."

My chest tightens as I wonder what alternate universe I'm living in. How does one of the sexiest men alive think that I'm in any way special? I'm average on a good day. He's extraordinary on a bad day. This is crazy.

"You can't mean that."

"I mean every single word. I've never chased a girl like this. I've never showed up at her house—repeatedly. I haven't felt like this in a long time."

No one has ever said anything like that to me, and suddenly, every reason to make him leave vanishes. I can't think of anything to say in protest. Plus, I've always believed that actions speak louder than words, and he's here. Even though I've done nothing to further his advances, he keeps coming back.

I shift a little, trying to break the physical touch because I'd be lying if I said I didn't feel something. When he touches me, I tend not to think straight. Eli makes me forget just how broken I am. I don't need to forget.

"Now," he prompts as he drops his hand. "What do you want to know about me? I don't want you to have that excuse anymore."

"Okay," I say with apprehension. "When did you get back?"

"I landed an hour ago, and I needed to see you."

"You landed and came straight here?" I shake my head in complete disbelief. "You can't possibly feel these things for me. You have no idea the mess my life is in, and I don't have time for games."

He retracts his arm from behind me and squeezes the back of his neck, "I'm not playing a game. We're not kids, Heather. We're both too old for that shit. If you don't want me here, I'll go." He moves to stand, and I panic.

"No!" I yell and then clasp my hand over my mouth. Why did I say that? Ugh. I'm giving off mixed signals everywhere.

Eli settles back down next to me, and the green in his eyes darkens. "No?"

"I don't know why I said that. I know I'm being complicated and stupid, but you have to understand my anxiety."

A shiver runs up my spine and I gasp. He gets to his feet and steps in front of me. "I think you're scared because you know what I'm saying is true and you feel it, too."

"I don't." I put as much steel in my voice as I can. He's right, though. Because when he said that he'd leave, I knew he would, and I want him to stay. Eli is the first man to make me feel anything since Matt. He looks at me without any pity or sadness. He doesn't know what I struggle with, and I'm not broken to him.

He looks at me the way I used to look at myself, and I can't help but want that.

"Tell me you don't think of me at all," he commands. "Tell me that in the week I've been away that you haven't wanted me to come here. Make me believe I'm the only one who feels this, Heather. Tell me, and I'll walk away right now. You'll never see me again."

Eli's hand cups my cheek as I get lost in his eyes. The desire swims on the surface, allowing me to forget all the reasons why I should push him away.

"I can't." The truth on my lips stuns me. "I can't say it because it would be a lie."

His lips move closer to mine, and my heart thumps erratically behind my ribs. He's going to kiss me. I *want* him to kiss me. There's no excuse of alcohol tonight. I won't be able to play this off as some drunken mistake. I'm sober, and I want him to make me feel again.

"I didn't think you could," he says before his lips press against mine.

Gone is the worry about my life, all that exists is us. Eli's mouth moves against mine, and his hands hold my cheeks. He keeps me firmly against him as our lips stay fused. It's everything that I remember and more. My fingers grip his shirt, holding him as much as he's holding me. It's reckless to be with a man that will never stay, but I don't have the energy to care.

Right now, he's here.

Right now, he's real.

Right now, he's kissing me.

And for right now, that's enough.

He slides his tongue against mine, pushing his way into my mouth. I've never been kissed like this. There's no way I'll ever kiss another man without comparing them to this one. Eli kisses me like he's been starved for it, which is completely absurd, but that's what he makes me feel.

Too soon, he pulls back and looks at me, his eyes blazing with heat as they dance along my features, his lips red from kissing me. If I pinch myself, would I wake from this dream?

"Tomorrow," he says in a strained voice. "I'm going to be here in the morning to pick you up."

"No," I say, shaking my head quickly.

There are so many things that I can't do with him. I can't get caught up in some tabloid scandal. I can't have my life get flipped upside down because of him. I can't date some celebrity who is only going to break my heart. More than anything, I can't seem to push him away.

"Do you have to work?" he asks.

"No, I mean I can't date you. I can't even think about whatever this is. I can't be hurt again, Eli. I wasn't kidding when I said I'm a mess."

Hurt flashes across his face before he masks it with a grin. "Who said anything about dating? I promise that no one will see us together. We'll talk about the mess you are and figure out how you're going to deal with me in your life."

"I'm not having sex with you again."

He laughs and kisses me. "Whatever you say. Wear sneakers and a bathing suit."

Before I can respond, Eli is halfway down the stairs. "Why are you fighting so hard to see me? I'm clearly pushing you away. What is making you keep coming back?" I ask.

He stops, rushes back up the stairs, and pulls me close. "Because you're not like every other girl. You're the first person I've met in what feels like forever who doesn't seem to want something from me." His hand pushes the hair back off my face. "You look at me like I'm just a guy, not a meal ticket. You're gorgeous, stubborn, and there's something more that I can't explain. I'm not saying this will work, but I'm willing to take a chance and see what this is, are you?"

Every word he said was exactly the right one. I'm not looking for anything from him. Maybe this won't work, but I don't know that I'm strong enough to say no.

"No strings?" I ask.

"No strings. Just a chance."

I'm not a fly by the seat of my pants kind of girl—I'm a planner. I like my life to have order because there's too much chaos everywhere else. I can't make my sister's disease fit into a box, but I can make my schedule solid. It's my only way of being able to control my life when everything else is spiraling. There was no way to plan for my parents to die when I was twenty-one, but I can make sure that each Thursday I'm at the youth center to teach self-defense. Eli is a variable, though. He won't fit into a box, so I won't let him become a fixture in my life.

I know without a doubt, he'll be the extra card that sends my house tumbling down.

The clock reads four in the morning, and I groan. There's no way I'm going to get back to sleep if my mind won't stop running through all the possibilities of what Eli has planned. I didn't think to even ask him what time he's coming to get me today. For all I know, it isn't until late morning, which is going to leave me keyed up all day.

I decide to be ready for whatever will happen. I won't be caught off guard again and look like ass.

No, today I'm going to look as hot as possible. So, I climb out of bed and start a pot of coffee.

Two hours later, I'm showered and wearing my deep purple bikini, white off-the-shoulder top, and black lace shorts. I wanted to look like I didn't spend an hour trying to select my clothes. I've curled my blonde hair in loose curls, and I actually put makeup on. Nicole would be proud.

I grab my phone and dial her number. It's only six, but I don't care. She's the one who convinced me that I needed to let loose, so she can deal with my neurotic ass.

"Hello?" her voice is hoarse and sleepy.

"Wake up!" I scream.

"What's wrong?" she asks sounding more alert. "Are you okay?"

"I have a date with Eli! That's what's wrong!"

She groans, and I hear some rustling in the background. "For real? You call me at the freaking ass crack of dawn for this?"

"Well." I huff. "It was your genius idea I sleep with him, and now he keeps showing up, kissing me, and forcing me on random dates."

Nicole snorts. "Yeah, forcing you. I can imagine how hard it is to say yes to one of *People*'s Sexiest Men Alive. The torture."

Maybe "force" is the wrong word, but this outing wasn't my idea. I have no idea what we're even doing, except I need a bathing suit, which probably means my eyeliner was a stupid idea. I'm so not equipped for this. I'm much better when I'm in control.

Like at work.

"Not the point. And that was three years ago. Look, you need to come calm me down. I'm going to end up on the floor from a panic attack."

"I thought you didn't like him," she tosses back at me.

"I don't!"

I totally do.

I like everything about him so far. The only thing that keeps me hung up is the whole famous and wealthy thing. He lives on Harbour Island, and I don't even have enough money to dream of stepping foot there. Hell, the only time I've ever been there was on a call.

Panic starts to take hold, and my breathing becomes labored.

"Heather?"

"I . . ." I gasp. "Can't."

"Okay." Nicole's voice turns soft and controlled. "Breathe.

Just relax. Think about the fact that he's chasing you. You're gorgeous, funny, and own a gun. You can shoot him in the dick if he upsets you."

Slowly, I gain control as I laugh at the last part. "What am I thinking?"

"You're thinking about yourself, babe. It's a good thing. You deserve to be happy and have some damn fun. Why are you overthinking this?"

My biggest worry is that I'll get swept up in this pretend life, and when reality comes crashing around me, I'll be broken.

Life isn't full of rainbows and sunshine. It's cloudy days and tornados that twist everything I love away.

"What happens when he finds out about my insane life and leaves?"

"What if he stands by you?"

It's my turn to laugh. "Yeah, what man doesn't love a woman who has no time for him?"

"Then you *make* time! You worry about shit that probably won't even be an issue. If he doesn't understand your life, then he doesn't belong in it."

"You're right."

Nicole sighs. "I know I am. Look, you're my best friend, and I love you when you don't call me before the fucking sun is up."

"Sorry." I lie back on the couch, hating my weakness. Self-doubt is a bitch.

"Don't be sorry, be Heather. Be the girl who is fearless, full of confidence, and knows what an amazing woman she is. Because that's who you are. You're not what Matt turned you into."

Another reason to hate him. When he left me, I started to wonder if I was worth anything. I know in some part of my rational brain that he's the idiot, but I couldn't help but doubt myself. I gave him my heart, and he tossed it away as if it meant nothing.

All because my sister needed me more than he did.

I've spent a long time trying to convince myself that he left because of his own issues, but the truth is, I wonder what's wrong with me.

"I wish I knew where that girl went," I admit.

"You'll find her. What time does he get there?"

"I have no idea. I forgot to ask."

Nicole bursts out laughing. "Well, this should be a fun day."

After Nicole gives me more of a pep talk, I get my emotions under control, and they are sent right back into meltdown mode when Eli knocks.

I take three deep breaths before opening the door.

Eli stands there in his mirrored aviators, white T-shirt, and dark blue board shorts. His dark hair is pushed to the side, and if I thought he was hot before, today he's on fire. In front of me is the man who every woman drools over. He drips with sex appeal.

And today, he's my date.

"Morning." I let his husky voice wash over me and try not to let it fry my nerves.

"Good morning."

"I'm glad to see you're awake."

I smile. "You never told me a time, but I get up early even on my days off."

It isn't a total lie, but I never would be awake at four in the morning.

Eli pulls his shades down and grins. "You ready?"

That's a loaded question. I'm ready in terms of being dressed, but ready to go on a date with him? No, not even a little bit. I'm not ready for any of this. I'm terrified of what today could lead to.

However, I'm more afraid of walking away and regretting this moment.

Instead of telling him any of that, I nod. "I am."

"Good."

"Can you tell me where we're going?" This is the only part of this whole thing that has me mystified.

"Nope," Eli says, his eyes dancing with mischief.

"Okay," I draw out the last syllable. "What do I need to bring?"

"Nothing."

This is so not how I function, but I've decided to go with him today, so I need to let it go. I grab my purse, leaving my gun in the safe, and try not to get lost in his smile.

He holds his hand out, and I take it, knowing that today, I'm going to let him lead.

The black Bentley is nowhere to be seen. Today, he walks me to a gray Audi Q5 sitting in front of the house. He opens the door, and I climb in. When he sits beside me, I can't help but look at him again.

His scruff is growing in, giving him a darker look than the first time we met. I like this so much more.

Eli's head turns, and I quickly look away. When my eyes shift back again, it's clear he caught me.

"So, how many cars do you have?" I ask after the silence between us has stretched to almost uncomfortable.

"A few."

"A few like three or a few like thirty?"

Eli smiles, focusing on the road. "Somewhere in the middle of that."

I shouldn't be surprised, his net worth is on Wikipedia, but still. It's hard to comprehend that he makes my yearly salary in a week.

Needing to shift topics again, I go with a safer question. "What was in New York?"

"I had to sign a new contract. *A Thin Blue Line* was renewed for another season."

"Oh, that's awesome!" I heard rumblings on a few of the news outlets that the show might get dropped. "I really hope you're finally able to get a new partner. I don't know why they keep pushing that story line. Tina is not a good match for Jimmy. Brody and I have been riding together for almost seven years, and I would punch myself in the face before I ever kissed him. The show needs to give Jimmy a woman who he saved or something. That would be an interesting plot. Also, your brother on the show *has* to stop sleeping with that model. Twitter went nuts when he went back to her. She's a bitch."

Eli's gaze shifts to mine, and he chuckles. "I thought you didn't watch the show."

Crap. I did say that. I chew on my thumb and shrug. "I guess I've seen a few seasons." I say the last word under my breath, hoping he didn't catch it.

"Seasons?"

No such luck.

"Whatever. It's just to see how bad you butcher my job."

Eli shakes his head and grabs my hand. His fingers thread with mine and then he gently squeezes. "Sounds like you're a little more invested than that."

"Fine," I admit. "I watch it religiously."

He brings my hand to his lips and kisses my knuckles. "I knew you liked me."

I laugh and hit his chest with our entwined hands. "You're crazy. I like your show, but seriously, tell the writers they need to clear that up."

"So, you and your partner have never . . ."

"Eww!" I twist in my seat. "Never. He's married first of all, and I was married to our lieutenant so that was never going to happen on Matt's watch, but . . ."

"You were married to your boss?" he questions.

I guess I haven't really been very forthcoming with information. Not that we've had a ton of time to get into much. I mentioned my ex-husband but didn't go into any great detail. "Yes, I was married, but we've been divorced for almost five years. It was amicable to a point, I guess. Not sure whenever a marriage dissolves that it's ever on good terms, but Matt and I see each other every day, so we're civil."

"You still see him every day?"

"He's still my boss. Unfortunately, it means that I have the pleasure of dealing with him almost daily. I hoped they would transfer me or him, but Matt has a lot of pull in the department."

Eli tenses, but he does a good job at hiding any further reaction. He has to know that I come with a past, just as he does. Might as well get some of this out in the open.

Besides, I'd much rather know what kind of man he is before we get too deep in a relationship or whatever this is. Matt couldn't accept my relationship with Stephanie, and she's a non-negotiable. If Eli can handle the Matt thing, I'll brave telling him about my sister.

"I can't imagine being around my ex. Especially with access to a lethal weapon."

I laugh. "In the beginning, it was tempting, but Matt is a selfish prick. He isn't worth the jail time."

His thumb rubs back and forth, leaving my skin tingling in its wake. Sure enough, we pull up to the gate on Harbour Island. Here's the contrast of my life to his. Eli scans the card that allows us access.

My anxiety starts to climb as the reasons why I should've said no start to swim back into my mind. I'm in his second of whatever number of vehicles, going through the metal gates to houses I couldn't afford to rent a bathroom in, and I'm completely out of my element.

I was crazy to think he and I were ever a possibility. I don't fit in this world.

As we drive down another road, the houses get grander, and my despair deepens.

The car stops, and he turns toward me. "You okay?"

"Yes. No. I'm not really sure," I finally settle on.

He releases my hand and turns to face me fully. "Care to explain?" His voice is light, but the concern is clear in his eyes.

My heart lurches when I see the house we're parked in front of. I point to the incredibly large mansion in front of us. "This. I live in a rundown house that could fit in your drive-way. This is just one of the reasons I pushed you away. We're from different worlds, and this scares the shit out of me."

Eli sighs, exits the car, and walks around to my side.

Well, that wasn't what I expected. Is he going to tell me to get out of his car? Am I supposed to call a cab? Is he leaving me here?

My car door opens, and he grabs my hands, helping me out of the car. After releasing a heavy sigh, he speaks. "I didn't bring you here because I wanted to show you we come from different worlds. The truth is, I lived in the other side of Tampa, but I think you knew that already. Money doesn't define who we are, it's what's inside us that matters."

"I didn't mean it like that." I'm not sure if I could hate myself any more than I do in this moment. Eli has done every-thing right, and my insecurities are getting the better of me.

"I want us to spend the day together, talk, and it's private here. I'm just a guy, Heather. At the end of the day, no matter what you think I am, I'm a man."

"I'm truly sorry," I say immediately. "I didn't mean to freak." Our bodies are close, almost touching, and I pull one of my hands from his so I can cup his cheek. "You're more than just a guy to me. You're a man who reminds me that I'm a woman. You look at me as if I'm special, and that's difficult to accept. More than that, you're a guy that I spent my entire life dreaming of, but right now, you're real."

Eli's arm tightens around my back. "I want to be Ellington today. Not Eli Walsh the actor or FBD member. Can we do that? Can we just be . . . ourselves?"

It's a grand idea. To let go of the bullshit around us and just be two people getting to know one another. I want nothing more than to see who he really is. "Just the two of us?" I ask.

"No one else will be here today," Eli says and brushes his lips against mine.

"Then it's nice to meet you, Ellington."

His name falls from my lips, and I sigh.

"You, too, Heather."

I push forward, pressing a sweet kiss on his mouth. His smile is warm against my lips, and he releases his hold on me. Eli takes my hand as we walk toward the house.

He opens the door, and my jaw drops. This is beyond words. As we step inside, I look around, trying to take it all in. The foyer hosts two huge staircases that lead to opposite ends of a balcony. There are two rooms off to each side at the bottom, one of which is a library. I'm not talking about a few books on a shelf, either. The entire wall looks lined. We walk deeper, and the other room opens to what looks like a more formal living room.

"Wow," I say with awe.

"I bought this house a few years ago. I like to visit my mother here in Tampa, and Randy lives in Sanibel Island, so this is a good medium."

"There's nothing medium here, Eli. This is super-sized." My voice cracks a little as he continues to lead me down the hall.

I try to stop counting rooms because it's beyond what I

thought it was from the outside. It's at least three times the size I assumed. The house seems to get deeper and deeper, and when we reach the back area, there are huge windows that overlook the water.

"Do you need anything before we go?" he asks.

"Go?"

"Yeah." He laughs and points outside. "That's my boat. We're going to spend the day on the water."

My eyes turn to his, and I plaster a smile on my face. I love the water. Some of my favorite memories of my dad are from when he would take me boating when I was a kid. His boat wasn't anything like the huge one currently docked to the pier, though.

Eli moves closer, and he pushes my hair back. "Is that okay?"

I nod. "It's perfect."

He shows me to the bathroom, where I put more sunscreen on, check my makeup, and say a few silent prayers that I don't get sea sick. It's been a long time since I've been on open water, and that would be my luck.

We get on the boat, which is equipped with two damn bedrooms, a kitchen area, bathroom, and a sitting area, therefore it's a house with a hull. He shows me around, and then eases the vessel out onto the water.

I watch him command the boat and fight back a sigh. Everything he does is sexy. The way his muscles flex when he turns the wheel. How his brow furrows when he's concentrating on steering. I don't want to do anything but watch him, so that's what I do. My focus is so singular, that I don't notice when we're out of the channel.

"Want to drive?" Eli offers, dragging me out of my staring.

"I've never driven a boat before."

"I'll help you." He gives an encouraging smile and steps back so I have room to stand in front of him.

Too excited to say no, I move toward him and slip into the space. My hands grip the wheel, and I glance at him over my shoulder.

"Good, hold it steady and move the wheel a little if you want to go in a different direction." Eli stands with his chest against my back, and I lean into him. "You're doing great," he says in my ear.

"I don't really know what I'm doing," I admit.

"Let's go right. There's a sweet spot for fishing over that way."

Eli's hands come around and settle atop of mine. He isn't steering, just holding on. I could close my eyes and get lost right now. Our bodies are so close, and his strong arms make me feel safe.

We stay like this for a while, not actually driving so much as drifting along together. Eli slows the boat and pulls me onto his lap as he holds the wheel. "It's like we're completely alone out here," I muse as I stare out into the ocean.

He kisses my shoulder. "We are."

I look back at him with a smile. "Let me get this straight, you're a sailor, singer, actor, and fisherman?"

"I'm a man of many talents."

My laughter is free and unabashed. "You're something all right."

"Come on, let's see if you can catch our lunch."

Eli and I move to the bow of the boat, where he has two fishing poles waiting for us. After we thread our lines and bait our hooks, we cast out into the water and stick the poles in the holders to wait. I settle back onto one of the benches and look out over the water. Deep blues and greens reflect the sunlight sending little bursts of light around. The cloud cover is light today, but they're big and fluffy. I turn to point out a cloud that looks like a dinosaur, but I can't speak. Eli stands there shirtless and my mouth waters.

Dear. God.

His body is exactly like I remember from our night together. Only now, I'm not in the dark. The sun shines on his perfect skin, giving me the most breathtaking view possible. I watch him move around the boat, securing a few things on the deck as I admire his chest. The tattoos etched on his arms, shoulder, and hip only make him look hotter. I swear that tattoos have never been sexier. My hands itch to trace the ink on his skin, the firmness of his muscles, feel his heat, and get lost in his touch.

"Come sit with me." Eli holds his hand out, and I force myself to drag my eyes away from his body to take it. He leads me to a couch under a retractable awning and takes a seat in the corner, pulling me down next to him. It's natural for me to rest my head on his chest, allowing the salty air and clean breeze to fill my nose.

"I'm glad you came." His deep voice seems to vibrate through me.

"Me, too."

"Tell me something," he requests.

"What do you want to know?"

"Something true. I don't get a lot of truth from people."

A wash of sadness comes over me from his words. I can't imagine what it's like to be him. Constantly battling the feeling of people trying to get a piece of him in some way. He probably doesn't get a lot of people being honest or just wanting to know him. I hate that for him. It must be lonely.

I sit up so I can look him in the eyes. "I won't lie to you. You can ask me anything."

He smiles and pushes himself closer to me. "Why do you keep saying you're a mess?"

I sigh and look away. "There are a lot of things going on in my life."

"Your ex?"

I laugh humorlessly. "I wish it were just that."

"Heather," Eli says my name with softness. "I want to know you. Really know you. I'm sure you know what the tabloids say about me, but that isn't who I am."

"Then who are you?" I would much rather hear more about him than air out my own life.

"I'm a brother, uncle, and son. My father died a few years after walking out on my mom. We were poor as hell, and I've done everything possible to make sure I never live like that again. Most days, I love acting more than singing, but I can't imagine not having Four Blocks Down in my life. I'm old as hell, tired of being so damn angry at things I can't control, and this is the first time I've ever had to chase a girl this fucking hard. Especially after giving her the goods."

I let out a soft laugh and lightly slap his leg. "I wasn't kidding when I said I don't do stuff like that. I don't date. I don't have time for men. I kind of gave up the idea of being with anyone after my ex left."

"Me, too," he says earnestly. "We all have our things, Heather."

I remember a few years back there was talk of Eli getting married, but you can't believe a thing you read. My curiosity spikes a little, and I have to swat away my inner cop who wants to interrogate him about it. "You had someone once, right?"

Eli shifts, bringing my attention fully back to him. "I don't talk about it much. She was playing me, though. Penelope was really good at it. I found out she was screwing my former agent when I came home early from a trip to surprise her. We were dealing with some personal stuff, and instead of coming to me, she went to another man. She fucked me up pretty good."

"I'm so sorry. That's awful." I squeeze his hand in solidarity.

He releases a deep breath through his nose. "I won't lie. I had no intention of ever having more with a woman, which is probably where all the rumors about my being a player come from. I don't fuck around and play games, but I'm not known for having relationships. It's been easier to keep my distance, and I'm always honest with the girls I've been involved with."

I've heard all of that, which is what leads me to wonder what we're doing here. Not that I need the promise of something magical, but I don't need a guy who has a girl in another city, either.

My heart races as I prepare to ask my next question. "Then what do you want with me?"

His eyes are open, allowing me to see all his emotions. "More. I want more."

"And what if you realize I'm not worth more?"

He shakes his head. "What if you're worth it all?"

"You've spent a few hours with me, Eli. You can't—"

"I'm giving you my truth," he interjects softly. "All I'm asking for is a little of yours."

The fear of falling for him is real. My mother and father left me, my husband left me, my sister will leave, and the last thing I want is to love someone else who will do the same. Eli doesn't know anything about me at this point. Nothing past the superficial things. If I give him my truth, I'll be giving him a part of me.

Fuck it. Not like he can go anywhere while we are still in the middle of the ocean. Plus, if I'm going to do this, if he wants to try, he should know.

"My sister is dying. She's twenty-six and has Huntington's disease, it's a rare degenerative disease."

His eyes widen as he sucks in a breath. "I don't even know what to say. Is there anything that can be done?"

I shake my head. "No, it's terminal. Stephanie's disease has become my whole life. *She's* my whole life."

Eli takes my hand in his. "I'm so sorry. I can't imagine how hard it is for you."

"Ha!" I laugh sardonically. "It's excruciating. She was diagnosed at nineteen and since then, we've been on a downhill slope. My husband left me because Stephanie needed full-time care. I guess I wasn't enough of a wife to him because I was too busy taking care of my dying sister."

"That's why he left?" Eli asks with disgust dripping from his words.

I look in his emerald eyes and sigh. "He couldn't handle it."

"He sounds like a fucking prick."

That's a nice way to put it.

"I'm telling you this now because whatever this is that we're doing here can't interfere with what I have to do for my sister."

Eli's hand tightens, and his head jerks back. "Interfere?"

"Yes, I won't be able to follow you around to New York, and I can't afford to spend time away from her. I can't get caught up in this . . . thing with you and miss spending what little time I have with Stephanie. It's what scares me. Well, that and the fact that you're . . . you, and I'm not in your universe. I can't allow myself to have regrets when it comes to my sister."

"I would never want you to. I'm not asking you to give anything up. And as for your ex, he's a piece of shit for making you think you should choose between your sister and a man. That's ridiculous. I have a brother, and if it were him, I'd be at his side."

A part of my bruised heart heals a little. I look in his eyes and wait for some kind of change in his thoughts. Anything to tell me that he's lying, but it never comes. "You can't be this perfect, Eli."

He laughs. "I'm far from perfect, baby."

"You're kind, funny, and unbelievably hot."

"Don't forget a God in the bedroom."

I shake my head. "Egotistical."

"Keep going with all my stellar qualities," he nudges.

Instead, I lean forward and touch my lips to his. "Don't make me think you're great and then break my heart."

Eli's fingers thread in my hair. "Don't make me keep fighting so hard to win you."

My defenses fall to the floor as he pulls my head closer. "What are you doing to me?"

He smiles. "I'm making you feel how you make me feel —helpless."

CHAPTER THIRTEEN
ELI

Kissing Heather is like nothing I've ever felt before. I've kissed a lot of girls, but she makes me lose track of the world around us. It's as if time is suspended when she's with me. The first night we slept together, I thought it was the endorphins from entertaining.

I figured that once I'd gotten her out of my system I would be able to move on.

Now, it's worse.

She's opening herself to me, showing me who she is and it's fucking beautiful. Everything about her brings me to my goddamn knees. How anyone can walk past her and not stop, blows my mind. The idea of her dickless husband leaving her is asinine. Who would walk away from someone as gorgeous as she is? It's more than just her beauty, though. She's smart, funny, strong—sometimes a little too strong, and she gives me a sense of hope that I haven't felt in a long time.

"God, you kiss good," Heather breathes, and then her lips are back on mine.

I hold her golden locks in my hands and plunge my tongue deeper. I taste the mint from the gum she was chewing. Heather's soft hands slide up my chest to cup my jaw, and I lean back, taking her with me. I'm practically lying flat so I can enjoy her weight as it settles on top of me.

Our tongues push against each other, giving and taking in a constant battle for control. I don't let up. I fight her for dominance. I struggle for her to let loose and give it over to me. The truth is, the harder she resists, the more turned on I get.

I tighten my grip in her hair, loving the moan she makes in my mouth. Her noises spur me further, wanting her so bad I think my dick is going to explode from fucking kissing. Because that wouldn't be embarrassing . . . I can see it now: "Pop Star Blows His Load While Making Out" on page seven. Thankfully, I'm able to keep myself in control because the only place I'm blowing my load is inside her. I might actually die if that doesn't happen soon.

My lips glide across the skin of her neck and down to her shoulders. "You're so beautiful," I rumble against her skin. "Every inch of you is perfect. I can close my eyes and see your body as if it's that night all over again."

She lets out a low moan as my hand cups her perfect breast. I let the weight of her fill my hand, and I roll it around, just brushing the nipple.

I'm a boob guy, always have been. Tits are like gifts from God. There's a reason men don't have them—if we did, we'd play with them all day. I would take a shit and cop a feel. I'd be showering and just rub them. I don't care if that sounds crazy, it's true.

"Tell me this is real," she demands.

"It's real," I say as I untie the knot of her bikini. I hold it there because I want her to lead this. If she wants to have sex and run away again, she's going to be swimming because there's nowhere to go.

She moves her hand to mine and pulls the strings down, giving me the view I am desperate for.

My mouth waters as I stare at her tits. I'm dying to taste her again. I shift our bodies so she's straddling my lap, and push my dick against the warmth of her pussy, wanting nothing more than to bury myself in her heat. My mouth latches onto her nipple, lavishing it as she holds my head where she wants it. The feel of her hands, controlling me has me sucking her harder.

Her head falls back, her long hair brushing the tops of my thighs as she grinds down hard. "I want you," she confesses.

I want her more than my next breath. I just don't want to scare her away. Yesterday was a turning point for us in some way. She didn't tell me to leave or push me away hard. It was almost as if she was finally agreeing to whatever this is.

The last thing I need is to go two steps back. However, I'm not going to tell her no, either. Not when my dick is so hard it could cut glass.

"Look at me, baby."

Her eyes meet mine, and I see the desire burning in her gaze. More than that, I see worry.

The way she looks at me stops my heart, and I feel like a prick. I may kick myself in the ass for this, but there's no way I can do this to her. If my whole goal is to get her to stop trying to get rid of me, I have to earn it. She has to trust me enough that, when I look in her eyes, the only thing I see is want and need. Not doubt.

The words feel foreign, but they're exactly what I know I need to say. This isn't a line of bullshit I'm spoon feeding her, it's the truth. "I want you. I want you so much that it's going to fucking kill me to say this, but I don't want to just fuck you."

"What?" Her eyes widen, and she quickly covers her chest.

I'm definitely kicking my own ass later.

"I feel like we're making progress, and I promised you we wouldn't have sex. I said we were going on a date."

Heather eyes me curiously, probably wanting to pull my man card and toss it overboard. Hell, I want to pull it myself, but I see something else.

Maybe hesitation.

Maybe a little doubt.

I also see a hint of respect.

For the first time in a long time, I revel in that last one.

She unhooks her leg and scoots off me so she's sitting next to me again. I watch as she re-ties her bikini, which makes me want to cry a little, and wait for her to say something. When she finally looks over, she smiles. "Thank you."

"Don't thank me yet, I'm seriously regretting it." I smile. I am, but I go for a more joking tone.

Heather giggles nervously, shifting again so her legs are under her. "I don't think you know what you just did truly means to me, Ellington." My cock strains against my board shorts when she says my full name in her soft voice. "I would've . . ." She stares off at the horizon before looking back. "I wouldn't have stopped you, and I probably would've hated myself for being so weak when it comes to you."

"I'm not sure it's you who's weak."

That's the truth, right there. I'm the fool who is chasing around a girl. Heather wasn't the one who showed up at my house, repeatedly, forced me to go on a date with her, or spent a week trying to negotiate a deal, only to take less money so she could get the fuck home to Tampa. I can lie and say it wasn't because I wanted to see her, but I won't. It felt like there was a magnet pulling me back to where she was. Heather may not see it, but I'm clearly fucked here.

"I keep waiting to wake up from this dream. That a guy like you could even look twice at a girl like me. More than that, I want to be close to you, even when I shouldn't."

Heather sighs and then gets to her feet. "Don't mistake my pushing you away to mean that I'm not weak to you."

I get to my feet and pull her into my arms. "I don't. I know you want this as much as I do. I know that even though you keep fighting me off, you're fighting yourself more. I heard what you said about your life, but I'm not running away."

Her hands rest on my chest, and she tilts her head back to look at me. "I hope you mean it, because I'm kind of liking the idea of you sticking around."

"Ahhh," I squeeze her tighter. "I knew I'd wear you down."

"I guess I have a thing for actors who were once upon a time in a kickass boy band."

"Once upon a time?"

She shrugs. I'll give her once upon a time. "I'll have you know I'm multi-platinum. I'm more than kick ass."

"If you say so." She smirks.

She's going to pay for this.

"That's it." I move quickly, bending to hoist her into my arms. Then I walk with her toward the edge of the boat. "Say you're sorry!"

"You wouldn't dare!" Heather yells.

"Wouldn't I?"

I wouldn't throw her in, but I would jump so we both went together.

"Eli!"

"Say it, Heather. Say, 'Eli is the best singer in the world and every artist should bow to his talent.'"

I'm laying it on thick, but I want to hear those words from her lips.

"You're insane!" She laughs, and I move her closer to the edge. "Eli! Stop! Please!"

"This could all be over if you just say the words," I admonish her playfully.

She clutches the waistband of my shorts and yells again. "Please, I can't swim!"

I quickly put her down and grip her shoulders. "I didn't know. I wouldn't have really done it."

She bursts out laughing, clutching her stomach. "Who the hell lives in Florida and can't swim? You're so gullible!"

I move forward, but she moves quickly to the side. We play cat and mouse for a few more minutes before I finally catch her. Then, when her lips touch mine, I realize the girl I can't seem to get out of my head, is cementing herself in my heart.

"HELLO," I smile to the woman at the front desk. "I'm visiting a few patients today, one is Stephanie Covey," I say hoping it's the same last name as Heather.

Her eyes bulge as her jaw falls slack. I stand there, waiting for her to recover before she sputters out her words. "Oh. Oh, wow. Umm, Eli, I mean, Mr. Walsh, of course." The front desk nurse types on the computer, trying to hide the blush on her cheeks with her hair.

"Take your time." She glances at me, and I give her the panty-dropping smile that I use for concerts and photo shoots.

She bites her lip and then lets out a nervous giggle. "Stephanie Covey, yes. She's in room 334."

There are some serious perks to being famous, one of which is people tend to forget certain things like patient confidentiality. It's probably why I'll always have private care if I ever need it.

"Thanks, doll." I place one of the flowers from Stephanie's bouquet on the counter in front of her and wink. I don't know anyone that actually winks in real life, but apparently, if you're famous, it's a sure-fire way to get women excited.

The nurse clutches the flower to her chest with wide eyes. It really does work every time.

After I dropped Heather off, I started forming a plan. I have a big event coming up, and I want to do something special for her. She's a giver. She sacrifices everything for the people she loves.

Her ex-husband is a fucking moron, but, I'm kind of glad for it because it allowed me a chance to meet her. One man's mistake is another man's fortune and Heather is the fucking pot of gold at the end of the rainbow.

I grab my phone and text her.

> Thinking of me?

HEATHER

Oh my God! You did not save your number under the name God's Gift to Women!

I had to program my fucking number in her phone after our boat date. She refused to enter it, claiming she liked the arrangement where I randomly show up.

> Well, I am. However, you still haven't answered if you were thinking of me.

HEATHER

Nope not once actually. Who are you again?

I laugh.

> Liar. And you know exactly who this is, baby. My ears were itching or ringing . . . whatever it is when someone is thinking of you . . . I figured I should do something about it.

HEATHER

You should see an ENT about that. Sounds like a medical condition.

> You wound me.

I love that she has no problem giving me shit. So many girls would be falling over themselves, but not her.

HEATHER

> Actually, I was thinking of you before. I had a call, and this girl was going crazy over how much she loved Four Blocks Down. She was good people.

> See, if you would've taken my number and I didn't have to trick you, you could've called me. I would've made her a very happy fan.

HEATHER

> Good to know. I'll be sure to call you each time someone talks about the God that you are. *eye roll*

I can picture her saying it and almost hear the sarcasm in her voice. Could I like this girl anymore at this moment? Doubtful.

> I'll be picking you up on Thursday at seven in the morning.

HEATHER

> You will, huh?

> I will. I have something I want to show you.

HEATHER

> Well, I guess I can squeeze you in.

> I'm honored.

HEATHER

> Seriously, though. It depends on if Stephanie is released, can we play it by ear?

I will never stand in her way with her sister, which is why I'm here. It's one thing to say the words and another to actually follow through with action. She should never doubt me, I'm hoping to prove this to her now.

> Of course, I'll be in touch.

HEATHER

Thanks, Eli. I really was thinking of you. (Don't let that go to your head.) *wink*

I have a shit-eating grin on my face as I push off from the wall I was leaning against and start walking. Nerves that I don't normally feel start to build as I approach Stephanie's door. What if she doesn't know that her sister and I are . . . whatever we are? Am I going to seriously piss off Heather?

Instead of getting ahead of myself, I say fuck it and do what I came here to do. I knock on the door and hope for the best.

"What?" a hostile voice calls from the bed. "I'm sleeping."

"Sorry," I say, and then she looks over and lets out a high-pitched scream.

"Holy shit!"

"Hi, Stephanie. Can I come in?" I ask.

"Oh. My. God!" A younger, brunette version of Heather yells. "You're Eli Walsh! The one who my sister slept with!" I guess that clears up whether she knows about me. "Shit!" Stephanie clasps her hand over her mouth in a very Heather-like gesture.

"I'm one and the same, unless she goes around sleeping with other guys named Eli Walsh?"

She shakes her head with her hand still covering her lips.

"I wanted to come by and meet you, I hope that's okay."

It's clear that Heather's sister is her number one, and I want her to know I get it. Unlike her piece of shit ex-husband.

She tucks her hair behind her ears and sits up a little. "Of course! I mean, yeah. I can't believe you're here . . . in my hospital room. And you know my name."

"Your sister talks about you a lot," I explain.

"She needs a life."

I ignore the comment because it isn't my place to say shit. I know how easy it is to immerse yourself in whatever is going on in life. "So, tell me, how are *you* feeling?"

"Umm." She hesitates and scrunches her face a little. "Me? I'm having a good day. I'm going home tomorrow."

"That's good. I know Heather thought you'd be done today."

Stephanie chews on her lip while looking out the window. "They're keeping me one more day because I had a rough night last night."

Shit. Maybe this won't work. "I'm sorry to hear that."

"It's fine. My medication was causing my heart rate to spike, but the last twelve hours have been steady. Please don't tell my sister that last part. If I say anything about having a bad day, it's a yearlong lecture on all the reasons I should call her when things like that happen. As if my life isn't a series of freaking medical issues, I guess she just wants to be on the phone all damn day." Stephanie says the words so fast it almost comes out like one giant sentence.

My lips turn up, and I stifle a laugh. There isn't a doubt in my mind that Heather would be okay with that. She has a big heart, and her protectiveness of Stephanie is clear. My brother is the same with me. Randy may come off as an asshole, but if I needed him, I know he will be there.

"Your secret's safe with me." I move toward the side of her bed and extend the flowers. "These are for you."

"I can't believe you brought me flowers. You must really like my sister."

"I do. I like her a lot."

I never understood the saying, "You know when you know." I always thought that was some line of bullshit an idiot came up with. Yet, the older I get, the more reality I see in it. I've always known in some part of my head that the girls I was spending time with weren't worth it. They weren't going to be the girl brought to meet my mother.

Maybe it's because I'm old.

Maybe it's because it's her.

No matter what the reason is, I just know.

Stephanie's smile is wide, and I can feel the happiness rolling off her. "She needs someone to take care of her. I know she doesn't act like it, but she does."

It's clear that these two have each other's best interests at heart. Here Stephanie is worried about her while Heather is always trying to help her.

"We all do, right?"

She nods. "As much as I'd love to pretend you're here because I'm so amazing and you needed to know more about me, tell me what really brought you here."

I lean in closer and grin. Heather has no idea what's in store for our date, but I'm hoping it shows her there are other sides to me. I do a lot that has nothing to do with music or Hollywood. I'd like to have her sister be there as well as a surprise.

I can't wait to see Heather's face when I pull this off. "How good are you at lying to your sister for a good cause?"

CHAPTER FOURTEEN

"What do you mean you didn't want me to stop by?" I ask Stephanie as I try to organize her room the way it was a week ago. She came back to Breezy Beaches yesterday and refused to let me do anything last night. She said she needed to be alone and practically threw me out the door. Today, I didn't care what she said, I came anyway even with her bitch-o-meter being at an eleven out of ten.

She sits on the bed, glaring at me. "You never fucking listen to me! I don't want you to come! I'm tired, I'm finally back home and I want to just . . ." She pauses and then groans.

Today is a bad day. She's struggling to string words together and is getting frustrated.

I wait and then the words burst out. "Settle in! I want to be in this hellhole alone."

"I am listening. I haven't really been with you a lot lately." I try to explain. "I love you, Steph."

She starts to cough and swats my hand away. "You were at the hospital every single day. I'm asking for a d-d-day to myself! Why is that so hard for y-you? Why can't you let me be alone?"

I sit on the edge of the bed and sigh. "I'm sorry. I'm trying here. I'm doing the best I can."

It breaks my heart when she's like this. I never know what will happen, and fighting with her literally kills me. If tomorrow never comes, I don't want this to be our last conversation. Whenever it goes down this path, I have to swallow my hurt and anger. I hide the pain and do what I can to try to turn this around. I know what regret feels like, and I never want that for us.

Stephanie goes quiet for a few minutes, touches my shoulder, and then releases a heavy breath. "I hate this f-f-fucking disease!" Tears fill her eyes, and I pull her in my arms. "You sh-shouldn't have to be around me. I'm mean!"

Rocking back and forth with her in my arms allows me to keep my own tears at bay. It isn't her fault that she's having a bad day. It's the way it goes. Her symptoms are worsening, and we both know it. The outbursts have become more frequent over the last few months, her speech is declining, and the medicine isn't doing as much for her tremors. Yesterday, the doctor told me frankly that this is the beginning of the decline.

"You're not mean, you're doing the best you can." I know this isn't her fault.

"I didn't want to come back here. I wanted to stay at the hospital for longer."

"Why?" I ask and take her hand in mine. "You hate the damn hospital."

"I miss Anthony. I liked seeing him every day. I liked knowing he'd stop by the room and talk to me like I wasn't this poor d-dying girl. He saw me as a girl, woman, whatever . . . the point is that he saw *me*, Heather. Not the tremors, locking joints, problems remembering . . ."

I hate that anyone sees her that way at all.

"Did you call him?" I ask.

Anthony has been good for her. He was in her room after his shift each day, bringing her comic books and flowers. The bouquet of varying shades of vibrant purple and pink roses with plush hydrangeas mixed in that he brought her was breathtaking. I tried not to make a big deal of it, but the fact that Anthony cared so much made my heart swell.

"No, I'm not going to make him watch me die." Stephanie is stubborn. She always has been, and I worry she'll push him away without a chance of any happiness. On the other hand, I can't imagine what knowing she is dying and having people she loves watch feels like to her.

What can I even say to that? She's allowed to make her choices, and I have to understand that. Even though I think she's wrong.

"I wish you'd tell him how you feel. He brought you flowers, and by the looks of it, he cares for you."

I understand that Stephanie has her own set of issues, far more than I can comprehend, but it doesn't mean she should just give up.

She snorts. "Okay, whatever. First, the flowers aren't from him, which I've said three times. I told you they just appeared in my room. Second, is that what you're doing with Eli? Are you telling him how much you want to spend time with him? Are you giving him even the slightest inclination of how much you actually like the guy? No? I didn't think so." Gone is the anger in her voice, all I hear now is challenge.

I guess it's like the saying about glass houses and throwing stones. But it's different for me. He's complicated, rich, famous, and doesn't live here. Why am I going to let myself get tangled in some crazy mess? I'm not.

Do I like him? Yup.

Do I wish I didn't? Yup.

Does he listen to anything I've said regarding what he can expect? Absolutely not. He wormed his way in, and I'm pretty sure he has no intention to leave.

"It's not the same. He's got too many question marks around him."

"You're allowed to love again. You love me and I'm a giant unknown."

Loving Stephanie was never a choice, it was absolute. Even with knowing the ending of our story, I wouldn't make different choices. With Eli, I'm not there yet. I don't have to let it get that far. Loving another gives them power, it can be beautiful, fulfilling, and as easy as breathing, but if I lose it again, it will destroy me.

I twist the fabric of my shirt in my hands, feeling the threads loosen and notice the similarities in my own life. Each time I think I'm together and secured, something starts to break the bond, and I tear.

"I won't let myself fall for him, Steph. I like him, I won't lie, but he's leaving soon. His life isn't in Tampa. I'm not moving. I'm not leaving you."

"It's going to be me who leaves you, Heather. I don't know when, and I don't know how, but we both know it's coming." A tear falls down her cheek and another follows suit.

"Don't say that." I beg.

"It's the truth, and you have to come to terms with it."

Tears spring in my eyes. I don't want to lose my sister. The thought of living in a world without her is intolerable. I've lost more than any person should, and life isn't done taking from me yet. Stephanie, she's mine. I've cared for her, watched her grow, packed her lunch, dressed her for prom, and the idea that I won't have her in my life is too much.

Sometimes it's all just too much.

"We have time." I will the words to be true.

"I'm saying that when I go, I want to know you're okay.

Don't you get it? As much as you love me, I love you more. You are my whole heart, and you have no idea how much anger I have inside me about this d-d-disease. It's taken everything from you, Heather. It took your money, your husband, your whole life! I need to know you have someone!"

"Stop it! Stop it right now!" I yell back at her, swiping the tears from my cheek. "We're not going to do this."

"We have to do this. We have to talk about it."

I don't want to. I want to forget and enjoy what time we have. I get to my feet and move around the room, trying to stop the tears that keep falling. I turn my back to her, looking out the window. Maybe I'm weak, but it's easier than facing her. "I can't lose you." My voice cracks with so much pain that I could splinter.

"Heather, look at me." I turn and meet her blue eyes that shimmer with unshed tears. "You will never lose me. We didn't lose Mom and Dad, we just can't see them anymore."

This time, it's my hands that are trembling. I move closer and reach out to touch her face. "I love you so much."

"I know," she murmurs.

"I hate this."

"Me, too."

"Do you forgive me for yelling? Are we good?"

Steph smiles and takes my hand. "If you want me to be good, you have to promise me you'll stop pushing everyone away. You have to tell me that you'll let your heart be open. Can you do that?"

I've never lied to Stephanie. It's one thing that I've always prided myself on. I tell her the truth, consequences be damned. Words matter and promises are meant to be kept.

"I promise to try."

Stephanie's eyes narrow. "Try?"

"Yes, I'll try to be open. I'll try to let Eli in a little, or if not him, some other jackass who will only fuck with my head."

That's really what it comes down to . . . men are liars. They say they're one thing and they never are. Matt said he loved me, that he'd honor and cherish me, and the first time shit got rough, he bailed. Cherish my ass.

"I swear, the older you get, the more dramatic you are. I think he's different."

"Based on all your time with him?" I challenge. She's never met him, so I don't know why she's so quick to defend him. Maybe because he's the first guy to actually try since Matt.

"No, based on the way your face lights up when you say his name."

I don't do that, do I? No. I don't think I do.

She laughs and points at my face. "You even do it when you think of him."

"Whatever." I'm going to have to work on that. I really hope he doesn't notice. He's good at getting me to do things as it is, if he has a read on me, I'm screwed. I think back to our last date and how sweet he was. Not many guys turn down a chance to get laid, but he did. I fell a little bit for him in that moment.

It was the first time in a long time that anyone put my needs above their own. I'm usually the one who has to sacrifice, and it was nice to have the shoe go on the other foot.

"Earth to Heather!" She waves her hand in my face.

"Sorry, I was just thinking."

"Uh-huh. Can you help me?" Stephanie asks.

My arm hooks under hers, and she slowly climbs out of bed. For the last month, her physical therapist has been pushing her to use her muscles as much as possible. She was in a wheelchair for four months, and with a lot of work, she was able to walk a little with the walker. That progress seems to be deteriorating as well. She sits up and stretches her limbs.

I watch my baby sister bite down whatever discomfort

she's feeling and get to her feet with shaky legs. I quickly move to support her. Her eyes say everything her voice doesn't. The appreciation that I'm here and sorrow that she needs me shines as bright as the full moon outside the window. She and I take a few steps and grab the walker. We move without hurry through the halls as she tells me more about Anthony.

After another hour, I can see the exhaustion settling into her features.

"I'm going to head home. Can I see you tomorrow?" I know that I'm spending the day with Eli, but I need to see her. After the conversation earlier, I think we are both coming to grips with the future. My mother used to tell us to hold on to the things we can control and let everything else go. She insisted that wasting time was never a good thing. She was right. I can't control Steph's disease, but I can control how I handle the time we have left together. I'm going to make the most of it, cherish it, and hope I don't break when it ends.

Steph smiles and touches my arm. "I think that can be arranged."

"Do you think on our next date we can do something in the afternoon?" I ask Eli, who's standing in my living room while I pour another mug of coffee. Last night was tough. I couldn't fall asleep until after two, and not wanting to look like crap, I was up early fixing my face.

"Oh, we're going on another date?" Mischief is laced in his deep voice. "I thought you weren't into me? I thought you friend-zoned me? I knew you couldn't resist."

I walk out of the kitchen and roll my eyes. Damn him and all his arrogance. "You're the one who keeps calling these

dates and showing up at my house. If anyone is into anyone . .
. it's you who is into me."

There. Take that. I'm not chasing him, and I'm going to
remind him of that.

He shrugs and pulls me against him. "I've never hidden
the fact that I'm into you."

My arms rest on his shoulders, and I smile. "Sometimes I
still think this is a dream."

"Would you believe me if I said I feel the same, too?"

I shake my head, because I can't see why he'd think that.
Eli *is* the dream come true. He's the wish upon a star that girls
spend their nights hoping for. Yet, he's in my living room. I
can't tell you the nights I would dream about this very thing
happening.

"Well, I keep waiting to find something about you that I
don't like, but even the things that would normally annoy me,
like trying to push me away so damn hard, only make me
want you more. I'm just glad you're starting to cave."

"Who said I'm caving?" I goad him a bit. I enjoy our
banter.

"I'd say the boat was a good indication I'm no longer
friend-zoned."

"I can put you back there if you'd like?"

Not that whatever we're doing is serious. It's only been
two dates and one hell of a night. But it's definitely more than
friends. I mean, Brody is my friend, and we sure as hell don't
rip each other's clothes off. We've gone fishing, and not once
did I end up grinding against him.

Eli's arms tighten, forcing my body to be even closer to
his. "I don't think I was ever there, and I don't think friends
do this."

In an instant, his lips press against mine, and the flutter in
my belly grows stronger. Eli's musky cologne envelops me,
and I commit it to memory. I want to remember each detail

regarding this moment. How his lips feel against mine, the way the callus on his thumb roughly grazes the skin on my cheek, and how he tastes. It's cinnamon and the hint of toothpaste. If this doesn't work out, I'll have this memory to hold on to.

His tongue seeks entrance, and I give it willingly. I don't even pretend to fight him. I want it. When he touches me, I can't help but find myself craving everything he'll give. I tell myself, and everyone else, that there's nothing here, but when he's close, I can't pretend. Eli breathes life into a heart that was deflated. A heart that never thought it would beat again is once again thumping at a steady pace.

He kisses me hard, forcing my feet to move with him. My back presses against the wall, and he pours himself into each movement. I'm trapped between the cool wood panel and the heat of Eli's body.

Everything is a contrast between wanting more from him and wanting things to end before it's too late to walk away.

I need him to leave, but I'm desperate for him to stay.

I say there's nothing between us, and yet the idea of him leaving is enough to make me scream.

I drop the mug to the floor, not caring that it shatters. My fingers grip his neck as I hold his lips to mine.

I drown in this kiss.

I die in this kiss.

I come to life in this kiss.

Eli pulls back and gives me a cocky smirk. "Do your friends kiss you like that?"

Instead of telling him the truth—that no one kisses me like that—I inhale and then sigh. "You know, I'm not even sure that was a kiss. It felt . . . a little . . . weak."

"Weak?"

"Yeah, it was okay, but you know . . . nothing to write home about."

"Really?" He pushes his hips forward, allowing me to feel that he's very affected by our kiss. My head falls back, and I use every ounce of strength inside to keep up my bravado. "You think so?"

"I'm just telling you how it is."

I'm playing with fire and I welcome the burn. I see the heat in his eyes, and I'm more than willing to dance closer to the flames.

Eli studies me like a lion about to strike his prey. Each movement is calculating, and I know I'm going to be one happy gazelle. His lips hover above mine, washing his warm breath over my own. I keep my eyes open, playing the part I've created. My pulse races as he stares at me.

His hand grazes my neck, sliding down my shoulder before he runs his fingers across my arm. "I know you're lying, baby. I know because of the way you kiss me." His lips barely touch mine before he retreats, and I smother a whimper. "I know because I can feel how hot you are. I can see the way your body is asking for me, even if you're not. If I touched you, Heather, would you come? Would you fall apart at my touch?"

I could come just from this. "Maybe you should find out." I dare him again.

Eli smiles and leans back so we're no longer touching. His hands frame my head, using the wall to keep him upright. "I have plans today for us, but tonight, baby . . . tonight we're going to find out a lot."

I move forward, kissing him softly. "We'll just see about that."

CHAPTER FIFTEEN

"Busch Gardens?" I ask with a groan. I love this place, don't get me wrong, but Eli isn't just a guy. He's Eli fucking Walsh. Everyone knows him, and I assumed today was another private or semi-private day. For some reason, I figured he wouldn't take me where a million people with cell phones would see us.

"Relax." He takes my hand, twisting his fingers with mine.

"Eli, I'm not ready for this."

He tilts his head. "Ready for what?"

I sigh, not wanting to spell it out. "For us to be public when we're not even sure what this is."

"I promise, this isn't what you think."

I eye him carefully, not sure what the hell that means. "It's an amusement park that's always filled, what could I be misinterpreting? I'm not ready to be public. You have no idea what that'll do to me. To be exposed to the world when I'm not even sure what we are. If people see us, they'll know. I don't have the life you do. I'm a poor cop, living in a broken-down house, and I have a dying sister. My life isn't glamour, photos, and money. I just wish you would've warned me."

His thumb grazes the top of my hand before he lets go and exits the car.

I freaking hate that he does that. I like knowing what's coming, and Eli likes to keep me in suspense. I'm going to have a talk with him about this.

After a few minutes of trying to get myself prepared, I exit the car. He's leaning against the bumper and looking off toward the gates.

"Eli?"

"I know my world comes with a crazy amount of shit. I get that your life is pretty simple in that you have privacy, family, friends, and a job that doesn't come with paparazzi." There's a little bit of sadness in his voice. "I thought long and hard about today. I didn't come to this decision easily, and I assure you, your privacy won't be compromised." When I take another step closer, he moves back. "I have other sides that makes me who I am, Heather. Things that I want you to see and be a part of. Things that I value and have nothing to do with boats, houses, and cars."

He lets me move toward him this time and guilt twists in my stomach. I never realized that he may feel judged by me. That's never been my intention. I'm not one to judge anyone, and Eli has never made me feel small or less.

"I'm so sorry," I say as I touch his arm. "I shouldn't have said those things. I don't think your life is just glamour, and if I insinuated that, I'm truly sorry."

His eyes meet mine, and he rocks back on his heels. "I want you to see *me*, Heather. I want you to see the things that make me who I am, and they're not fame."

"I never thought that's who *you* are, Eli."

He extends his hand, and I don't hesitate to take it. He's right—this isn't about whatever people are going to think, it's about Ellington and me. It's about the man who keeps coming around, making me smile, and making me feel special.

Eli kisses my cheek and lets out a heavy sigh. "Let's go."

For the first time since we entered the parking garage, I look around. Where are all the cars? I count a total of twelve. Twelve cars on a Wednesday at Busch Gardens? I know it's a weekday, but this place is always packed.

"Where is everyone?"

"I told you it wasn't what you thought."

Did he rent out the damn park? My heart starts to race as my mind goes crazy. What did he do? "Eli," I say his name tentatively. "Why is no one here?"

He smiles and squeezes my hand. "I know your cop senses are flashing, but for once, just trust me and relax."

Cop senses? Huh. Now that he says that, I guess I do have them. I'm naturally untrusting and always want information. It's power in my job and allows me to stay safe. If I'm not informed when I run into a call, I might get shot, which would suck.

"I can do that," I say with as much conviction as I can muster.

Eli chuckles, which I ignore. He doesn't realize that I may have cop senses, but I'm also extremely competitive. If he doubts my ability to do something, I will find a way to do it. So, he wants me to relax, game on, buddy.

We get to the front gate, and they let us right in. I open my mouth to ask him another question and quickly close it.

We wait in the front and a man comes over. "Mr. Walsh, good morning. I'm Mr. Shea, I'll be making sure today goes smoothly. Your publicist called and gave all the names over, they've all been added to the list. Timothy should be here in the next ten minutes."

"Great." Eli's voice is full of authority. "This is Ms. Covey, she'll be with me through the day, and I'd like to ensure whatever she needs or wants during the day will be tended to."

Mr. Shea agrees. "Of course."

"Timothy is obviously my main concern. I want him to have the time of his life. Have the harnesses been acquired?" Eli questions. I probably look a bit crazy as my attention bounces back and forth between the two.

"Yes, we have everything that his team listed."

"Timothy?" I ask aloud. Does he have a kid? Am I meeting his son? Panic starts to flood, and Eli grips my hand tighter.

"He's an eleven-year-old kid from the Make-A-Wish Foundation. Timothy has terminal cancer, and one of his wishes was to meet me and ride some roller coasters. So, I rented out the park for the day so Timothy and I can ride until he's content. We have a big day in store for him."

That isn't at all what I expected, and it makes my heart sputter. Each emotion possible hits me all at once. Sadness for Timothy mixed with awe for Eli. He took time, and God knows how much money, to ensure this little boy has a day to remember.

I've been so wrong about him.

He's nothing like I could've ever known. He's everything.

Without thinking, I face him, grip his face in my hands, and kiss him. It isn't long or passionate, it's just all my emotions. I needed to kiss him because words wouldn't explain what I think.

His eyes shine with adoration, and his smile almost knocks me on my ass.

"Told you it wasn't what you thought." He taps my nose.

Mr. Shea shows us to the area where Timothy will be coming in. He has no idea that Eli is here or what the day is. Just that he's coming to the park. Eli made arrangements for his family and ten of his friends from the baseball team he played on before he was sick to come to the park, too.

We stand in an obscure part of the entrance so he doesn't

see Eli until it's time. "Thank you for letting me be a part of this," I say when we're alone.

"You may not thank me if you're not big on rides." He laughs.

"I haven't been to an amusement park since Stephanie was a kid."

"Really?"

I nod. "She got sick when she was in her first year of college. It's kind of hard to fit in roller coaster rides when you're shuffling between doctor appointments and testing. Plus, sometimes, she loses control of her hands and legs."

Eli looks away and sighs.

"You okay?" I ask.

He looks back with a sad smile. "Yeah, just thinking . . ."

"He's here." Mr. Shea appears before I can ask what he's thinking about. "We'll lead you out this way if you're ready."

Eli pauses to glance back at me. My own excitement spikes at the thought of how happy he's about to make this kid.

"Go." I smile. "I'll be right behind you."

He follows Mr. Shea out, and I follow. I can't wait to see this. I've seen these things on television but never in person.

Timothy's family all have big smiles as they see Eli come into view. I stay back, not wanting to miss a thing. Timothy's back is to us and Eli moves quietly. A few kids see Eli, and their eyes get big, jaws go slack, and they point. Timothy spins his wheelchair around and covers his open mouth with his hands. The joy, surprise, and awe are bursting from this child.

Eli moves quickly and crouches in front of him. Timothy's arms wrap around Eli's shoulders and tears fill his eyes. He keeps shaking his head and looking back at Eli. I stand here with tears falling from my face. I think about my sister and how this family feels. The small amount of joy Eli brought them in a life filled with so much heartbreak. Knowing that

Eli made this little boy's dream come true crumbles the last defensive wall I have against this man.

Eli takes the time to hug the kids and shake everyone else's hands. The boys jump around and snap pictures of him with Timothy.

His eyes meet mine, and I swipe my face, praying I don't have mascara running. He motions me over, and I plaster a smile on my lips.

"Timothy, this is my friend Heather. She loves roller coasters, too."

I squat and shake his hand. "It's nice to meet you. Though, I have to be honest, I'm a little scared of heights," I admit. "Do you think they'll be too scary for me?"

He grins. "No way, that's the best part, when you want to puke because it's so high."

"Good to know," I joke.

He looks back at Eli as if he's the coolest thing he's ever seen. "Eli, you're not scared, right?"

"Not a chance. I think we should try to make Heather as scared as we can. Maybe we can make her ride so many times in a row she gets sick," he says conspiratorially.

Timothy's eyes light up. "That would be so fun!"

Great. Now I'm going to have not only Eli but also Timothy and his friends trying to get me to puke.

"How about we go have some fun, bud? The whole park is ours so there are no lines!"

"Awesome!"

It is pretty awesome. If I were a kid, I would think this is like Christmas morning. To get an entire amusement park to myself and my closest friends would've been the best thing ever. He and his friends make a plan on the most efficient way to get all the rides in as the adults try to get them to focus.

Timothy's mom, Cindi, walks over, wraps her arms around Eli, and cries while letting out a laugh. "I can't thank you enough for this. He never could have handled a day with crowds, and you're his idol."

"I'm happy to do it. He seems like such a great kid."

"He watches your show each week. He can tell you everything you've done to save the day."

Eli laughs. "I used to watch cop shows with my dad as a kid."

"He always wanted to be a police officer." She looks wistfully at her son. "I hate that he'll never be able to do that."

Eli places his hand on her shoulder and squeezes. "If there's anything I can do."

Cindi shakes her head. "You have no idea what this will mean to him. To hang out with you and have a day where it isn't about cancer. He can just be a kid today."

The parallels I feel for his mother are everywhere. I know the fear, the hate, and helplessness she feels. Watching her son smile because of the man in front of me will carry her through the dark days. He has no idea that this gesture will not only mean the world to Timothy but also to all those around him.

He turns back to me, taking my hand in his. "My girlfr—" His lips press together, stopping the word. "Heather is a police officer, I'm sure Timothy will love hearing real stories from her."

She smiles at me. "Oh, if he finds that out, you're in big trouble."

I laugh. "I'm happy to take him on a ride along if I can get clearance from my boss."

Her smile is huge, and she pulls me into her arms. "Bless you both."

"Mom!" Timothy yells, breaking the moment the three of us were sharing. "You gotta see this, Mom! Eli, are you coming?"

"I'll be right there, dude. I just need to take care of something."

Timothy waves, and his friends run with him in the wheel-chair all screaming and laughing.

Eli turns back to me and grins. "Are you okay with this being our date today?"

"Oh my God, I'm more than okay with it. Thank you for letting me be here."

His hand cups my cheek, and I lean into his touch. He looks over my shoulder and then back to me. "I have another surprise for today."

"You do?"

His gaze shifts, and I follow it.

Never in a million years would I have guessed this would be the surprise.

But sure enough, my sister is coming toward me with a huge smile. Anthony pushes her in the wheelchair, and I gasp.

Stephanie holds her arms out, and I run to her. "I told you I'd see you!" She laughs.

I hug her tightly, overcome with another wash of emotion. "How?" I pull back. "How are you here?"

She smiles and lifts her chin, motioning to Eli. "He came by the hospital and told me about today."

I turn to him, eyes wide and full of tears. "You met Stephanie?"

"After our boat date," he admits.

"You went and spent time with my sister?"

"She's important to you, and she's pretty cool."

I move quickly, jumping into his arms and wrapping my legs around his torso. He catches me and laughs. I lean back and plant my mouth to his. He'll never truly get that this means more to me than anything else he could've done. I don't need fancy things. I need someone to care. I need to rely on someone, which isn't something I've had since I was eighteen.

Here Eli stands, caring about me enough to take time to go on his own and meet Stephanie.

"Get a room," Stephanie jokes.

I slide down his body and kiss him again. "Thank you."

"You're welcome, sweetheart."

We all enter the park, and Mr. Shea radios to find out where Timothy is. As we make our way there, I'm smiling so hard my cheeks hurt. My sister is with us, and we have the entire park to explore. Eli offers me a little bit more of his heart, and I give him a piece of mine.

As we all make our way to the first ride, I grip Eli's arm and stop him. I feel like I wasn't clear enough about how much I appreciate what he did. "I don't think I thanked you properly."

He smiles. "I think you leaping into my arms was clear."

"No." I shake my head. "I don't think you understand how much it means to me. For you not only to meet my sister but also to bring her here to something without me saying anything . . ."

Eli turns, cups my face, and presses his forehead to mine. When he pulls back, his eyes are filled with something that simmers on the edge of love. "She's important to you, which means that if you and I have any chance at a future, she's important to me, too. I wanted to meet her and let her see what I'm doing isn't a game. I'm not a guy who fucks around with people. I've always been honest of my intentions when it comes to you. I want your heart and your trust."

"I think you're going to win it all." The admission falls from my lips with ease.

He grins. "I sure plan on it."

I don't doubt he will, either. My heart races as I look in to his eyes, the determination stuns me. I'm not sure why this gorgeous man has decided he wants me. It baffles me, but I'm not questioning it anymore.

He's sweet, thoughtful, considerate, and I know that my heart has no chance of resisting him.

"Eli! Come on! We need to get Heather on this ride!" Timothy yells, and Eli laughs, breaking away from me.

"We're coming," he informs Timothy and takes my hand.

We walk toward him, and then Eli stops, grabbing his leg and massaging his calf.

"You okay?" I ask.

"I'm fine, I'm just getting old."

I laugh and pat his back. "Aww is the big sexy rock star not able to keep up?"

He pulls himself upright and smirks. "I'll show you later."

Heat pools in my core at the promises he's made about tonight. But Timothy cuts off my response.

"Come on, guys! I bet Heather is going to cry when she sees this one!"

Eli chuckles and looks at the roller coaster in front of us. "I bet she will, buddy. Wonder if the big bad police officer is too much of a chicken," Eli taunts me by using the words I just did.

I rise to the challenge. "Twenty bucks say you both scream like little girls!"

"Game on."

The rest of the day, I ride more rollercoasters than I care to admit, most of them for Timothy's amusement. He laughs each time my face pales at the peak of the incline and laughs hysterically each time I have to take a minute to settle my stomach. However, Timothy thinks that because I'm a cop, I have no fear. He eggs me on, and I agree because it's pretty impossible to say no to this kid.

Our day is perfect. I sneak kisses in with Eli and laugh with Stephanie after she actually does puke after the Scrambler ride.

She and Timothy take long breaks together, talking about their stays at the hospital and how much they hate needles. It's the first time in a long time that I've gotten to see her through the eyes of a big sister. Just as any good little sister would, she coerces Timothy to ask Eli to sing for the group.

"Please, Eli," Timothy whines. "I didn't get to go to your concert last time because I was in the hospital."

"Come on," Stephanie pipes in. "Timothy really wants to see this. You wouldn't want to disappoint him, would you?"

Eli lets out a nervous laugh and stands. "I don't have my group or music, though."

"Who cares!" Timothy says. "I have my phone!" He grabs the phone from his pocket and puts on the song Eli sang to me at the concert.

I smile at the memory of the night we met. It seems like so long ago, but it's only been three weeks. It's crazy how fast my feelings for him have changed. I giggle as he spins and does his best to entertain the crowd in a private concert.

Apparently, Eli isn't content being the center of attention, and decides to embarrass the shit out of me by pulling me out of the group. Once again, Eli serenades me. Only this time, it's much more intimate, and I'm not drinking. He gets on his knees in front of me, belting out the lyrics, and in true fashion, I turn bright red. My limbs are numb and each time I try to move away, he pulls me closer.

The song ends, and he bows as the group erupts with applause. Timothy claps the loudest and I bury my head in his chest, shielding myself from seeing anyone's face.

Once it's over, we go back to the rides for a while more. The sun begins to set, and I wish I could freeze time. If today could last forever, I'd be happy. It's been a day of celebration. It isn't focused on what the people who are suffering can't do, but all the ways they still live.

Stephanie wheels herself over to Timothy, who looks so tired I think he may fall asleep right here. "So, did you have fun?" she asks him.

He opens his eyes with a smile. "Today was awesome."

"I agree, kid."

"The cancer makes me so tired, and it's in my bones now."
He rubs his arm and winces.

Stephanie reaches her hand over, touching his. "I understand. I'll need a lot of sleep tomorrow."

"It was worth it." He yawns. "It was the best day of my
life."

Stephanie smiles at me and Eli. "Anthony and I have to go.
I'm exhausted and need to rest. My head hurts, and my
muscles are tight."

"Do you want me to come with you?" I ask.

"No!" She pretty much yells before dissolving into a
giggle. "No, I'll be fine, Heather. Stay with Eli and come see
me tomorrow or the day after, okay?"

Eli kisses her cheek, and her hand covers it. "Thank you. I
really hope you stick around."

He grins. "I plan to."

"I love you," she says to me.

I kiss her forehead and smile. "I love you more."

I watch as Anthony fusses over her as they exit, and then
we move over to Timothy hand in hand.

"I'm glad I got to spend the day with you," I say to him.

"Me, too," Timothy says and then looks at Eli. "I had so
much fun."

Eli pulls his small body into his arms and holds him tight.
"Thank you for giving me today, Timothy. I'll never forget
spending the day with you."

Timothy looks up with tears in his eyes. "When I go to
Heaven, I'm going to tell God about today. I'm going to tell
him how meeting you was the best day of my life."

My hand flies to my throat, and I work hard not to fall
apart. Eli doesn't do as well. He pulls Timothy to his chest
again and shakes his head. "I hope that day is a long time from
now."

Cindi, who has been watching the exchange, is crying as her family holds her tight. We all know the truth is that day is coming sooner than it should.

Eli tenderly places him back in the wheelchair before whispering something to him and kissing the top of his head. Then he makes his way to Cindi and does his best to comfort her. She thanks him repeatedly, and then he's at my side.

We watch as they leave, neither of us moving as he grips my hand.

After a few minutes, I turn into him. His arm is around my shoulder, and I hold his waist. "Today was . . ." I'm not sure how to express it, but I want to try. "It was everything. Not because you did something extraordinary for me, but because of the whole day. Seeing you with Timothy and his family, I can't tell you how much I'll cherish this."

Eli's gaze moves to mine, and I'm almost startled by what I see. There's an openness that is a gift. He's giving me access to his soul, and it's the most beautiful thing in the world. "I meant it, I want you to know me. I want to spend every possible day we have together in Tampa with you. I want to win your heart, Heather." He wraps his arms around my waist. "I'm forty-two and this is the first time in my life I've wanted to share myself. Randy used to say I was wasting time by not settling down, I think I was biding time until I found someone worthy."

I touch his cheek, waiting for him to disappear like an apparition. Guys like him don't exist, do they?

"And you think you were waiting for me?" I question.

"I think you make me feel like no one else has. I know that I want to give you things I've never given anyone else and make you proud to know me. It's a foreign feeling."

"You're not the only one who is feeling things that are foreign," I explain. "I promised myself after my ex that I wouldn't let another man in my heart. I lose everyone I care about. Until I met you, I was doing a great job keeping that promise. I've been able to shut it down before, but with you, I can't."

Eli has a way of making me forget that I'm not supposed to like him. He's leaving. He's famous. He's a heartbreaker . . . and yet, here I stand, wanting him anyway. The fact that he's so much more of a complication than I could ever want is scary, but maybe I need the fear. Maybe the fear is my way of knowing he's worth the chance.

His thumb brushes my lips. "I'm glad you can't."

"I'm starting to be as well."

Eli stands on my doorstep and I know without a shadow of a doubt what I want. I want to be with him. I want to be with him in every way.

"I'm going to see my brother next week, I'd love for you to come meet him," he says as I fumble with the lock.

Our ride home was quiet but comfortable. I was thinking about the events of today. How he orchestrated everything and cared to make it special for me. It's something that I still can't get a handle on.

"I'd like that. So, since I'm willing to meet your brother then you have to meet my friends."

"Do I?" he tilts his head to the side.

"It's only fair."

"I wouldn't want to have the scales tipped in my favor now."

He's too much. "One of my best friends, Danielle, has her big annual barbeque this weekend. I'd really love it if you'd come."

I don't have a big family for him to meet, but my girls are just as important to me. We're kind of a package deal and I want him to know them. It's also about time they learn about the relationship that's happening between us.

"You're inviting me to something?"

"It would appear so."

"For an event in a few days?"

It's amazing how much fun he seems to have giving me shit.

"Yes, Eli, an event, with my friends, in three days."

"I knew you liked me."

I smile and shake my head. "I guess you're kind of a keeper."

Eli's hands slide up my back and grip my shoulders. My hands tremble, and I finally get the door open. "Heather," Eli's voice is low with a hint of desire, "why are you so nervous?"

My eyes meet his. "Because I want you to spend the night." I blurt out before I lose my nerve. "I want you to stay."

"Are you sure?"

"Yes."

And I am. I've never been more sure of anything. It isn't only the emotions of today—it's him. It's everything about this man that has me so torn up. Eli wanted me to see him, I did, and now I want all of him.

He moves quickly, lifting me and then carrying me over the threshold. I press my lips to his as he kicks the door closed. My hands are buried in his thick brown hair as I kiss him.

"Bedroom?" Eli grunts as he bumps into the table.

I giggle and point. Our smiles are bright as he moves us. His mouth finds mine again, and he crashes into the wall. "Ouch." I laugh.

"Sorry. I promise I'll make it up to you as soon as we find your damn bed."

"Promises, promises," I tease.

"You know I make good on them."

Oh, yes, I do.

We get to my bedroom without further injury, and he places me in front of him. The moonlight shines through the windows, illuminating the planes of his face. My fingers lift, rubbing the stubble on his cheek. Slowly, my hand drifts to the other side, memorizing his features. The tip of my finger touches the small beauty mark under his left eye and then to the faint dimple on the right before moving across his lips.

I meet his gaze, and it feels like a thousand words pass between us. So many questions, promises, and worries, but I put my arms around him. I hope that, while we're wrapped up in each other's arms, we'll find the answers.

"I know you've been hurt, but I won't hurt you, Heather. I want to be the guy you can count on. I'm not sure how to make this work. But I'm not going to let you go. Not without one hell of a fight."

"I worry about tomorrow," I confess.

Eli brushes the hair off my face and kisses my lips. "We can't worry about tomorrow, we can only own tonight. And tonight, I'm going to make sure you never forget how good we are. When you want to run away, I want this to be what you remember."

I don't doubt I'll ever forget those words. There's moments in my life that I've cherished, and this will be one of them. The way he looks at me eradicates all the doubts I've held onto. The tenderness in his touch extinguishes the fears of our future together.

Even if this is the last night we ever share, I'll never regret it.

"I don't want to run anymore." My words are filled with honesty.

"I won't let you."

I hold his face in my hands, bring our lips together, and kiss him. Eli takes control, brushing his tongue against mine.

Both our breaths are heavy as we drink each other in. This man can kiss like no other.

Eli pushes me to my back, and my heart takes off in a gallop. I watch his hands move from my hips, up my chest, and then he removes my shirt. "You're the most beautiful thing in the world," he comments while looking down at me.

My nerves bubble up, but the look in his eyes stops them. There's no mistaking the passion there, but under that layer is so much honesty, it knocks the wind out of me. "The way you look at me . . ." I mutter.

"Is the way you make me feel," Eli finishes my half statement.

Every thought in my mind is gone. I can't hold on to anything long enough for it to make sense. The only thing I know is that I need him. I need to touch him and make him feel everything I'm feeling.

"Kiss me," I request.

He doesn't make me wait, his mouth is on mine in an instant. His hand cups my cheek, providing the tenderness to offset the force of his lips. I try to pull his shirt off, needing the skin-to-skin connection, but I can't remove it.

Eli does that guy move where he reaches behind his back and pulls his shirt off in one move. God he's sexy. I love watching the muscles tense as my fingers explore him.

I stare at the ink I've come to love so much. The arrows on the inside of his bicep, the words on his hip and his arm, the cross on his shoulder, and wanting to see the birds on his back. My hands glide across the one that goes from his side down over his hip. "Tell me about this one," my voice is soft.

"It's to remind me that I don't have a right to judge anyone. To each his own."

"And the birds?"

Eli moves my hair from my forehead and hesitates. "To remind me that even though I feel caged, I'm free."

A part of my heart breaks at the sullen tone in his voice. "Do you feel caged?"

"Not when I'm with you."

"I'm glad." I move my fingers higher, loving that he allows me to touch him freely. "This one?" I graze along his shoulder following the shape of the cross.

"Perspective."

I regard him with bewilderment. I definitely didn't expect that answer, and I'm not sure what it means.

Eli seems to sense my confusion, and he gently brushes his nose against mine. "When things in life get hard to deal with, it's easy to be angry, blame others, and forget all the good. Each day I see that tattoo, it gives me strength, humility, and drive to live the way I want."

"Why do you have to be so perfect?" I ask.

His fingers slide against my neck and his lips brush against mine. "It's only because you're meant for me. I'm not perfect, baby. We're just perfect together."

His mouth crushes down on mine with so much passion I feel it through my toes. The power in his touch rocks me to my core. Our connection is so much stronger than the night of the concert. Tonight isn't about hooking up with Eli Walsh. It's about Ellington, the man that is stealing my heart so effortlessly. The man I'm quite possibly falling in love with.

He pulls the straps of my bra off slowly, placing soft kisses on my neck before fully removing it. Our mouths find each other again as his hand moves to my breast. Pulling the nipple between his fingers, rolling it, causing me to moan.

"I love the sounds you make," he declares as his mouth moves lower.

"You make me feel so good."

He groans, peeking at me as his tongue glides around my skin. "I love the way you taste, too. I'm going to savor you all night long."

Gone is the sweetness in his eyes, desire has burned it all away.

"Eli," I breathe his name as he licks around my nipple before taking it in his mouth. My hand is in his hair, fisting it and holding him there as his other hand moves to my shorts. Without much effort, he has me fully naked beneath him.

He moves back to my mouth, kissing me hard while he drives me crazy with his hands. I gasp when his finger finds my clit and he makes a circular motion. My body responds, causing warmth to flow through my veins. Everything he does feels so good. I move against him, wanting more and yet wanting to go slower.

"You're so fucking sexy when you're like this," he murmurs against my ear. "When my hands are on your body, making you feel good, it's so hot, baby."

Eli increases the pressure and then inserts a finger. My head lolls to the side as he continues to drive me crazy. "Please," I beg.

"Please, what?" he asks as his teeth nibble my lobe.

I don't answer him because I really don't know what I'm asking for. Just him. I need more of Eli. My fingers tangle in his hair while he continues to finger me and rub my clit.

My mouth falls open as I'm right at the pinnacle of my orgasm, and then I plummet over the edge. He moans against my neck while I scream his name.

Eli looks at me with a self-satisfied smirk.

The need to make him feel as good as he makes me feel takes over. I want to make him go crazy. My hand slides down his chest, and I remove his shorts quickly, freeing his cock. He allows me to push him onto his back with ease.

"Fuck," he grunts as I grip him.

"I want to hear you make noises this time, baby."

I pull my blonde hair to the side and kiss my way to his

abdomen. My tongue leaves a trail leading to where I plan to go.

He leans on his elbows, keeping his eyes on me as I move lower. "I want to watch you suck my cock." His voice is thick with longing.

"Well . . ." I kiss all the way down his six-pack. "It looks like you're going to get your wish."

Eli does exactly what he wanted, he watches my lips kiss the tip of his cock. I want him to fall apart because of me. As much as he wants me to remember this night, I want the same. Our relationship is filled with obstacles that we'll either hurdle or trip over. I'm fully aware there are no guarantees, but I can give him this. I can give myself this.

I wrap my lips around his cock, pulling him deep into my mouth as I bob up and down, paying attention to the underside with my tongue. The noises that fall from his lips are exactly what I want to hear. He mumbles and moans as I take him deeper.

Hollowing out my cheeks, I force him to the back of my throat. Eli's fingers grip my hair, pulling just enough to spur me harder. I love that he's losing control. I bask in the fact that it's my body, my mouth, and our connection that's stealing his restraint.

"Heather! Fuck. Baby! Fuck! You have to stop." He groans. "I want to be inside you."

No arguments here.

He pulls me off him and flips me so fast I'm not even sure how it happened. But he throws my legs over his shoulder, and now it's my turn to watch. "First, I'm going to taste you. I'm going to make you scream my name while I bury myself in your pussy."

Dear God.

Eli does exactly as he promised. His tongue flicks my clit over and over, while I fist the sheets. He varies from fast to slow, drawing another orgasm to build. "Oh my God," I breathe as he continues.

I never want this to end. I fight it off, wanting tonight to last as long as possible. If we can make love all night, I'd be happy, but Eli has no intention of delaying my orgasm. He licks and sucks the bundle of nerves until I'm panting incoherently. Then his finger enters me, curling up, and I fall to pieces. "Eli!"

A sheen of sweat covers my skin, and I fight to catch my breath. The aftershocks of my second orgasm seem to be unending. I hear him tear open the condom wrapper, and when I open my eyes, he's braced above me.

I touch his cheek, and he kisses my nose.

Eli lines himself up, ready to enter me. "I need to be inside you. I can't wait another second, tell me you want this."

It's more than want, it's beyond that. I know that when we connect this time, it'll be different. This is me giving him so much more than just one night. This is special, meaningful, and a part of my soul will forever be his. I won't be able to brush this off, and I don't want to. No matter what tomorrow brings, I know that tonight, he owns my heart.

"I want you. I want this. I want us."

Eli fills me completely. My body, my heart, and my mind are consumed by him. The intangible connection that has been between us since the first moment, grows stronger, brighter with each stroke.

Our eyes stay trained on each other's as we make love. It's the most open I've ever allowed myself to be. There are no walls around us right now as we share ourselves. My every emotion is his to have and he shares the same gift.

I tip my hips back, drawing him deeper inside me than seems possible. Eli's jaw clenches as he picks up the pace. "Baby," he grunts. "Fuck. I can't hold back."

There's no way this can be happening, but it is, I build

again. "Don't stop," I request as my body pulsates with pleasure.

Eli's hips slam into mine, driving himself harder. The sweat drips down his face, and his finger finds my clit. I close my eyes as I shatter apart, calling out his name as his release rocks though him at the same time. "Heather!" Eli yells and then collapses on top of me.

Moments pass, and I can't bring myself to open my eyes as I feel him slip from the bed. He isn't gone long, and when he comes back, he gathers me into his arms. Our legs are tangled together, my head rests on his chest as his fingers make patterns on my back. Neither of us says anything, we lie here, lost in all that just was.

In all my thirty-eight years, I have never experienced sex like that. It was truly two people coming together as one. We were one heartbeat, one breath, one moment in time where there was nothing other than us.

"You okay?" Eli asks.

"I'm more than okay. What about you?"

Eli makes a humming noise of contentment. I twist my head to look at his face. "That good, huh?"

His eyes open and he winks. "I'm pretty sure you've ruined me."

I laugh. "You ruined me right back."

It's completely true. I'll never recover from this night.

"Are you hungry?" I ask as his stomach growls.

"I'm not moving right now," he informs me.

Works for me.

I rub my hand on his shoulder and sigh. "I like this."

"Cuddling?"

"Cuddling with you."

He chuckles. "You could've had this the first night, but you ran out."

My cheeks burn, remembering the frantic way I threw my

clothes on and rushed off the bus. "Because I had sex with you!"

"We had sex just now," Eli reminds me as if I could possibly forget.

"So not the same."

"We can't go backward this time."

I brush my thumb across his lower lip. "Please don't make me care about you if you're going to leave me."

That is the bottom line to all my issues. When I care about someone, they're gone. If I fall in love with him and lose him, I don't know if I'll endure.

"I'm not going anywhere."

"Good."

"So, was tonight better than the first time? Or do I need to go again to be sure?" His brow raises, and I smack his chest.

"Yes, Eli, your performance was stellar."

"Medal worthy?"

I push onto my elbow, but he pulls me back down. "You're such a guy."

"I damn well better be. I'm pretty confident I just proved it as well. How many orgasms was that? Two?"

Three, but I'm not telling him that. His ego is already inflated. "You should know if you were gifting them out."

"I'm like fucking Santa Claus, only I come every night with your presents."

I burst out laughing and roll off his chest. He shifts so he's braced over me and gives me a brilliant smile.

"You're really lucky you're so hot. If you keep saying shit like that, no woman is going to stick around."

Eli's emerald eyes pierce mine. "There's only one woman I'm worried about right now."

I smile, wrap my arms around his neck, and pull him in for a kiss. "Good answer."

His stomach growls even louder than the first time. He

pulls back with a different need in his eyes. "On second thought . . . what kind of food do you have?"

"How do you feel about junk food?" I ask.

I throw on Eli's T-shirt and hop out of bed. I'm a closet junk food freak. There's something about cookies that I can't quit no matter how many hours I have to spend at the gym to burn off the calories. We make our way into the kitchen, grab a few things, and plop on the couch.

"No judging." I point at him. "I like food."

His hands rise. "None here."

I take the first Double Stuffed Oreo out and twist the cookie apart. The obvious thing would be to lick the icing before eating the cookie part, however, that isn't how I roll. Instead, I grab one of the Chips Ahoy cookies and place it between the two halves, making an Oreo and Chips Ahoy cookie sandwich. I like chocolate chip cookies, and I love the icing from Oreos—so, this is my perfect cookie.

Eli watches as I take a bite, a moan filling the silence. Heaven in my mouth.

"Did you just orgasm?" he asks with a throaty chuckle.

"Wouldn't you like to know?"

I scarf down two more cookies that way without feeling self-conscious at all. Eli doesn't make me feel guilty or as if I shouldn't be eating these things. Matt would always remind me that I wasn't in college anymore and my figure wouldn't remain. Just another vast difference in them.

"Your sister looked good," Eli says before he pops a chip in his mouth.

I nod. "Today was a good day, yesterday wasn't."

"Does she have more good than bad?"

I sigh and drop the Frankensteined Oreo I'm making. I wish I could tell him that she did, but the last few months have definitely been weighted toward bad. "Huntington's doesn't usually get better. It gets progressively worse. Because

Steph was so young when she presented, we were told the decline would most likely be like falling off a cliff."

Eli takes my hand in his, probably hearing the pain in my voice. "What does that mean?"

"That once she starts to go downhill, it'll be very hard and fast. There won't be weeks and months of her suffering, though. That's the one thing she says is her silver lining. I don't know if it's better or worse that way. I've had a few years with her symptoms being pretty mild, but I can't say watching her struggle isn't the worst part. I don't know how I've survived so far. When my parents died, we didn't have a warning. There was no time to worry. With Stephanie it's the opposite, I'm literally watching her life slip away. I've been doing it with no one to help me keep it together."

His fingers go limp and he pulls his hand up, rubbing it with the other. "I wish I could say something to make this easier for you."

I shrug even though nothing we're talking about feels casual. "Tell me you're not going to leave me, Eli. Because I can't let myself keep falling for you if this is only going to end with you walking out the door."

"Come here," he says as he opens his arms. I don't waver, I move into his embrace, allowing him to hold me firm. "I'm not going to leave you."

Being vulnerable is a scary thing. It's hard to give anyone, let alone Eli, unfettered access to my biggest fear. I've been alone for a long time, and I've learned to handle it. This, though? I have no idea how to handle. Having a taste of Eli's affection is enough to make me an addict. The more time we spend together, the more I crave him.

"You're leaving soon."

It's the elephant in the room. We can pretend all we want that Eli isn't who he is, but there is a reality we need to face. He has to go back to New York in less than two weeks. Our time is fading before my eyes as well. I know it's his job, I would never ask him to stay, but I'll be without him. Three weeks ago, I could've said goodbye and walked away, but when my heart entangled with his, it complicated things. Why can't I fall for a normal guy? Why do I pick the one man who literally lives every single one of my insecurities? Because I'm dumb, that's why.

Eli's arm tightens. "That part sucks, but it won't be that long. We take breaks during filming, I can come here or you can come spend time in New York. I meant what I said, Heather, we'll make this work."

"I have work, too. And Steph."

"I know, I'm not asking you to give up anything, just make room for me."

When he says it like that, it seems so simple.

"Nicole, Kristin, and Denise?" I ask, trying to get the names right. Heather's best friends are her family, and I'd like not to look like a total douche in front of them.

"Danielle, or Danni for short. That's whose house this is." She corrects as she parks in front of a house in West Chase. It's a modest two-story house on a cul-de-sac, complete with a picket fence and all.

I'm adaptable, but my life hasn't ever been normal. I'm not sure what the hell I was thinking agreeing to this.

Heather watches me, and then I remember why—her. She wanted me here to meet her friends, and that's exactly what I'm going to do. "Are you okay?" she asks.

"It's going to be great, baby. Do they know I'm coming?"

I should've asked this earlier.

"Umm, well, I kind of didn't say anything."

I'm not sure if this is because she didn't think we'd make it to the weekend or because she didn't want her friends to freak. Well, here goes nothing.

I take her small hand in mine and smile. "Let's go surprise them."

Her one friend, I remember. Nothing specific, but she was who came back stage and urged Heather to come with me, I make a mental note to thank her.

There are a few guys standing over by the front of the yard, pointing at something on the ground, and the smell of food cooking on a grill fills the air. I'm in suburbia and completely out of my element.

We exit the car and the two guys who were shooting the shit stop and look. "Heather," guy number one calls her name.

"Hi, Peter." She smiles and waves.

They both head over and Peter extends his hand. "Hi, I'm Peter Bergen."

"Eli Walsh," I say, shaking his hand.

I watch as recognition sinks in. "Right, of course." He looks at the other guy. "Eli, this is Scott McGee."

We shake, and Scott stares me down. What the fuck is wrong with him? "Nice to meet you both." I try to keep my instant dislike to myself.

I wrap my arm around Heather, pulling her into my side. I don't like these guys, well, the one at least.

"Same here. The girls are around back," Peter says to her.

"Thanks." She smiles, but it isn't a real one. It seems I'm not the only one who doesn't care for these dickheads.

"What's their issue?" I ask once we're out of earshot.

She laughs. "Nicole and I hate them. Scott is the worst, but Kristin just makes excuses for him. Peter isn't that bad, he's just a sheep and follows what the first idiot says."

We make our way around the back of the house, and I take it all in. Kids run around in all directions, spraying each other with water guns. The women all have their backs to us, laughing and arranging the food table. It's exactly like the parties my mom threw when Randy and I were kids.

"Heather!" one of her friends yells and then drops the bowl she was holding. "Holy fuck!"

Heather steps forward, pulling me with her. "Danni, this is Eli, I hope it's okay that I brought a date?"

I flash one of my million dollar smiles and move toward her. Her eyes haven't moved from my face, and I'm pretty sure she's shaking. "Thanks for having me. Heather said you have the best party of the summer."

"I-I-I," she stammers. "You're . . . you . . . in my . . . Eli."

Heather laughs and nudges Danielle. "I wanted you guys to meet him officially."

The girl I remember comes walking straight up to me. "I'm Nicole, we met briefly, you may not remember because you were kind of busy trying to get in my best friend's pants, which you did. Good job on that."

"Thanks." I laugh. "And I remember you from climbing the fence."

She huffs and gives Heather a dirty look. "Yeah, she's an asshole for that, but it seems you found your way over it as well. Don't fuck it up, and I won't have to blow your nuts off."

"Nicole!" Heather screams and turns to me. "I'm so sorry. I should've warned you about her. We think she has a mental disorder that affects her ability to think before she speaks."

I burst out laughing. "I like her."

"Oh, God." Heather covers her face. "Don't feed the animals, Eli, they bite."

I say hello to her other friend, who I assume is Kristin since she stands there like a statue without saying a word. Her gaze moves from Heather to me and then back again. I've never understood the awe of famous people. We're normal and have the same issues that everyone else does. The only difference is that I travel, have no friends, and I deal with other famous assholes. It's not all it's cracked up to be.

Heather and two of the girls head inside to get some food together and probably talk about me. Nicole laughs when they ask if she's going to help, and instead, sits beside me with a beer in each hand. "You're going to need this." She hands me one of the bottles.

"Thanks."

"I want you to know that Heather is special."

I guess since there's no father or brother in the picture, I'm going to get the speech from her best friend.

"I agree."

She takes a swig and nods. "I think you're good for her. I've known her my whole life, and there's something different about her since you came around."

"Aren't you breaking some kind of girl code?" I ask.

I'm not sure how these things work with chicks, but if I'm basing it off my experience with Savannah, they're all deranged. She and her friends talk in some alternate language that Randy and I tried to decode once. In the end, we gave up and decided being on the inside wasn't worth it. However, I know she's talked about never breaking the code. Whatever the fuck that means.

"She knows me too well. I don't have a code."

"Good to know." I laugh as I take a pull from my beer.

"I heard about what you did for her sister."

I know this is a test. What I say now will determine if Nicole helps or hurts me. So far, I think she's been pro-Eli, but that can change. I'm not a fool.

"What's important to Heather should be important to who she dates, don't you think?"

She smiles and then catches herself. "Not all men feel that way. Some think they should be most important. I'm sure in your world it's that way a lot?"

There are days when I wish people could see the shit I go through. It may look all wonderful on the outside, but it isn't when you live it. I get hounded by the press, followed by the paparazzi, and forget having any kind of privacy. The only reason I have an ounce of it with Heather is because I'm here.

Tampa is where I can be low key. But if Heather and I went to dinner in public, you can bet your ass I'll have photos taken, which will bring the headlines, questions, assumptions, and everything else. I don't think that was her point, though. I have a feeling it's about the loser she married before me.

I weigh my words carefully. "It can be, but not where the people I care about are concerned. Sure, the people who want something from me treat me differently, but if you met my brother or his wife, you'd know that's not the case. I'm fully aware of Heather's situation and only a selfish piece of shit would put her in a position to choose."

Nicole looks off at the kids running around and then back to me. "I'm protective of her."

"I'm glad."

"I won't let you hurt her," she warns.

"I don't ever want to hurt her."

Quite the contrary, actually. I want to be her protector, her sense of comfort, and the one who she can rely on. It's a primal desire to take care of her. I just don't know if she'll let me.

"Wanting and doing are two different things and people tend to protect themselves over another."

Her words strike me deep in my heart. Is that what I'm doing? Knowingly keeping things from her to protect myself? To be able to have whatever I can have with her at her expense? I hate myself in this very moment.

CHAPTER EIGHTEEN

"There you are," I smile when I find Eli still sitting with Nicole in the backyard. His eyes are filled with sorrow when they meet mine. "Eli?"

With a blink, the sadness is gone. "Hey."

"What's wrong?" I ask quickly and glare at Nicole. I'll kill her if she said something stupid.

"Don't look at me." She waves her hand. "I was warning Eli of all the ways I'll make his life miserable if he hurts you."

Seriously, I wonder if I can have her committed. I know she's being a friend, but Jesus, she's a pain in the ass. "Could you not scare him off so soon?" I ask.

Eli pulls me to his side. "I'm good. It takes a lot to scare me off. Besides, I'm pretty sure Nicole would like to meet a certain member of the band, right?" He kisses my shoulder, and I chuckle.

In one of our recent conversations, I told him the stories of Kristin's tickets, Danielle licking the poster, and Nicole's obsession with his brother. He called his publicist right away and got something special for each of the girls. I laughed hysterically when he told me they took a photo of Shaun licking his own poster for Danielle. I'm sure her dumbass husband is going to be thrilled.

"Shut up!" Nicole yells. "I can't believe you told him!"

I shrug.

She turns her gaze back to Eli and huffs. "I know he's married and all, but seriously, your brother has always been my favorite."

Eli and Nicole are sitting on the table portion of the picnic table, and he pulls me so I'm sitting between his legs. I rest my hand on his thigh as they talk about how his sister-in-law would laugh so hard she'd pee herself hearing people talk about Randy. He tried to tell Nicole that he isn't all that special, but she's a dog with a bone, and there's no changing her mind.

Nicole heads inside for another drink and then the guys come over, striking up a conversation with Eli. I sit, bored and then I encourage him to go look at whatever the hell they're talking about. The three guys walk away, and I can't wipe the smile off my face. He looks so domestic right now, and it's adorable.

"Look what I got," Nicole calls me over by holding the sangria she's famous for.

"You're the best."

I take the glass, and we both take a seat away from everyone. "I think he really likes you, babe," Nicole says as she watches me watch Eli.

"Yeah?"

She smiles. "He's a good guy. Keep your heart open to him. I know you guys have a ton of obstacles, but he passes the best friend test."

I think Nicole forgets we're almost forty, and I don't need her approval. Still, I'm glad I have it. She tends to see through people's bullshit easier than anyone else. She also would never say it if she didn't mean it.

"I love you." I pull her close.

"I love you even though I'm jealous you're sleeping with a God each night."

"What about your threesome?"

She scoffs. "I'm over those two, I think they wanted to fuck each other more than they wanted to fuck me, and if I'm taking two men to bed, I better be the center of the world. I have my eye on someone else."

My jaw falls slack, even though I'm not sure why. This is Nicole. She's always been this way, and I'd be worried if she weren't. "I can only imagine what the hell you're up to now."

Danielle comes over and touches my shoulder. "I can't believe you kept this from us."

I wanted to keep Eli to myself for as long as possible. Plus, I don't talk to them as much as I talk to Nicole. They're in marriages that are hanging on by a thread, and their advice is always so off base.

"Oh, please," Nic pipes up. "Wouldn't you want to keep that a secret? Look at him, he's Eli Walsh. If I had him in my bed, he'd never leave, maybe bathroom breaks, but then back to the good stuff." She winks at me and grins.

"Well, cat's out of the bag now, tell us every glorious detail," Kristin says through a giggle.

We sit like we're kids again, gossiping about our first kiss, and I divulge my last few weeks with Eli.

"HOW ABOUT WE go to my place tonight?" Eli offers.

So far, he's stayed at my house each night. I don't know if it was him trying to fit into my world or show he's fairly normal, but I've appreciated it. Tonight, though, I want to show him the same. His world and my world will need to mesh, and that won't happen by forcing him to fit only in my space.

"I'd like that."

Eli takes my hand and kisses the top of it. "I'm going to like seeing you in my home."

I like that he wants me there at all. I want to make him happy, too. Today was amazing. I knew he was uncomfortable at first, but he joked with my friends, did his best to put up with their husbands, and was all around perfect. I'd catch him watching me, smiling, or finding little ways to touch me. He was taking care of me without me even realizing it.

"Thank you for today."

"I had fun, your friends are great."

"They're something all right."

Eli laughs. "Nicole genuinely loves you."

"I'm lucky to have her." As much as she drives me batshit crazy, I could never imagine life without her. "All of them really, but Nicole and I have always been the closest."

I tell Eli a little about our childhoods, which makes me laugh. We were not all that bright back then. I don't know how we didn't land ourselves in jail. My mother would've beaten my ass if she knew half the dumb stuff we tried. Kristin was always the goody two-shoes out of our clique, and our parents allowed us to do anything as long as she was there, too. I guess they hoped she'd somehow talk us out of it, the problem was, we usually talked her into things.

"Wait, you actually tried to hop the fence to get into Busch Gardens?"

"It was a dare." If you told Nicole and me that we couldn't do it, we found a way. "Nicole's boyfriend worked there and said it was impossible."

"Did it work?"

We pull into Eli's driveway and he parks the car. He looks over, waiting for me to answer.

"You saw firsthand how well we climb fences. We're no better now than we were then."

Eli's deep laughter fills the car, and he slaps the steering wheel as he lets it out. "That was the best thing I've ever seen."

I roll my eyes and cross my arms. "It was self-preservation." It was dumb. I know it, and I can't imagine how ridiculous we must have looked to someone else. At least I wore pants that day, otherwise, I'd have been even more mortified.

"From what?"

"From realizing I just slept with you."

Eli shakes his head at my rationality. "I'm not sure if I should be offended. It was definitely a first for me, though. Having someone sneak out after I gave them multiple orgasms."

I wish I could go back in time to change many things, but that isn't one of them. Sure, I could've done things differently, but my last few months would be very different.

"Let me ask you this, if I'd stuck around that night, would we be sitting here today?"

He goes quiet and runs his hand through his hair. "I wish I could say yes, but you walking out that night is what made me determined to know you. I've never had that happen."

"No one would dream of running from the Sexiest Man Alive."

He chuckles. "You did."

I lean over the center console so we're face to face. "I would do it the same all over again."

"Yeah?"

"Yup, because I'm here with you now, and I know if I'd stayed in that bed, you wouldn't have chased me."

Eli's eyes soften, and he gives one of his cocky smirks. "I guess we'll never know." He moves closer until our breaths become one as we both take in this moment.

I lift my hand, tangling my fingers in his brown locks without moving my gaze from his. I see the shift from content-ment to fear and then to adoration. Is he afraid of us? It's twice today that I've seen something troubling him. There's a part of me that wants to ask him, but I pretend I don't see it.

My gut fills with dread because I know it's the wrong choice. I've felt this before, and I acted on it. I used to beg Matt to talk to me, to tell me what he was feeling. Each time I tried, he pushed me away more. Doing the same thing and expecting a different result is the definition of insanity. For all I know, it's nothing, yet somewhere inside me, I don't think that's the case.

Eli leans in, touching his lips to mine. I work hard to let whatever I saw go and focus on right now. Our futures are undefined, and if I set us on the wrong path, we'll crumble. I have to walk it with him and hope that we can endure the potholes and detours.

He pulls back, resting his forehead on mine. "Let's go inside. I want to get you in my arms."

"Sounds good to me."

We exit the car, and he seems to be back to normal. The sun has set, and strategically placed lights illuminate his house. It looks like a freaking palace. The grandness of it all hits me the same way it did the first time. I don't think it'll ever fade. With my hand in his, we tour the house again, only this time he shows me all the rooms.

On the second floor, he shows me his six guestrooms, all are double the size of my master bedroom at home, with a bathroom, and decorated with extreme detail. There's no way he chose this stuff, I can only imagine how much fun Nicole would've had in here.

When we enter his room, I almost pass out. It isn't a bedroom; it's a small house. There's a sitting room at the far end with a full living room set up, off to the left is a fireplace that's see through on both sides. Eli leans against the wall watching me as I walk around the room, trying to take it all in.

"This is incredible," I say with awe.

I continue looking around the other side of the fireplace. There's a master bathroom, if you can call it that, that leaves me speechless. The Jacuzzi tub sits off to the right, and there's a shower taking up the entire back wall. I swear at least ten people could fit in there.

Eli clears his throat, causing me to turn quickly. "You look good here."

I shake my head in disbelief. "I doubt that."

He moves forward. "One day, you're going to see how beautiful you are."

"One day, you'll realize that you need glasses." I try to joke, but it falls flat. I've never thought I was ugly, but I'm nothing special. It's still crazy to me that Eli thinks differently.

He wraps his strong arms around me, and I sink into his embrace. Just like that, Eli can make me feel whole. When I'm with him, my world doesn't seem so bleak. Sure, the issues are all there, but with him, shouldering them doesn't feel so hard.

"Let's go to bed." Eli's words are mixed with double meaning.

I smile at him. "I'd like that."

We both get ready for bed in the massive bathroom. I internally laugh at how vastly different this is from my house. I have one sink in my bathroom, and the double vanity occupies three quarters of one wall.

Once we're done, we settle into the king-size bed. As much as I love the space, I kind of like that we snuggle in my smaller bed. Eli puts his arm out, and I nestle into his side. "I like when we're close like this."

He makes a low rumbling sound in his chest as I drape my

arm over him. "I never realized how much I like it until it felt like you were miles apart on your side."

"Aww, you like being close to me," I say, teasingly.

"I like being *very* close to you."

I grin and kiss his torso. "I like that you like that."

"Are you trying to seduce me, Officer?"

I look at him through my lashes and bat them. "Me?"

He twists, hoisting me so we're even. "I don't mind if you are."

"Are you seducible, Mr. Walsh?"

Eli's lips move to my ear so he can trace the shell with his tongue before gripping it in his teeth. "Maybe you should find out."

I move my hand under the covers, skimming over his hard body, until I find his erection. I love that he's always ready and I never have to wonder if he wants me. There are many benefits to sleeping naked, this is one.

Eli groans as I wrap my fingers around him and my lips find his. He roughly grips my hips, digging into my flesh as I start to jerk him off.

My phone rings in my bag across the room, but I'm too lost in his touch to care.

His moan is low, and I swallow it as we kiss. I feel his hands on my breasts, kneading the skin and pulling at my nipple. The sexual chemistry we share is unlike anything I've had before. I'm not the most experienced lover, but Eli pushes me. I want to please him. I love knowing it's my body he's seeking, claiming, and worshiping.

"You make me crazy," Eli admits before his mouth is on mine again. His hands exploring my body until his fingers brush my clit.

The phone goes off again. "Maybe you should get that," he practically growls against my lips, and I groan.

I drop my head on the pillow and curse the phone. "Don't

go anywhere," I warn and hop out of bed. I glance back at him as he rests his head on his hand, watching me as I prance across the room.

My phone has six missed calls from a number I don't know. I didn't realize it rang that much. Something is wrong, I can feel it in my bones. No one calls me that much unless it's an emergency, and my dumbass ignored the call. "Hello?" I ask with a shake in my voice.

"Heather, it's Anthony."

"Anthony." My eyes shoot to Eli's, and he's already tossing the covers off him. "What's wrong?"

He pauses and dread fills my body. "You need to come to Tampa General. Please don't wait."

"Is she—" I choke the words as Eli's hands grip my shoulders. I can't say the words. I can't ask if she's gone, because if he says yes, I'll lose it.

"Just get here."

The phone drops to the floor, and Eli's arms encircle me. Everything I thought I knew about how I'd handle this moment is false. I feel my body start to protect itself. My mind goes to a place where I can't feel or do anything. I'm not sure how I got to the bed. I don't know how my shirt is on my body. Nothing is real right now. It's as if time has ceased to exist for me.

I feel hollow and lifeless.

Eli lifts me in his arms, carrying me like a child down the stairs. He barks orders to someone as we move to the car. He must be on the phone, but I truly can't process anything around me.

The car is moving, but I can't see anything passing by. I didn't need Anthony to tell me she died and I wasn't there with her. I can feel it.

My world is without my sister.

I'm alone.

"We did everything we could, Ms. Covey. I'm truly sorry for your loss." The doctor explains as I stand with a steady stream of tears trekking down my cheeks and dripping off the tip of my chin.

My sister has drawn her last breath.

Three days ago, we were at an amusement park. We were laughing, enjoying our time together, and now she's dead. No warning, no time to say goodbye, nothing but agony.

Now I stand in a cold, stark room while they try to give me some kind of answers.

"How did this happen so fast?" I ask. "I thought there would be a warning, something to tell me it was coming."

Anthony comes forward. "She begged us not to tell you."

"Tell me what?"

Dr. Pruitt touches my arm. "Stephanie was being treated for pneumonia after her seizure. It's why we kept her a few extra nights. The antibiotics weren't working, but she demanded we stop all treatment and discharge her. We did the best we could with the parameters she set."

Anger floods my veins, searing the pain in every limb. She

chose this? She knew? They were lying to me? Don't they know what this cost me? My chest heaves as I struggle to understand how this could happen.

I look to Eli and then back to the doctor, and I erupt, "I don't understand! How could no one tell me? How didn't you think I should know?" I scream at them. "I was her caretaker! She wasn't thinking straight! I'm her sister! I should've known."

Eli pulls me into his embrace, and I wail. I smack his arm and then his chest, angry at everyone. Angry at him because I was with him when this happened. Angry at Stephanie because she didn't tell me. I could've had another three days with her. If they'd kept me informed, I never would've allowed her to come to a fucking amusement park. I would've pushed her to have treatment, not let it kill her. There were so many things I could've done, and now, it's too late.

My rage turns to Anthony. "You knew!" I rage at him. "You knew she was sick, and you brought her out!"

His head drops, and when he looks back at me, his eyes are brimming with tears. "I know you don't believe this, but I cared about her. She asked me if I would help to keep her stable so she could have that day with you. She wanted one day of normal with you. Your sister knew she was dying and didn't want to drag it out. I was there with her, holding her hand, and giving her what she asked for."

"You knew her for what, a week? I was there every single day throughout the last seven years! I should've been the one beside her. You took that from me."

A lone tear falls down his face, but there is no room in my broken heart to feel anything but hatred for him. "Believe me, your sister loved you so much that she wanted to spare you. It was all from love."

I hate myself. I hate him. I hate everyone, and I can't breathe.

I gasp for air as Eli rubs my back. "Easy, baby."

I look to him, his image blurry. "She's gone and I didn't say goodbye. I wasn't there, Eli. I wasn't with her."

"I know."

The doctor clears his throat. "We had specific instructions from Stephanie in her medical directive. They were followed to the letter. I'm truly sorry for your loss, Ms. Covey. Take as much time as you need."

He and Anthony both walk away, leaving me to do the last thing I ever wanted to do . . . say goodbye to my baby sister.

Eli and I walk down the hallway with his arm around my shoulder. I want to push him away, be alone and wallow in my grief, but I can't seem to do it. He's the only person here who didn't spend the last however long lying to me. I hold onto him as we move, following the line on the floor. We don't speak because there's nothing to say. I can't go back in time. I can't change the way everyone handled this. Once again, I've had the choice stripped from me.

The door is open, and I glance at her lifeless body lying there. I'm not strong enough for this. I've been fooling myself by believing I was prepared. There's no preparing for grief. Instead, I'm thinking of how I wasn't with her in the end. No, I was lying in Eli's bed, wishing my phone weren't ringing. I should've been holding her hand, telling her how loved she was. My beautiful little sister is gone, and I hate that she didn't hear my voice telling her all the things she needed to know.

Eli's hand is on my back, and I spin, crumple against his chest, and twist my fists in the fabric of his shirt. "No, no, no, no!" I thought maybe this was a lie. Somewhere deep inside I hoped she'd be alive, but she's not. "I'm not ready for this!" I cry. "She can't be gone. Please, God, give her back to me!"

He murmurs words of comfort and support, but they don't matter. There's no way to soothe the torture I'm feeling. Grief, guilt, anger, and desolation consume me. "Do you want to go in? You don't have to."

I know I need to. Even though she isn't really there, it's all that's left of her. "Yes, I do." I say to him and straighten my shoulders, finding a tiny bit of strength in his warm hand on the small of my back.

"I'll be right here."

My feet shuffle forward, and I pull the chair closer to the side of her bed as my heart splinters. Eli stays back, allowing me some privacy. I lift my hand, brushing the dark brown strands off her face. She used to love when I did this. In the beginning of her disease, it was the only thing that calmed her. I would spend countless nights running my fingers through her hair.

I close my eyes, not wanting to see her face, and repeat the motion. "I'm sorry, Stephy. I wasn't here, and I'll never forgive myself for that. I'm your sister, and I was supposed to be beside you. I don't know if you were scared or if it hurt. I don't know if you were looking for me —" A strangled sob breaks free.

Eli moves, but I put my hand up to stop him. I need to do this alone. Even if she isn't alive, I pray she can hear me.

"I would've been here, baby girl. I should've been by your side. You were my whole world, Stephanie Covey. I don't know how to go on. I love you more than my own life. You were the best sister in the world. Each day that I had you was a gift, and I wish it never ended. I wish I could tell you a stupid joke right now." The tears come so hard I can't see. "I wish I could hold you and tell you how special you were. Because you were everything good in this world." I wipe my face and suck down a breath. "The world was a better place with you in it. I was a better person because of you."

My head falls on the side of the bed, and I grip her lifeless hand in mine. I cry without restraint. It's ugly, full of pain, and I don't have the wherewithal to care. "It should've been me who was sick! You didn't deserve this."

I have no idea how long I stay hunched over the bed clinging to her. I never understood loss until this moment. I thought when my parents died that was the most grief I could've felt, but that was a splash in a puddle. Now, I'm drowning in the ocean, the current pulling me farther out into the murky waters.

I need air.

I can't breathe.

My lungs struggle to function. I gasp, trying to find any oxygen in the room, but there is none.

"Easy, baby. Easy. Look at me, Heather." Eli's kneeling by my side and cradling my face as he wipes the tears with his thumb. My eyes find his, and he stares until I calm down. "That's it. Breathe. Just breathe. I'm right here."

"She's gone."

"I know, baby."

"She won't come back."

His own eyes fill with sadness. "I'm so sorry."

The sound that escapes my throat is filled with despair. "Take me home, Eli. Please. I can't see her like this. I couldn't save her, and now she's gone!"

His arms become a vice around me as I fall apart. I want the numbness back. It didn't hurt when I didn't feel. The knowledge that tomorrow, I can't call her, text her, or touch her leaves me so bereft that I'm not even sure there's a way to live past this moment.

Eli tucks me against his chest, holding me as we move. I hear him talking to someone, but I've found my way back to the darkness. This is where I want to stay.

I focus on nothing.

The only thing that registers is Eli's arms wrapped around me as I close my eyes and drift to where not even death can touch me.

"HEATHER," a soft voice calls to me. "Wake up, honey."

Stephanie? Is she here? My eyes fly open, hoping to see my sister, but it isn't her. Instead, Nicole is leaning over me. Disoriented, I look around and realize I'm not in my house. A big bed sits in an enormous room. I'm at Eli's. When did we get back here?

"Hey." She stares at me with red-rimmed eyes.

She knows about Stephanie.

He must've called her.

"Nic—" I choke her name out, and she reaches for me. The minute she touches me, I break. The tears I cried before seem small in comparison.

The pain is back with a vengeance. Nicole rocks me back and forth, and I hold on to her for dear life. "Oh, honey. It's okay, let it out," she encourages. "Just let it out."

There's a connection between two people who understand each other. That's Nicole and me. We don't have to speak to know what the other needs. Sometimes, it's just falling apart in the comfort of your best friend's arms.

Nicole leans back when I quiet down. "Better?"

"No. I don't know that there is a better."

She wipes her own tears and nods. "It's going to hurt, but you're strong, Heather. Stephanie loved you so much, know that."

"She kept it from me." All the emotions of the night continue to assault me. My sister knowing that she was going to die and that she was sick. The fact that she hid her condition so we could have the day at Busch Gardens. "All at her own expense. If she were alive, I'd beat her for it. She should've stayed in bed, got better so that . . ."

"So she could just get worse again?" Nicole challenges. She loved my sister as if she were her own. Stephanie was always around when we were young, wanting to be exactly like us. I can remember finding Stephanie trying on my clothes and talking to her "best friend Nicole." It was annoying back then, if only I had the gift of foresight. "Is that what you'd really want for her?"

My gut reaction is to yell: Yes!

I open my mouth, but Nicole glares at me, daring me to say it. "I . . . I don't know."

I pull my knees to my chest and wrap my arms around them. I wish I could crawl inside myself and disappear. Living hurts too damn much.

"I know you, and you didn't want that. I can't imagine how you'd feel if this was months of her in agony."

Sure, I guess there's some comfort in that, but not much. The last seven years of Stephanie's life were a series of ups and downs. We struggled with everything, and she suffered through it all. I watched her life start to fade the day we got her diagnosis.

My eyes move to the doorway where Eli leans against the frame. In his hand is a glass of water and a plate of food. He hesitates before moving forward. I gaze at him, tears welling in my eyes.

"You've been sleeping for a while." His deep voice is filled with emotion. "I thought you should eat."

My lip trembles, thinking of how happy I was before I got the call. We were together, loving each other while my sister took her last breath. I wish I could go back in time. I would've gone to see her after the barbeque, but I was so wrapped up in him.

My heart aches thinking about the minutes wasted

because I didn't answer the phone. The what-ifs are tearing me apart.

Nicole touches my arm. "Eli called as soon as you got back. I came right over, but you've been sleeping for about fifteen hours."

"I'm tired."

Eli and Nicole share a look, and she gives me a squeeze. "I'm sure. You need to eat, though. Do you want me to call Matt and tell him you'll be out for a few days?"

"Tell him I don't know when I'll be back."

Right now, I can't deal with anything. The idea of riding in a squad car and talking to people is too much.

"I'll tell him a week, and then you'll handle what comes after that." Her tone is firm, and I know what she's trying to do. The same thing I would do if she were giving up.

I'd push.

But you can't push someone out of a hole. You have to hope they'll claw their way up enough for you to help them. There is no strength left in my hands to help me move right now.

"Do you need me to stay?" she asks Eli.

"No, I'll take care of her."

I glare at both of them as they talk about me as if I'm not here. All I need is to go back to sleep and wake up when this isn't my reality.

Nicole kisses my forehead, and then they both leave the room. I grab my phone, scrolling through the texts and missed calls.

> DANIELLE
>
> I love you. I'm here if you need me.
>
> BRODY
>
> Rachel and I send our love. Let me know what I can do.

Nothing. You can't do a damn thing.

KRISTIN

I talked to Nicole, I'm so sorry, Heather. Do you want me to come over?

I reply to Kristin right away. I don't want to see anyone.

Thanks, but I'm not up for company.

It doesn't matter that I'm at Eli's house. She'll show up. That's Kristin's nature, she's the caretaker in our group, and I don't want to be mothered. I don't want anyone to make me feel better right now.

I try to remember what it was like when I lost my parents. Was I this devastated? I think I was, but I had Stephanie to worry about. I didn't focus on the sorrow. I had to be strong, give her hope, and make sure we would be okay. My friends were around, but we were also college aged. It wasn't like now.

Eli enters the room, and I use all my energy to stay upright. I tighten my arm, hugging myself together.

"Did you eat anything?" he asks.

"Not hungry."

The bed shifts slightly as he climbs in next to me. "Okay."

I look up, not expecting that. I figured he'd fight me to do something other than drown in my pain.

"Don't look surprised. You have to grieve the way you want. I'm just trying to be here in whatever way you need."

Tears fill my eyes, blurring him out a little. I lunge forward into his arms. I don't know why or what comes over me, but I need him to comfort me. He falls back, taking me with him and wrapping me tightly in his arms. The tears fall silently as I listen to the beat of his heart.

He's been here every second since it happened. Even when

I couldn't care for myself, he made sure I was okay. I turn my head so that I can see his face. Eli gives me a sad smile, and appreciation overwhelms me. These have been the worst hours of my life, and he's stood by me.

"Thank you, Eli."

He threads his fingers in my hair. "You don't have to thank me."

"We haven't been together all that long."

"It doesn't mean that what we feel for each other isn't real. I told you I wasn't going anywhere, and I meant it."

I close my eyes and another tear escapes from the corner. "I'm going to be sad for a bit."

I might as well warn him now, let him run before I fall even harder. It would have to be him leaving, too. I don't think I'm strong enough to walk away even if I wanted to.

"Baby, look at me," he urges. I open my eyes, and he sits up, causing me to have to do the same. "You should be sad. I didn't know Stephanie like you did, and I'm sad. I don't think you understand how I feel about us . . . about you. I'm not going to leave you because you're sad. I'm not walking away, I'm staying here with you."

"You leave in a week," I remind him.

His hands grip my shoulders and then move to my neck. "I told my producers I'm not coming next week. I'll go to New York after we figure this out."

My fingers wrap around his wrist, and I press my forehead to his. "I don't know what to say."

"You don't need to say anything," he murmurs. "Just let me take care of you."

His lips brush mine with hesitation, and I make the movement to connect us. It isn't about passion. It's about something deeper. Our kiss is soft, sweet, and comforting. In all the sadness, he gives me hope that the sun will shine again. It's a brush of lips that tempts me to believe he'll combat the clouds and ward off the storms so I can feel the warmth of the rays again. I hope he's ready for Mother Nature's fury.

CHAPTER TWENTY
HEATHER

It's been seventy-six hours since my sister died. I've been cocooned in the comfort of Eli's home. He's been patient, kind, loving, and attentive. When we first met, I would've laughed if someone told me this is what he'd be like. I assumed he was a rich, selfish, arrogant prick who only cared about his wants. Because . . . that's the illusion of a celebrity.

I was wrong.

Eli is none of those things, except rich. He's definitely that, but he's never selfish with me. We've watched television, had takeout, and he's held me as I've cried.

I wrap my arms around him and snuggle closer, inhaling his scent. I love the mix of soap, sandalwood, and musk that is him. He's asleep, but he instinctively squeezes me tighter. I watch his face as whatever he dreams of makes him smile. I trace the lines on his cheek with the tip of my finger, grazing each little spike of his scruff.

"Hi." He smiles as his eyes flutter open.

"Hi."

He shifts a little lower to his side. "Did you sleep?"

I'm not sure that I've really slept since that first night. It isn't for lack of trying, but my body won't relax. The second night, I woke Eli with my sobs. I relived the entire event at the hospital, only this time I made it in time to watch her fade away.

My mind played every scenario out in the worst way. I don't know now if it's a good thing that I wasn't there. If it was anything like I imagine, I know I wouldn't be just mourning. I wouldn't have survived. I was never more grateful for Eli's presence than I was when I woke, covered in sweat and tears pouring down my face.

"I think I did."

"Good. How about we grab some food?"

I haven't eaten much, and thinking about food makes my stomach growl. "I guess I am hungry."

He laughs. "Come on, I'm starved."

I follow him into the bathroom and almost scream when I see my face in the mirror. My eyes have dark circles under them. Makeup is now dried on my skin, and I'm not sure if it's somehow become permanent. I won't even talk about the mess that is my hair. Jesus. I glance over at Eli, who looks as perfect as always. His hair only looks sexy in its disheveled state, there aren't any dark circles under his eyes. The deep lines of his hips are more prominent as the basketball shorts hang loosely.

Eli's eyes move to mine, and he appraises me. "What?" he asks with a grin.

I think he knows I'm checking him out, but I shrug, not caring that I got caught. "Nothing."

He comes closer, pressing his lips to mine. "You look at me like that, and I can't help but kiss you."

"Like what?" I ask.

"You'll figure it out soon enough." His kiss is quick and silences me from asking what the hell he sees in my eyes.

When he pulls back, I open my mouth to get my question

out, but he moves toward the shower, slowly removing his pants. I stare at his broad shoulders, the way his muscles tense on his back, his now bare ass, and I can't speak.

For the first time in three days, I want something more to ease my pain. Not food, or him holding me. I need him to make me forget who I am. I feel alone, broken, and Eli has pushed me to stay out of the numbness.

I want to get lost in his green eyes and have him make me feel pleasure. He's spent every minute ensuring I felt safe. I think back to what Stephanie said: *You have to promise me that you'll let your heart be open. Can you do that?*

She was asking so much more than that. She was practically begging me to let myself be vulnerable enough to love again.

"Are you coming in?" Eli asks as he stands in the shower, water dripping down each delicious inch of him.

A thought strikes me, halting my feet. I was never more vulnerable than I have been the last three days. I let him see me at my lowest, and he's still here with his hand outstretched, calling me to him.

I step toward the man who I never thought I'd feel anything more than lust for. Each stride forward cements what I already knew was happening — I'm falling in love with Eli Walsh.

The steam circles around us as we stand in front of each other. My heart races with the knowledge of my deepening feelings. How did I get here so fast? Is it true that when two people are right for each other, time is irrelevant? Out of all the people in the world, is he really who I'm meant to be with?

His green eyes fill with wonder, as if we're sharing the same thoughts, and I know . . . I love him.

I lift my hand and place it on his chest. His heartbeat quickens as we both gaze at each other.

"Tell me what you're thinking." Eli's voice is heavy with confliction.

I'm terrified that if I say the truth, he'll laugh. I'm frightened that I'll lose him, like I lose everyone else. The crippling fear keeps me from saying it, but I give him what I can. "That I'm not alone because of you. That I'm afraid of losing you."

His arms wrap around my shoulder, clutching me as the water falls on us. "I told you, baby. I'm not going anywhere."

I tilt my head back, believing what he says. "I want you to make love to me."

He tenses, probably scared that I'm not ready. Each touch we've shared since that night has been in comfort, and he'll never grasp the intimacy he showed in that.

"Heather . . ." He hesitates. "I'm not . . ."

"I know." I put my hand to his lips. "I'm telling you that I need you. I need you to make me feel alive. I want you to make love to me because I *want* to make love to you."

His eyes don't leave mine, and I see the mix of desire and surrender. His fingers slide down my spine as I grip his neck. Both of us move in perfect harmony, and our mouths collide. Eli takes control of the kiss, entering my mouth, and pouring himself into the moment. Each swipe of his tongue solidifies my heart to him.

My hands move down his shoulders, over his thick arms and firm muscles, and then back up again. I love the feel of him beneath me. The way he emboldens me to give myself over.

The kiss continues as we touch each other. It's as if I'm experiencing him for the first time. His mouth moves against my throat, kissing me as his lips find purchase where it drives me wild.

He moves back to my lips and takes my head in his hands. My gaze meets his, and I see it all. He's as in love with me as I am with him.

Just as I was too afraid to say it, he doesn't utter the words, either. However, I know, and I show him the same love back.

The intensity of his stare is too much. My breathing becomes shallow, and he drops his grip and takes my hand. "I want to do something," he admits. "Will you let me take care of you?"

"You already have."

I'll give him anything he wants. I trust him more than I've ever trusted any other man.

Eli fills his hand with soap, turns my back to his front, and starts to wash me. He starts at my neck, lathering the soap and moving ever so slightly down to my shoulders. "You have no idea how you make me feel," he says against my ear. "How much I want to take away your pain. I want to make you smile, baby. I want to give you everything."

I lean back against him, as he moves to my chest. "I need you so much," I admit. "It scares me how much you mean to me."

He spreads the soap across my body with care. We're both naked, but it's more than foreplay right now, it's filled with meaning. Once he's done washing me, I'm desperate for him.

I need him inside me. I need to feel whole. I need him to fill me with life.

His gaze is brimming with hunger. Neither of us can wait any longer.

He presses my back against the wall and his mouth finds mine. I pour out every ounce of love I feel from my body. I want him to feel how deeply I'm in love with him. My hand reaches for his dick, trying to line it up. I can't wait. I have to have him right now.

"Heather," he says against my skin. "We don't have a condom . . ."

"I have an IUD, and I'm clean."

His head drops to my shoulder, and he moans. "I'm clean, but are you sure?"

I look up, watching his green eyes beg for me to say yes. But there's only one thing that falls from my lips. "I love you, Eli. I want you to make love to me."

I stun myself with my admission and wait for him to freak out.

He pushes the wet hair from my cheek and smiles. "I love you. I loved you the day we were on the boat. I loved you the day your face was covered with paint. I might have even fallen in love with you when you screamed my name at the concert."

The tears that fall this time aren't from grief, but from hope. I'm not alone or lost, I found my home.

"YOU KNOW, I've spent my entire life in Tampa, and I've never been here," I state.

Eli chuckles as we continue walking on the trail. "I love this park, Randy used to take me here to fish when my dad was too drunk to be around."

After our intense shower, Eli told me he wanted to show me something. I wasn't in the mood to leave our safe haven, but he wasn't budging, insisting that we were leaving the house before we had to meet with the assisted living director.

"Tell me about your parents." He doesn't talk much about his family. I know his mother lives in Tampa, but he hasn't mentioned her.

He sighs. "Not much to say. My father was a drunk, smacked my mom and Randy around. I don't remember if he hit me, but Randy says he took the hits so I didn't have to. From what I'm told, he lost his job and then left."

"Wow, is that why you and Randy are so close?"

"Yeah, my brother was more of a father than anything.

Even though he's only a few years older, he took me under his wing. When we found out our dad was dead, that was when Randy really made it his job to take care of me."

It mirrors the relationship between me and Steph. When my parents died, I became the parent figure. It was different because we lost both Mom and Dad, but still, I can imagine what Randy experienced.

I rest my head on his arm as we continue through Lettuce Lake Park. The trees provide shade, allowing us to walk comfortably. It's Florida, so it's always hot and humid, but today is bearable. "What about your mom?"

"She's here in Tampa, but she spends half the year in New York visiting her sister. They do the whole snowbird thing. I don't get it, but they've been doing it for years." Eli stops in front of the opening by a small pond and grabs my hips. "I want you to meet them."

I give a small smile. "I'd like that."

"My brother is up my ass about bringing you to his house. I'd love for you to meet my niece and nephew."

A sharp pain slices through my chest. Eli having a family shouldn't hurt me. I know it's a little irrational for me to be jealous, and a part of me is angry with myself for thinking that way. In my heart, I know all of this, but it's there.

He rocks my hips back and forth when I don't say anything. "Yes, of course. I'm sorry I spaced out there." I try to laugh it off. "Maybe next week?"

"There's no rush, babe."

"Okay, I do want to meet them, though. Your niece sounds great."

I love that while the media portrays Eli as big and bad, he's a man with a beautiful heart. The fact that he's so smitten with his niece is proof. I can only imagine how much she rules his world.

Eli tosses his arm over my shoulder, tucking me into the

crook of his arm, and we continue walking. I've been around tall and strong men my entire career and never felt secure. I've always been able to hold my own and am proud of that. With Eli, I can almost relax. I'm not looking for the next bad guy, I'm just happy to be in the moment with him.

"It's so peaceful here," he muses.

"I'm glad you brought me here. Stephanie would've loved it."

He smiles down at me, kisses my forehead, and rubs my arm. "That's the first time you've talked about her since the hospital."

"It hurts to think of her," I admit.

"Maybe talking will help."

I don't know that anything will help, but I know I don't ever want to forget her. If that's how I can keep her memory alive, I'll endure the pain. My sister loved when we'd talk about the funny things my parents did. She would tell me that by whispering their names in the wind, it brought their spirit to life.

I lean into Eli, needing his support. "Stephanie wanted to be a professional gymnast when we were kids. One time, she was practicing doing flips on the bed in my room." I smile as I remember how disastrous it was. "She missed the bed and her tailbone hit the wall, leaving a big ass imprint."

He laughs, and I giggle.

"My mom was so mad because we tried to cover it with pillows."

"Pillows?"

"Yeah, like we could hide the giant butt in the wall and she'd never know."

Eli shakes his head and grins. It was one of the stories Stephanie loved to tell. I ended up getting grounded because she lied and said it was me. Since it was my room and my bed, my mother never believed me when I told her Steph did it.

She was always doing those kinds of things, taking my clothes, mixtapes, and any toy I loved. What I wouldn't give to be able to have that all back, I'd give her anything she wanted.

"You ready to head back?" he asks. "We need to meet the director."

This is going to be impossible. Collecting her things and getting rid of anything we don't want . . . I don't know how I'm going to do it.

"I guess—" I start to say but a woman shrieking stops me.

"Oh my God, oh my God, oh my God!" A jogger who is no longer running starts to yell. She stares at Eli with her jaw hanging open. "You're! You're Eli Walsh! Like, I love you. I'm your biggest fan!"

"Well, thank you." He flashes a smile and drops his arm.

This is the first time we've had this happen. I watch as the woman starts to prattle on about how amazing he is and how hot he is in person. A knot in my stomach starts to coil. I know he's hot, and I get that he's famous, but when we're together, it's so easy to forget.

"You have no idea, I've loved you forever. I know you're from here, and I kept waiting to meet you! And now you're here!" She screeches, and I barely contain my flinch.

Eli reaches his hand back, twisting his fingers in mine. "It was great to meet you, but I need to be going," he smoothly explains.

"Can you take our picture?" she asks me.

The last thing I want to do is be a photographer, but I have to remember *this* is part of who he is. To me, he's Ellington, the guy who watched awful comedy movies with me the last two days. He carefully picked each one to ensure nothing would trigger me breaking down again. He made sure I ate, slept, and functioned. He's the man who held me together when I was breaking apart. I don't share that man with these women, but Eli is a superstar. He doesn't belong to just me.

"Oh, sure." I grab her phone, and he shoots me an apologetic look.

The woman gushes some more, touches his arm, and doesn't even glance at me again. I take the photo and watch her hug him once more. She runs off, glancing back at him a few more times. What is wrong with these people? I know that I did that with Eli, but I was drunk and at a concert where I never thought he'd actually hear me. If I had been sober and in a normal setting, I would have waved or smiled, but telling him I loved him? No. That's ridiculous.

I love him. She doesn't even know him.

He walks toward me, and I can't get a grip on the emotions I'm feeling. "Hey," he says tucking his thumb under my chin. "I'm sorry."

"You have nothing to be sorry for." This is what his life is filled with, he shouldn't have to apologize for that.

"I brought you here because I wanted us to get some air, I forget that this can happen."

"How do you forget that?"

Regret flickers across his face. He reaches behind his neck, gripping it as he looks back at me. "When we're together, it's like I'm not that guy. You make me forget all of the shit that comes with singing and acting. I feel . . . normal."

"I was caught off guard, that's all. I'm pretty sure if this happened a week ago I wouldn't be acting crazy."

"You are not acting crazy, baby. Not even a little."

I don't trust whatever I'm thinking right now. It's a hint of jealousy mixed with a lot of grief. Not exactly the cocktail for sound decision making. I'm definitely filing this instance in my memory bank to recall later. I need to reconcile loving someone who I have to share. I'm not sure I know how to do that.

CHAPTER TWENTY-ONE
HEATHER

Today was the memorial.

It was the final formal event of my sister's life. Kristin and Nicole took care of the flowers and handled all the arrangements. Stephanie knew exactly what she wanted and laid it all out years ago. She had prepaid for the funeral home, memorial location, and casket, claiming that she knew I'd pick some ugly wood design and be too distraught to care. I thought she was being silly, but it turns out she was right.

I'm a mess and far worse than I thought I would be.

I figured because we knew it was coming, I would've been at peace. There's nothing peaceful about this.

When we got to Breezy Beaches the other day, I couldn't do it. As soon as Eli parked the car, I lost it. He went in, handled everything, and took me back to his house. He forced me to try to relax, so we had lain by the pool, and I read a book.

Well, I pretended to read because I don't think I absorbed a word.

Now, I'm back at my house, sitting on my bed, wondering what to do next.

"Knock, knock." Kristin pokes her head in. "You okay?"

After Stephanie's burial was over, I made a resolution to find a way to move on. My life has been my sister for almost twenty years. I went from being her guardian to being her caretaker. I don't remember a time when she wasn't my focus, and that hole is what I fear most.

What do I do when I don't have to worry twenty-four hours a day? How do I make choices that aren't regarding her needs? Where do I go after work or on Saturdays? My life has been her. Every choice has been made around her needs. I understand why Stephanie begged me to open my heart. She knew that I was going to be lost once she was gone.

"I'm doing a little better each day."

Kristin smiles. "I don't think we ever are any better, but we learn to accept it and find a new normal."

"That's what I'm hoping to do. I probably should decide what to do about going back to work."

"You have a lot of vacation days saved, maybe you should take some time for yourself. Go on a trip, do something fun for a change."

I can't remember the last time I went away. Maybe my honeymoon, but even then, we went to the Keys because Stephanie wasn't mature enough to be trusted. Nicole was going to watch her, which meant they threw a party in my house.

"Maybe. I don't know when Eli needs to be in New York. He was actually supposed to be there a week ago, but he didn't want to leave me."

Kristin grins and takes my hand. "I really love you two together."

"I told him I loved him," I admit aloud for the first time.

"That's big for you."

"I know." I sigh. "It took me a year before I said it to Matt. And I wasn't even really sure I loved him, but he said it, so I said it back. With Eli, I couldn't hold it in any longer. I had to say the words or I'd explode. But I haven't said it again and neither has he, maybe he didn't actually mean it . . ."

Kristin giggles. "You're such a freaking nutjob. You honestly think he doesn't love you? Think about it, the guy blew off his job, has practically moved you into his house, has taken care of you, and took care of all the expenses for today—"

"What?" I jump up. "They were prepaid, he couldn't have."

"I'm pretty sure that man can do anything he wants. He said he had all the money refunded a few days ago."

How could he do that? We took the money from the life insurance account that my parents left us. Stephanie didn't want us to use all the money on her care and leave me trying to scrape together funds.

I grab my phone and pull up my banking app. "Oh my God." My hands fly to my mouth. "It's all there."

My account is now ten thousand dollars heavier. He really did do it.

"A man doesn't do that for a woman he doesn't love. I see the way he looks at you." Kristin takes my hand. "Scott used to look at me that way. It isn't about what he says, Heather, it's about how he acts."

She's right. Since the very beginning, he's shown me how he feels. He doesn't have to say the words, because they've been in every one of his actions.

I'm such a fool to have been worried.

"I'm sorry that he doesn't see how wonderful you are." One day, I pray Scott will either do a complete one-eighty or she'll finally see her worth and leave.

"Don't worry about me." She taps my leg. "Tell me why you doubt your love at all?"

I tell Kristin about the park and the jogger. How I felt

invisible and was worried that once we left our bubble, our love would pop. It was nothing he did. Even when he was performing, he touched my hand as if saying he saw me. I'm naturally a worrier, and Eli has an entire new can of worms that I can't contain.

"Well, my best advice is to talk to him. If anyone can navigate a public life, it's him."

Once again, Kristin proves I'm a fool. "Why am I so dense?"

"Because you're emotional right now, babe. Stephanie might have been a sister to us, but she was almost a daughter to you. We expect to lose our parents and people older, but never anyone younger."

She pulls me into her arms, and I'm reminded why I'm blessed beyond words. My sophomore year of high school, I met Kristin in study hall. She had broken her foot and she sat at my table because it was closest to the door. To anyone outside, we were the most unlikely friends. She was on the honor society, I was barely passing. I played sports, she was not athletically inclined. Yet, we clicked. Our friendship was instant and completely unbreakable. She introduced me to Danielle, and I brought in Nicole, from there, our group was indestructible. I couldn't ask for better people than them.

"I love you, Kriss."

"I love you. So, I came in here because I have to give you something." Kristin fidgets. "About six months ago, Stephanie reached out to a few of us. She explained that she could feel changes happening in her, and that she was sure she wasn't going to last another year."

My heart begins to race, and my chest aches. "Why didn't you tell me?"

"She begged us not to. Nicole, Danni, and I listened to her, and she explained that she wanted us to help her. So, the three of us have letters—" Kristin's voice cracks as a tear falls. I want to jump her and find the letter from my sister, but I restrain myself. She clears her throat and continues, "We have letters for you. Brody has one, too, I believe. I'm supposed to be the strong one, so I got today. Clearly, they all misjudged me." She wipes her face before letting out a nervous laugh and pulling an envelope from her purse. "She asked that you read it after her service."

"Have you read it?" My voice trembles as I take it from her.

"No, it's for you, honey. Do you want me to stay?"

Kristin is one of my best friends, she knows me inside and out, but it's not my girls that I want right now. It's really astounding how when I gave my heart completely over to Eli, he became so essential to me, and I want to sit next to him as I read this.

"Would you be angry if I said I wanted Eli . . ."

"Don't even finish that thought." Kristin gets to her feet. "I would never be upset. I'll go get him." She kisses my cheek and walks out.

I stare at the envelope with my name on the front, and my stomach is filled with knots. I feel Eli's presence as he enters the room.

"Kristin told me before she came in." The sound of his voice eases a little of the fear. "You want me in here?"

"I do."

He sits beside me, and I place my hand on his leg. I feel tethered to Earth around him. I need him to anchor me so I don't drift into the pain of whatever I'm about to read.

My finger slides under the glue, separating the flap to reveal a single piece of paper folded inside. I let out a deep sigh and pull it open.

My Sister who became my Mother . . . my Mister,

If you have this letter, I'm dead. Don't cry. Although, I have a feeling my asking that is like telling the sky to be yellow. You were always so dramatic, even when we were kids. You should stop that. We all knew this was going to happen, and I know you won't understand this, but I'm glad it's over. I have no idea how long it'll be after I've written this until it's in your hands, but know that I was ready. I was ready not to be a burden on you anymore. I was ready not to be in pain. Mostly, I was ready to be free.

You never let me be broken after Mom and Dad were taken from us. You were the rock. It couldn't have been easy to become my parent. Especially when I was going through that goth phase, which I still think I rocked. However, I never worried if you'd be there. The day I got my diagnosis, I lost my life, and so did you. We went from being in this relationship where I hated you for telling me I couldn't go on a date with Tyler Bradley—who, by the way, was not a bad guy for smoking—to having to worry about painkillers. Our Saturday nights weren't movies and popcorn; they were tremors and numbness. I hated watching you go from being happy and married to divorced and depressed.

You can try to convince yourself that you didn't care, but no one is that selfless. And if you truly believe my disease didn't rob you of anything, then I'll tell God you should be the next Saint. Although, I'm sure he knows about the time you had sex with Vincent in Mom and Dad's bed. Yeah, I totally heard you . . . gross.

My point to this letter is that you're free as well. You don't have to worry anymore. I know that you'll think I'm being stupid and I can hear you saying how you don't want to be free, but I do. I want you to be free. I want you to go out with your friends and have one-night stands, because I can't. I want you to find someone who isn't a loser and wants you to be a Stepford wife.

I want you to know this above anything else. You were the best Mister anyone could ever have. You are the only thing I will miss when I'm gone. On a side note, don't think I don't plan to haunt you. I'm going to be an awesome ghost. I figure it'll be like that movie you made me watch where Whoopi teaches the ghost guy how to move objects. So, when the remote goes flying because you're watching that awful cop show, you know it's me telling you to find something better to watch.

I'm going to stop rambling, but seriously, I love you so much. Thank you for being my Mister and not Momster.

So, in order to ensure you live your life after I'm gone, there are three more letters. I figured Kristin was the weakest link in your group, so she got the first one . . . the next you'll get on your wedding day. Because you need to find love again. You need to have someone who will take care of you for a change. Go find him so you can hear from me again! I promise, it's a good one!

I love you always and forever.

Stephanie

I FOLD the letter back with a mix of tears and a smile. It would be just like my sister to leave me on a cliffhanger so I'd do what she wanted.

I look at Eli, who's studying me closely. "She was always such a ballbuster, it's good to know even in death she kept that about her."

"What did she say?"

I laugh, thinking about the one thing she wrote about him. "She thinks your show is crap and doesn't want me to watch it."

He laughs and tugs me against his side. "Yeah, she mentioned that I needed to find better acting jobs."

"Are you nervous?" he asks as we sit outside another ridiculous mansion on Sanibel Island.

"Of course I am," I chuckle. "I'm going to meet your family!"

It's been four days since the memorial, and while I've loved it being just Eli and me, I'm excited to spend some time with other people. I wish it wasn't the first time meeting them and it wasn't his famous brother's family. It's Eli's nephew, Adriel's birthday, so his family is having the adults over to celebrate.

"They'll love you," he assures me for the fifth time, and I know I can't put this off any longer.

When we climb out of the car, a little girl comes barreling forward. "Uncle Eli!" she screams as her brown curls bounce in the wind.

"Daria!" He scoops her in his arms and twirls her around. "I want you to meet someone." He moves over to me. "This is Heather, can you say hi?"

"Hello." She smiles sweetly.

"Hi, you are even prettier than your uncle said."

She giggles and tucks her hands under her chin. "Untle Eli always tells me I'm going to be big trouble."

Daria wraps her tiny arms around his neck and squeezes. "You already are trouble," Eli says before blowing raspberries in her neck.

"You're silly!" Her sweet laughter fills the air.

"Look who's late again!" A woman with long brown hair, dark brown eyes, and a loving smile comes walking down the drive. From what he's told me, I assume this is Savannah. She's much shorter than I imagined, though.

"Look who's busting my balls, as always," Eli retorts.

She rolls her eyes at him and then turns to me. "Hi, I'm Savannah, I'm so glad you came."

"Thank you for having me. It's really nice to meet you," I say as she pulls me in her arms.

"We're all huggers, honey. Be ready, this family is small but crazy as hell." I laugh, and Eli grumbles about her being the leader. "Anyway . . ." She dismisses him. "I'm so sorry to hear about your sister."

"Thank you." I do my best to give her a small smile, but bringing up Stephanie is like a knife to my heart.

"We wanted to come for the memorial, but Eli said it would be better if Randy wasn't in Tampa when he was. The press goes a little crazy when both Walsh brothers are around. One is much easier to hide. I hope you understand."

I never knew they had planned to come. He never mentioned a word about it, and it touches me more than she'll know. It also reiterates what Kristin said about him showing me how he feels. He told his family, and they thought I was important enough to him to come to my sister's memorial.

"Of course. I'm so grateful you even thought to come." I glance at Eli with surprise and then back to Savannah.

Eli puts Daria to his side and grips my shoulder.

"Savannah has a strong sense of family. She was adamant until I put her in her place."

She snorts, and her eyes narrow playfully. "You wish."

Their banter is hilarious to watch.

"You don't scare me, Vannah."

"Don't let him fool you," she whispers conspiratorially. "He knows who reigns supreme and it isn't either of the Walsh boys."

"Good to know." I laugh and jab his side.

"Everyone's out back," Savannah tells us and leads us through the house.

Eli holds my hand as I, once again, get lost in the wealth that he and his family have. This house is a little smaller than his, but it *feels* like a home. There are toys, warm colors on the walls, and it's clear a family lives here. Even with the size, it feels cozy.

We exit out back, and Randy puts his beer down and comes forward. "Heather, I'm so glad you could make it!"

"Thank you for having me."

Randy pushes Eli to the side and gives me a big hug. "Thank you." I look up, not sure what he's thanking me for until his gaze moves to his brother.

My cheeks burn, and I give a short nod.

"All right, asshole, stop embarrassing my girlfriend."

I won't lie, the fact that he called me his girlfriend gives me a thrill. Eli pulls me away from Randy, who chuckles over the possessive gesture. I meet his nephew, who reminds me of Danni's son, all proud and a total boy. He fist bumps Eli and gives me the chin lift.

Then Eli places his hand on my back and leads me over to who I assume is his mother. She has light brown hair, green eyes that match Eli's, and the sweetest smile. She's exactly like I pictured. Her hands are delicate, and she keeps them folded on the table. When she sees Eli approach, her entire face lights up.

"Mom." His smile is wide as he greets her.

She gets to her feet and takes his face in her hands. "Eli! My sweet boy!" His mother kisses both his cheeks before releasing him. "Are you eating? You look too skinny. I don't like you too skinny."

"I'm fine, Ma."

For the first time, he looks a little embarrassed. I didn't think that was something I'd ever see.

"He's all skin and bones," she says to the lady sitting next to her. When her eyes go back to him, she seems to notice me. She claps her hands together and then touches Eli's chest. "Is this her?"

"Ma, this is Heather, my girlfriend. Heather, this is my mother, Claudia."

Twice, but who's counting?

"She's so pretty." She's talking to Eli but looking at me.

"I'm so happy to meet you."

His mother walks over and takes my hands in hers. "I have waited a long time for Ellington to bring a girl to me, and here you are."

I'm not sure what that means, other than he told me that he hasn't really dated since his ex. Did she never meet her? I would've assumed they knew her considering how close to marriage they were.

I glance at Eli, and he rolls his eyes. "Don't start," he warns her.

"Oh, you hush. You don't date, and you don't call your mother. I have to read about your antics in those magazines. My Eli is too important to find a good girl. Makes his mother have to worry about being all alone without someone to take care of him."

I laugh as she gives him shit. He doesn't fight her back, he just tucks her in his side. "You love me."

She smacks his stomach and laughs. "Come sit, Heather. This is my sister, Martha."

I take the seat next to her, and Eli leans in, kisses my cheek, and wishes me luck. I watch him grin as he walks off. Asshole. Way to feed me to the lions.

His mother is absolutely perfect. She asks me a million questions about my job, my family, and her eyes fill with sympathy when I tell her about Stephanie. Her entire being is filled with warmth, and it's comforting being around her. Claudia tells me a little about Eli before he was famous, and I can't picture him that way. She talks about how scrawny he was, and that Randy was his only and best friend, which is something I assume followed him into adulthood.

He doesn't talk about any friends, and now, I can't imagine it's easy for him to trust anyone. When you're as successful as he is, it's probably impossible to figure out who wants to be your friend because they gain something from you and who genuinely cares about you. It's easier to shut them all out and not worry about it.

"You surviving?" Savannah says, handing me a beer before sitting.

"It's been such a great day so far."

"I'm glad. I have to tell you, we were shocked when Eli said he was bringing you to the party."

I'm not sure if I should be upset or relieved that he doesn't bring random girls here. I take a drink, hoping to mask my emotions. "I guess I was, too."

"Don't take that the wrong way." She gives me a reassuring smile. "We're all a little protective of Eli and haven't been a fan of his past choices. That said, judging by everything he told us, you're nothing like that. We were really

happy he was finally going to get his head out of his ass and
bring you around."

"Vannah," Claudia chastises her.

"You know you were happy, too, Mom. He's been so weird
since the she-bitch."

I nearly choke on my drink. I think I love this girl. "I take
it you don't like his ex?"

She lets out a loud laugh. "No. I hated her from the first
second I saw her. You know how it is, I'm sure, women can
read other women pretty easily."

"Oh, for sure," I agree. I feel like that's one of the advan-
tages that make me a good cop. I have a pretty good gauge for
whether someone is pulling crap or if they made a mistake.

"Guys are stupid and only care about one thing . . ."

Claudia scoffs. "Not my boys. They were raised right."

Savannah side eyes me and grins. "Yes, Randall and
Ellington would never care about that."

If she only knew that's what Eli and I did after knowing
each other twenty minutes.

Speak of the Devils, and they shall appear. Eli and Randy
walk over with a plate of burgers and hotdogs.

"Don't scare her off with your evil ways." Eli points at his
sister-in-law. "I'm watching you."

I inch closer to Savannah. "Don't be mean to my new
friend."

"Great," Eli groans. "Now I'm really screwed."

Laughter fills the air and then we dig in. The family
dynamic is fun and loving. They all make fun of themselves
along with each other, and the conversation flows effortlessly.
Randy dotes on his wife, showering her with little tokens of
love. It's clear where his brother learned how to treat a woman.

It's like watching Eli with me. He hands her a drink before
she asks, or takes her hand for no reason. Once again, the

Walsh brothers surprise me. People paint Randy as anything but a family man, but that's exactly what he is.

After the sun goes down, Savannah and I head inside to start cleaning up.

"You know that when your relationship goes public, things won't be easy," Savannah says as we wash dishes.

"I'm not sure what you mean."

She rests her hip on the counter, giving me her full attention. "It means that women are crazy, and Eli has been this attainable guy in some of their minds. You're not an actress or movie star, you're relatable to them, and you need to have some thick skin if you're going to get serious with him." She sighs. "I don't want to scare you, but I do want you to be prepared. Eli truly cares for you, believe me, I've never seen him like this. He may not understand this side of dating a famous person, but I do. I've been called horrible names, had photos photoshopped to make me look fat, and seen stories upon stories of Randy cheating."

"You don't think I can handle it?" I've wondered the same. I think back to the jogger and how uncomfortable I felt with her touching him. That isn't even what Savannah is talking about.

"I don't doubt you can if you want to. I'm sure there are awful things said about you being a female cop, right?"

I laugh. "You have no idea."

"Well, amplify that by a thousand. In the beginning, it'll be bad, but then it'll calm down. Just be ready, be on guard, and seriously don't listen to anything they say. It's truly disgusting the way the media portrays us, how people get a sick joy in watching famous people flounder. They will actually root for you and Eli to fail. Drama sells, and everything is about money in this world."

I hear the pain and disgust in her voice. She's been living

this for a long time and must've experienced a lot of hurt at people's hands. "How do you deal with it?"

She looks out the window at her husband and smiles. "I love him. For better or worse, that man is my entire world. I deal with it because music is who he is." Her eyes turn back to me. "It's who Eli is, too. So, keep your head down and be open with each other. If you love him, he's worth it."

Without a shadow of a doubt, I know I love him. The mere thought of walking away from Eli is enough to make me want to cry. It could've been easier to fall in love with anyone else, but nothing in my life has been easy. I've had to bury my parents, my sister, endure a divorce, and been so broke I wasn't sure I could afford to eat, so dealing with people hating me is a cake walk. Nothing will ever compare to the pain of losing my sister. If they want to hate me because I love him, then so be it.

He's worth the risk, he's worth it all.

Hours pass, and his mother takes the kids upstairs for baths. Eli, Savannah, Randy, and I have been playing rummy for the last hour. I'm kicking ass.

"Well," Randy tosses his cards down as I win another round, "on that note. Heather is clearly a hustler."

"Never!" I pretend to be offended.

"Liar." He laughs and then turns to his brother. "Eli, you should search her for hidden cards."

"Are you cheating, baby?"

My jaw drops. "I would never. I'm an officer of the law." Savannah and I have been passing each other cards under the table.

His eyes narrow, but he doesn't refute me. I watch him look over at Savannah, and he yells. "I knew it! You little cheats!"

Savannah bursts out laughing, and I follow. "You guys are so blind."

"Unreal, Ran, we've been played by our women."

Randy smirks at his wife and kisses her. "She's been playing me since we were kids."

"Mommy!" Daria comes running in wearing her pajamas, her hair still dripping from her bath. "Will you read me a story?"

Savannah hoists her daughter up and gives an apologetic smile. "It's that time, Randall."

"We're going to hit the road."

"Don't be a stranger, you're welcome here anytime," Savannah says and pulls me in for a hug. "He doesn't need to be present, we don't like him much anyway."

Eli snorts and then we all say our goodbyes.

Today was a day I'll never forget. It was a family welcoming me without knowing me at all. I had worried before that meeting Eli's family would remind me that I was alone in the world, but instead, it showed me the opposite. Once again, Eli provided me with something I didn't even have to ask for.

CHAPTER TWENTY-THREE
HEATHER

"I don't fucking care, then fire me!" Eli yells into the receiver. "Film what you can without me. I'm not leaving Tampa until I'm damn good and ready." The phone falls to the floor, and he grips his hand. "Fuck!"

I move over quickly as he presses his thumb to his palm. "You okay?" I ask as I pick up the phone. He winces in pain, shaking out his hand. "Eli?"

"Yeah, give me a minute to finish the call." He grabs the phone and moves into the other room. I've never seen him this angry, but he's livid. I hear him continuing to fight with whomever is on the line.

I sit at the kitchen counter, picking at the fruit that his chef cut up. I took off the rest of this week and the next when Eli said he wasn't in a hurry to go back. I want to spend as much time as I can with him before our entire relationship shifts. We discussed the fact that he was in breach of contract, but he was relentless in telling me not to worry about it.

It appears that I should've trusted my gut in worrying.

Eli returns to the kitchen about fifteen minutes later and tosses his phone on the marble countertop. He pulls the fridge open, mumbling about asshole directors and egos. I try not to laugh, but he's so cute when he's pissed that a short giggle escapes.

His eyes shift to me, he slams the door shut, and then he moves to me so quick I gasp. Then, his lips are against mine and I have to grip his arms to keep from falling back. The brute force of the kiss shocks me. This last week has been all tenderness. This is anything but that.

He hoists me out of my seat with one arm, lifting me so my ass is now on the counter. My hands move to his neck, holding him now that we're even in height. He pushes himself between my legs, and I wrap them around his waist.

As much as I love the gentle Eli, I really missed the sex-God.

"Ellington," I say as I break away for air.

"Say it again," he commands. His lips suck at the skin on my neck, and I hold his hair. "Say my name, Heather."

"Eli," I moan as he starts to move lower.

"No, baby, try again."

I know now what he wants. Eli Walsh is the man I share. Ellington is all mine. I pull his hair back so he looks at me. "Ellington."

I watch the fire burn in his gaze, and I melt for him. "That's who I am to you, baby. Only you."

"Kiss me," I request.

He seems to struggle with moving, but I don't let him pull away from me. I'm not breakable. Eli made sure that, no matter what, I had what I needed, and now he needs me.

Instead of letting him decide, I push my lips back to his. He moans against my tongue, and it's the sexiest sound ever. There's nothing I love more than driving him to the edge. To have influence over this man is exhilarating.

He stops quickly, taking two big steps back, both of us breathing heavily. "Why did you stop?" I ask.

"Fuck!" He bellows as he looks to the ceiling.

I hop down. "What happened? Are you okay?"

His eyes close, and he takes a few deep breaths. "I'm fine, just pissed, and I shouldn't've taken it out on you."

I touch his cheek and smile. "Did it look like I minded? If that's how you handle being pissed, then I may piss you off constantly."

He bursts out laughing and shakes his head. "I love you," he says without hesitancy.

We still haven't said it since that night. I didn't need him to, either, but my smile is wide. "I love you, too."

My hands rest on his chest. "I was worried I imagined that night."

"It's been a long time since I've said that to anyone. I'll be sure to tell you more often."

"You show me every day."

He kisses my nose and sighs. "That was my agent. The producer is livid, demanding I return to New York in twenty-four hours or I'll be hearing from their legal team."

I've been selfish to think he could keep this up. We've both been living in our own dream world. He's under contract. I can't keep him here. "I'm doing fine now. You don't have to stay for me."

"I'm not here because I don't think you're okay, Heather. I'm here because I can't leave you. I don't want to go to New York and not see your brown eyes when I wake up. There's nothing up there for me, and you're everything I need here."

I know he's an actor, but there's no doubting the sincerity in his words. Knowing that he wants to stay because he wants to be with me makes me fall even deeper. However, if he loses his job and has this big legal battle because of me, it could possibly cause a rift in our relationship.

"You used to tell me you weren't going anywhere, the same goes for me, babe. I'll be right here when you get back.

We have to trust that what we've found here is strong enough to endure a few months apart."

He starts to pace the room, and the air fills with his confliction. "I know that, but they're being fucking ridiculous."

There's nothing I'd love more than for him to stay, but it's wrong. I walk over to him, lacing my fingers with his. He needs to go, and I need to be on board with it. As much as he says he's not still here because he's worried about me, I know a small part of him is. Maybe he's not worried that I'm going to go catatonic again, but he's still concerned. I need to ease his mind and get him back to work.

"Eli, you have to go back to work. You've given them no timeframe so they're going to make threats. It would be the same in my department. I don't want you to leave, but we both know it's what needs to be done. I'm going back to work in a week anyway. With as amazing as our little world we've made is, the reality is we can't stay here." I hate the words because they're true. Our time together has been perfect. It's been what we've needed, but now we have other things that we both have to face. "I love you, and part of loving each other is trusting that we can handle this. You love acting, I love my job, and we need to build *our* life where we have balance."

Eli doesn't respond, he grabs the phone, dials, and waits. "I'll be in New York in one week. If they want to sue me, I don't fucking care. I'll be there next Monday ready for work. Let them know that I have other priorities now, and I'm going to be coming to Tampa on weekends."

The phone goes sliding across the counter, and I smile. He's going to come here on the weekends. Without a word, he takes my hands, guiding me upstairs. When we enter the bedroom, he pushes me onto the bed and climbs over me.

"I have seven days with you." His green eyes glimmer with

lust. "Let's see how many times I can make you scream my name."

Eli continues to surprise me each time we're together. I've never known the kind of pleasure like he gives me. He's rather proud of the fact that I scream his name multiple times. I'm not complaining, either.

Sated, he passed out quickly and I lie awake next to him, watching him sleep. I want to do something special for him. When he talks about his life, it's almost surreal. People are always doing things for him, but it isn't like they care about him. They do it because it's their job. No one ever really thinks about him.

Thanks to my Wikipedia stalking, I know his birthday is going to be in two weeks. Since I'll be back to work, and so will he, I want to celebrate with him early.

So, I leave a note on my pillow that says I'd be back after I run a few errands and head out.

My first phone call is to Savannah. I ask if they'd be willing to come to the house for a party in two days. Of course, she agrees and then goes on to give me a list of his favorite things and then offers to help make sure everyone can make it.

After I have a list, I head to the grocery store. Eli's favorite cake is German Chocolate, which is not exactly the easiest thing to bake for someone who knows what they are doing. I'm not that person. I love to eat cake, but I can't make it. However, I want everything to be made by my hands. I can't give him fancy things. I'm not rich or have people to call to get things done, all I can give him is my heart and my time.

My phone pings with a text.

BEST SEX OF MY LIFE

Hey, babe. Where are you?

He's ridiculous. I can't believe he changed his name in my phone again.

> A little full of yourself, huh?

BEST SEX OF MY LIFE
I have no idea what you mean.

> Really? The name in my phone keeps upping your game.

BEST SEX OF MY LIFE
Well, it's all true so far.

I laugh. It's these things. These little things that make him so endearing to me.

> I'm not sure about this one. I've had better.

BEST SEX OF MY LIFE
The hell you have.

> Wouldn't you like to know . . .

BEST SEX OF MY LIFE
I'll show you when you get back. Start stretching because it'll be one hell of a workout. Which leads me back to the first question, where are you?

I smile as I think about what his face must look like, the prowl in his eyes, and how his jaw is set. I know damn well he'll make good on his threat.

> I'm out. I'll be back soon. I love you.

BEST SEX OF MY LIFE
I love you. See you soon . . . naked.

I snort.

I finish gathering ingredients and then stop at my house to

unload them. I don't want to tip him off about anything. Not that I initially intended it to be a surprise, but if I can pull it off, I'd like to try. Eli and I have pretty much planned to do nothing but be together this week, but I can be creative.

I make my way back to his house—mansion—excited about my plans. I called my girls, inviting them as well. They love Eli, especially after seeing him with me these last few weeks, so they should be a part of his celebration.

"Honey, I'm here," I call out as I enter the house.

"I'm in the kitchen," Eli replies.

I move toward the back of the house where I find him walking to the fridge.

"You were gone a while, is everything all right?" Eli asks.

"Yeah, I had some stuff I needed to do, and then I stopped at my place for some clothes."

We've been staying here more than at my house, and I was running out of things to wear, even though we spend most of the time by the pool or in bed.

Eli moves back to the island and he winces. "You okay?"

"Yeah," he grumbles. "I did something to my foot getting out of bed."

"You really are getting old," I say in a joking voice. "You're falling apart, Gramps."

He cocks his head to the side and chuckles. "Keep it up, baby. You're not that far behind me."

"I am not old! I can kick your ass any day of the week and twice on Sundays."

Eli grabs the sandwich and takes a huge bite. "Try me," he says around a mouthful of food.

I think he forgets that I'm a cop. I've wrestled big guys in bar fights, taken down punks who try to run, and battled with prisoners who think they can take on the world. My training is vast, and I've worked hard to know my strengths.

Plus, most men don't want to hurt a girl. It's in their DNA.

I take full advantage of that. It is also in their genetic make up not to get their ass kicked by a woman. I need to remember that.

"So," I say as I plop on the bar chair. "What do you want to do today?"

"I was thinking we go on a date . . . a real date. Where you get dressed up, and I wine you, dine you, and then sixty-nine—"

"Okay!" I cut him off. "Romantic."

He shrugs. "I thought so."

"People will see us."

"Good."

"They'll know you're dating."

Eli puts the sandwich on his plate and leans on the counter. "Good."

"We won't be able to hide."

He moves around toward me, still watching my reactions. "It's not my life that will no longer be hidden, Heather. I'm ready for every woman to know that I'm not interested, the question is . . . are you?"

My mind recalls the conversation with Savannah. I know that as soon as we step out from behind our curtain, all of that will follow, but I meant what I said to him. I'm not going anywhere. His life and mine are becoming entangled, and I don't want to see what would become of me if the threads were cut.

"PEOPLE ARE LOOKING AT ME," I whisper as Eli looks over the menu.

"Yup." He grins. "You're kind of hard to ignore."

I tilt my head and sigh. "Don't be charming."

"Can't help it. You bring out the romantic in me." Eli shrugs and goes back to reading.

I try to stop fidgeting, but it's hard when I can feel people's eyes on me. At least when we were in the park, I was invisible to the woman. Here, it's the complete opposite.

I straighten my back and follow his lead. I can do this. People look at me when I'm in uniform, so this is no different.

The waitress takes our drink order, spending extra time attending to Eli's request for water. I swear.

"You look beautiful," he says, taking my hand.

I glance at my navy one-shoulder cocktail dress and then back to him. I spent extra time getting ready, making sure I looked like someone who belonged with him. My hair is curled and pulled over to the side, exposing my neck. The nude pumps I stole from Nicole six months ago are killing me, but I wore them. And even with the extra makeup, making me feel less like myself, I'm totally freaking out.

"I feel like I'm naked in front of a crowd." Once again, I look around at all the people, some of whom are whispering and staring.

Eli's mouth turns into a sly grin. "I would be perfectly fine with that as well."

I glare at him. "Funny."

"Relax, Heather." Eli gives my hand a squeeze. "People look, and people talk, but we're the only thing that matters right now."

He's right. I'm on a date with Eli, and we both love each other. This is a part of who he is, and that means, it'll be a part of my life. I might as well get used to it.

"Okay, I'm sorry."

"Don't be sorry, it's an adjustment, I'm sure. You get used to it."

Something to look forward to.

The waitress returns, giving me a sour look. "Wine," she places it in front of me while looking at Eli. I go to open my mouth to let her know she's brought the wrong wine, but she turns her back to me. "And for you, Mr. Walsh, we've selected our top-of-the-line bottle of cabernet, on the house."

"Thank you," he says politely and then his eyes meet mine. "However, my girlfriend ordered the Pinot Grigio, but you brought her red wine. Why don't you fix her drink first since I only asked for water?"

"Oh, I'm so sorry." She grabs the glass and walks away quickly.

"I think she might cry." I fight back laughing. Her face was priceless. It's clear she's a fan, or at least thinks he's hot, and he just dismissed her.

Eli raises and drops his shoulder. "Maybe if she didn't ignore you, then I wouldn't have to be a dick."

I've never had someone love me like this. Thinking back, I'm not sure Matt ever defended me. I always felt like I was on my own. With Eli, he looks at me as if I'm special and treasured. He wants to protect and care for me.

"Is it like this in New York . . . when you go out?" I question.

He chuckles. "No, it's like I'm a normal guy."

"Yeah right." I don't think Eli could ever be normal. He's sexier than any man I've ever seen, and he's impossible to ignore.

"I swear. Celebrities there aren't treated as if they're special. It's why so many of them live there full time. Plus, there's always a movie or show being filmed. It's a part of life there."

The waitress returns with the right wine and a plate of appetizers. We place our orders, and I smile when he rubs his foot against my calf as she stands there. I can't remember the last time I played footsie.

Our food comes, and we enjoy the meal. I understand now what he means by no longer noticing the people around us. I'm sure they're watching, but I don't pay attention. I'm here with him, and that's all I care about.

Eli and I chat about his time in New York as I sit enthralled. It all sounds so exciting. We finish the meal and are enjoying our bottle of wine. He tells me about his co-workers, and I can't help but fangirl a little over Noah Frazier. After Eli, he's my favorite character, and hearing about how they hang out makes me a little giddy.

"Is Noah as cute in person as he is on television?" I blurt out.

Eli nearly chokes on his drink. "What?"

"I'm a fan," I reply with innocence. "Of the show, of course."

"Oh, of course." The sarcasm in his voice tells me he clearly doesn't believe me.

"Jealous?" I taunt.

Eli leans back, crossing his arms across his broad chest. I use all my restraint to hold back my laugh because he looks adorable when he's being stupid. "Not at all."

"Good."

"It's not like you're asking me about another guy on *our* date."

I giggle a little and recover quickly. "Eli Walsh, do you not know that I think you're the sexiest man I've ever laid eyes on?"

He leans forward, resting his hands on the table. "Do you now?"

I move closer and reach toward him. "Yes."

"Tell me just how sexy you think I am."

I extend my hand, and he mirrors my movement. When we connect, Eli laces his fingers with mine. My mouth opens to tell him all the ways I find him sexy when his phone rings. He grumbles as he looks at the screen.

"Hello, Sharon. Yes. No." His eyes meet mine, and I see the worry there. "We're on a date . . ." Eli huffs. "I don't have to tell you beforehand." A pause. "Well, then do your job and handle it and make it clear what it means." He disconnects the call and then runs his hand down his face.

It doesn't take a detective to figure out what's happened. She knew we were out, which means someone has leaked that Eli Walsh is no longer on the market.

Living in our bubble was great, but we knew it wouldn't last. I'm grateful for the time we had. It allowed us the time to get to know each other and fall in love. If we had people following us around, we may have never gotten past the first date.

"Well, I guess we're official now, huh?" I smile, hoping to reassure him.

He studies me, and when he finds whatever he was looking for, he smiles. "Yeah, baby. We're official."

I nod. "Maybe this means women will stop touching you?"

Eli laughs without reservation. "I doubt it, but I promise not to like it."

"And I promise not to shoot them when they do."

I think that's fair. He doesn't like it, and I don't lose my badge or go to jail . . . win, win.

"There will be photos tomorrow." Eli grows serious.

"I figured as much, people have been staring all night while holding their phones."

Eli's eyes turn playful. "How about we give them a good one to post?"

I'm not sure what exactly that means, but the look in his eyes is enough to make me go along with him. He gets to his feet, makes his way around the table, and places one hand on the arm of my chair, the other on the table.

"I'm going to kiss you," he warns. "I'm going to tell the world that you're mine, right here and now."

Warmth spreads through me as his hand moves to my cheek. He leans down, presses his lips to mine, and publicly declares our relationship.

"Heather, where are the streamers?" Nicole yells from the living room.

"Check the bags where all the decorations were!"

Today is the surprise party for Eli. I'm shocked I've been able to keep him completely in the dark. His mother left for New York the other day and can't make it, but Randy and Savannah will be here. Nicole came over about an hour ago and started getting things ready.

I told Eli that Nicole needed some best friend time since he's been monopolizing me and asked him to come pick me up at eight.

"Found them!" She bounces into the room with a grin. "We only have about five more minutes till everyone gets here. What else do you need?"

"I think we're all set. The cake is done, the food is out, and we're decorated."

"Good. Now you can tell me about your big public date with Mr. Sexy Pants last night," she says as she flops on my bed.

Eli wasn't kidding when he said it was going to get crazy.

Within thirty minutes of the call from his publicist, we had about fifteen paparazzi outside the restaurant. Before we left, he told me exactly what to do and promised he'd shield me as much as he could.

It wasn't all that fun, but we survived. Once we got back to Eli's house, he encouraged me to call my friends and the police department to let them know. I couldn't believe he thought they'd care that much, but he's the expert on dealing with it. No one seemed to care, except for Matt. That was a fun conversation.

"I'm sure you read all about it," I say with my brow raised.

Nicole is a gossip column freak, so I'm sure she knew before I did that the story was going to break. "Not the same. But you're right. Tell me about what happened with Barney Fife instead."

Her and her names for Matt. "He was very short with me. Just one word answers."

"I'm glad he knows. I hope he hates himself for walking out on you."

Eli was not happy about that conversation. He knew he couldn't say much, but I could see how angry he was that I had to tell Matt. It's the part about my job that sucks. I wish I didn't have to deal with my ex-husband, yet I can't say I didn't enjoy having to tell him.

"Matt made his choice, and he has to live with it," I say as I put the last of my clothes away. Not being here much in the last few weeks has made me a little lazy regarding my home. "All right, let's finish up. They'll be here soon."

"Is that what you're wearing?" Nicole asks.

"Yes."

"Oh no," she admonishes me as she looks at my outfit. "You need to change."

I glance at the shorts and top I'm wearing, confused as to

what the hell her issue is. "There's nothing wrong with my clothes."

"Put a freaking skirt on."

"What I'm wearing is fine."

"No." She laughs. "What you're wearing is lame."

I'm not sure what the hell she wants. "What is the issue? Should I be wearing a ball gown for a party with friends and Eli's brother?"

She snorts and heads to my closet. "You need to dress a little sexy for the man. It's his birthday! I have two words — easy . . . access."

The one thing that will always be constant is that Nicole is always thinking about sex. I'm here, worrying about making sure the house is ready, and she's worrying about me getting laid. Nicole riffles through my clothes, and a few things fly from my closet.

"Here," she shoves a skirt and off-the-shoulder top at me. "Put that on, fix your face, you have like . . . two minutes."

Sometimes, I love this girl, other times I'd love to kill her, this is the latter.

Instead of arguing with her, I get changed. I don't think Eli gives a shit about what I'm wearing, but I want this to be special. After I get dressed, I check my makeup and decide Nicole is an idiot because I was perfectly fine.

A few minutes later, Kristin and Danielle arrive. Both of them left their husbands and kids at home. I explain again while it's the four of us that Randy will be here and they have to control their inner fangirls.

"I swear I'll behave," Kristin says. "I figure after Eli, this should be easy."

"I make no promises," Nicole says as she plops on the couch.

I glare at her. "I swear to God, if you do anything stupid, I'll pepper spray you."

Her eyes widen, and I know she's flashing back to the one time she accidently sprayed herself. Dumbass thought it wouldn't hurt and was acting like anyone could be a cop, she pushed the button, but it was pointed at her. After that, she's never even gone near my canisters.

"Not funny." She crosses her arms.

All of us laugh at her face. She's such a turd.

Brody and Rachel arrive a few minutes later, and I'm glad they made it. He got along well with Eli at my sister's memorial. They bonded over the Rays and their predictions for this season. I can't tell you how happy I was that Brody finally had someone other than me to talk to about baseball.

Five minutes later, the doorbell rings. Once again, a dose of fear hits me. I've only met Savannah and Randy once, and it was at their mansion on the beach, now they'll see my home. Will they think I'm a gold digger? What was I thinking having them come here?

I feel a hand on my shoulder, and I know it's Nicole. Sometimes our damn near telepathy is a blessing. "You'll be fine. No one is going to judge you, and if they do, famous or not, I'll kick their ass."

I nod and open the door.

"Hey!" Savannah says with her arms wide. "I'm so glad you gave us a reason to come out. I swear, Adriel is giving me gray hair."

"I'm happy you're here." I hug her back.

"Hey, Heather," Randy's deep voice booms as he pulls me into a hug.

"Savannah, Randy, these are my friends Nicole, Kristin, and Danielle. That's my partner Brody and his wife Rachel."

They all take turns saying hello and shaking each other's hands. It's clear that everyone but Nicole is nervous meeting Randy. However, Savannah's constant poking at him makes it easier to see he's just a guy. Brody and Randy grab a beer and head into the kitchen, leaving all the women to themselves in the living room. I love that my new friends and old are meshing so easily.

"So, what time will Eli get here?" Savannah questions as she scrunches her shoulders.

"Should be here in about ten minutes. I should text him to make sure."

I pull my phone out and search for the last name that he put himself as, but there is no Best Sex of My Life contact. I should've known he'd change it again. I scroll through the contacts from the start. Of course, he doesn't use his actual name, that would be too easy, so I continue checking each letter.

When I get to what is clearly the new name change, I burst out laughing. He's a mess, my mess, but a freaking mess.

Savannah looks at me with a mixture of humor and worry. "What's so funny?"

"He changes his name in my phone each time I forget to hide it."

"Oh, what has my idiot brother-in-law called himself this time?"

"Mr. Multiple Orgasms."

She doubles over with laughter, and I shake my head.

> Hello, Mr. Multiple Orgasms . . . seriously? I wanted to make sure you're picking me up at 8? I can't wait to see you.

MR. MULTIPLE ORGASMS

> Yup, I'll be there by eight. I'm leaving in five minutes.

My smile is automatic. I can't wait to see his face.

"He'll be here in about twenty minutes!" I tell everyone and go back to my conversation with Savannah. She laughs about the other names Eli's given himself, and then we all mingle.

Twenty-five minutes pass and still no Eli, so I shoot him another text.

> Hey, you almost here?

Another fifteen minutes pass, and he doesn't respond. Maybe he's stuck in traffic?

I mingle with my friends, watching the clock and trying not to jump to conclusions. I have to remember that not everything is a tragedy waiting to happen. Years of being preprogrammed to expect the worst is sometimes a curse.

It's now half past eight, and he's definitely late, and I'm undeniably concerned.

"I'm not sure where the hell he is," I say to myself as I make my way around the room. I shoot off another text.

> I hope you're okay . . . please text me back or call me.

Brody comes over, places his hand on my back, and drops his voice to a whisper. "What's the matter, Covey?"

I look over with surprise.

"Don't look at me like that," he admonishes. "I can read you. You're worried about him being late?"

I subtly shake my head. "I'm fine. He said he'd be here over a half hour ago, and we both know it doesn't take that long to get here. He isn't responding to my texts, either."

I wait for my phone to buzz with a response.

"Everything okay?" Nicole asks when she sees me whispering with Brody.

"She's just being Heather," Brody explains.

I shoot him a dirty look, and he shrugs. "He usually texts

me right back, and he's now forty minutes late. I'm wondering why he isn't responding."

"Maybe he fell asleep?" she suggests, which is ludicrous.

"After he said he was leaving?" I counter.

"Want me to check in at the station for reports of any accidents?" Brody offers.

I shake my head. "No, I'm probably being stupid. I'm going to call him now."

I can't explain it, but there's a niggling feeling in my gut telling me something else is keeping him. There are times that gut check has been the difference of life and death for me, I don't tend to ignore it, but I don't want to be a crazy girlfriend, either.

I make my way outside to see if maybe his car is here, but since there's no sign of him, I call. The phone rings and rings before his voice mail picks up.

"Hey, babe, I'm calling because it's been almost an hour since you said you'd be here, and I haven't heard from you. Give me a call when you can. Love you."

I disconnect the phone and start to pace the porch. My mind races from one extreme to the other as I go from fear to resolve. A big part of me wants to get in the car and head over there, the other says I have to trust him. He could be held up for a hundred reasons, and my being paranoid isn't going to be good for a long-distance relationship we're about to embark on. Not wanting to be dramatic, I convince myself to head inside and give him a little more time.

After another seven minutes, that niggling feeling is now a full-blown boulder threatening to crush me if I don't get in my car to go find him.

Randy comes outside, and I give him a fake smile. "You okay?"

"Eli isn't answering the phone or my texts, and he said he'd be here at eight."

He looks at his watch and back to me. "I'll go to the house and check on him."

I shake my head. "No, I mean, he has no idea you're here."

Randy's eyes flash with something, but I don't catch it. "You should do that . . . so it doesn't ruin the party . . ."

"Okay," I draw the word out.

"My brother has no idea how lucky he is."

I smile and shrug. "I think we're both lucky."

I'm fully aware of how blessed I am that Eli thought enough to chase after me. All those times I tried to get rid of him make me grateful that he doesn't like to be told no. Otherwise, I wouldn't know what real love is like.

I enter the house and explain to everyone that I'll be back. "I'm going to check on him. It's been an hour, and he still isn't answering."

I hop in my car, telling myself the entire way to remain calm no matter what. He's given me no reason to distrust him, and he's probably sleeping. Who am I kidding? He's not sleeping. The only reason I feel as though I'm a good cop is because of my intuition. It's something so many of us brush aside, but I believe it's a gift not to be squandered. How many times did I think Matt was unhappy and pretended I was being stupid? So many I lost count. I think back to when Stephanie's symptoms started, how the doctors told us she didn't need the extra tests, but I demanded they do them. I knew there was something we were missing, and I refused to budge.

Right now, my nerves are screaming that something isn't right, and he isn't where he should be.

I pull up to his house, and the lights are still on. I use the key he gave me and head inside.

"Eli?" I call out, but no one answers.

I hear noise coming from the family room off the kitchen. I turn the corner, but it's just the television. I check the pool deck before moving on to the rest of the second floor. This freaking house needs to be smaller.

My heart starts to quicken as I get closer to the bedroom. I don't know where he is, but each step I take makes my stomach grow tighter. I close my eyes, steeling myself for whatever I might find, and open the door.

He lies crumpled in the middle of the bedroom floor.

"Eli!" I scream and rush toward him. Sweat covers his body, he has a gash on his head where blood leaks from. His breathing is labored, and his eyes flutter open to closed. "Oh my God." My hands shake as I try to turn him over. "Eli, can you hear me?"

He struggles for breath, and I'm not sure if he's conscious when he mutters something incoherent. I lean closer, listening, and swear I hear the word "Help."

"Stay awake," I say as I tap the side of his face.

I dial 9-1-1, and my mind switches immediately into police mode. My voice shakes, but I'm able to give the dispatcher his address, my badge number, and a rundown of the situation. They instruct me to keep him awake if possible and to wait for help.

It shouldn't take long for the paramedics to arrive, but each second feels like hours.

I sit on the floor with his head in my lap. "Can you open your eyes?" I ask, but he doesn't respond. "Can you hear me, baby? Can you tell me what happened?"

"Heather," Eli's eyes open, and he starts to struggle. "Have to get . . . to . . . phone."

"I'm right here, Eli. Don't move, just stay with me," I command as I wipe a bead of sweat from his forehead. "Help is on the way."

He pants again, and I take his pulse several times, watching the clock move. His heart rate is all over the place. I hear the banging on the door below, and I now understand what it feels like on this side of the door. My fear of leaving him to let them in but knowing I have to makes my heart plummet.

"I'll be right back," I say, even though I know he probably doesn't understand.

I rush down the stairs faster than I knew I could move and throw the door open. Two of my fellow squad members, Whitman and Vincenzo, stand there.

"Covey?" Whitman asks with surprise.

"He's upstairs. Where are the medics?" I ask without answering the questions in their eyes.

"They're pulling through the gate now," Vincenzo replies. "Are you on duty?"

"Why aren't they here? He needs medical help!"

"Relax." Whitman touches my arm. "Wait, is this . . . this is . . ."

I don't answer him. I don't care if he's figuring out whose house this is and why I'm here. The man I'm so deeply in love with is going in and out of consciousness, and he needs help. My legs start to shake, and Whitman catches me as I start to crumble.

He steadies me, and I turn toward the staircase. I can't wait for help, I *am* the help. We need to get him to the hospital now. "You guys can transport him, fuck the ambulance. I can't carry him. I don't know what happened, but he needs help now!" I say with so much emotion that their faces fall. I'm not sentimental at work. I don't cry. I don't whine. I do my job and kick ass. I'm a warrior when I'm in uniform. Even through my sister's illness, I never once appeared weak. Right now, I can't hold it together. "He can't wait! I can't lose him!"

Tears spring in my gaze, and I can't stop them. I feel helpless.

"Heather," Vincenzo says in his calming voice. I know that tone. I'm the master at that tone. "They're almost here, relax."

"Go with her," Whitman instructs. "I'll get the medics upstairs. I'll radio when they arrive, okay?"

I know he's right. We can't take a patient with a head injury to the hospital in the cop car.

We rush back up the stairs and into the room where Eli still lies helpless on the floor. I move back to him, checking his pulse again. Tears continue to fall as I brush back his dark brown hair.

"They're here," I hear Whitman over the radio.

The paramedics enter the room, and I see the recognition as they realize they're in Eli Walsh's house. They look at both of us and back to him.

Questions are fired off as they try to gather information about his injuries and medical history. So many things I don't know . . .

"Is he taking any medication?"

"I don't know."

"Any medical conditions?"

"I don't know," I admit.

"Allergies?"

"I . . ." I shake my head. "I don't know."

"Has he taken any drugs? Been drinking?"

"No, I've never seen him take anything. And I wasn't here, so I have no idea if he drank anything."

They both look to each other and then ask more questions that I can't answer. It takes me three minutes to realize how much Eli and I don't know about each other. He has no idea I'm allergic to penicillin or that I had surgery eight years ago for an ovarian cyst. We're so in love and so oblivious.

He groans as they roll him onto the backboard and then carry him down the stairs. I grab my phone and keys off the front entry table and they're already closing the doors.

I quickly try to lock up, but my blood-covered hands are shaking so bad I can't get the key to go in.

Whitman comes over, places his hand over mine, steadying it so I can turn the key. "I'll drive you over," he says, guiding me to the cruiser.

I don't say anything, I'm in shock, and my mind can't fully absorb anything. I climb in the back and twist my hands together.

The only thing that goes through my mind is that I can't lose him. Not like this. Not so soon after Stephanie. Not when we haven't had enough time. We deserve more time.

Please, God, give me more time.

"RANDY!" I rush forward as he sprints into the hospital. It's been twenty minutes since we arrived. I was told to take a seat and they'd let me know something, but no one will answer me. They keep saying I'm not family. "They're not telling me anything, but they're working on him."

"Okay, I'll find out." Randy heads to the desk where the nurse grabs a file and then escorts him back.

Savannah's hand touches my shoulder, and I turn to her with tears streaming. "It's okay, Heather. Eli is strong."

"I don't know what happened. There was blood on the carpet from the bathroom to where I found him. I guess he hit his head and stopped there?" Now that I've had time to think, I'm trying to piece together the scene. My best guess is that he fell. I know his foot was giving him problems, so maybe he tripped? Either way, he hit his head, and then either fell again . . . or something. Why was he dripping with sweat? Did he have to drag himself from the bathroom? I don't know. "I couldn't tell the paramedics anything. I don't know what caused this or if he takes any medication . . . I called as soon as I snapped out of it."

Savannah guides me to the chair, and she's silent. "So, you

and Eli haven't really gotten to that share everything point?" she asks after a few minutes.

"No, I guess not. We happened so fast and so strong. It was like this tornado that swooped us both up. Plus, I was dealing with my sister's disease, and he was trying to be there for me. I don't know."

She takes my hand in hers. "Randy should be out soon, he'll let you know what's going on."

"I should've gone and checked on him earlier."

Hindsight is a bitch. I had a feeling when he wasn't responding. I ignored it, and he needed me.

Randy comes into view, and we both stand. "He's going to be okay. He's confused, but he'll be fine."

"Oh, thank God." I sigh. The weight lifts from my chest, and I can breathe again.

"He wants to see you, but he needs a few more tests."

"Okay." I'll sit out here and wait forever if it means he'll be okay. He's going to be okay. I knew I was afraid, but I hadn't realized how tightly the fear had gripped me until it was gone. "Do you know what happened?"

Randy looks to Savannah and then back to me. "The details are fuzzy, but I'm sure he'll explain what he remembers."

"I'm going to call your mom," Savannah says and kisses his cheek.

"I'm glad you checked on him," Randy says as we take a seat. "I don't know what would've happened if you hadn't gone there. He's really lucky to have you, Heather. I hope you know how much he loves you."

It's weird hearing this from his brother. We've only met twice now, but Randy seems to understand Eli at his core. He clearly loves his brother, and it's a bond I can understand completely. What he said is something I would've felt toward someone loving Stephanie.

"I love him, too."

He nods. "I believe you do."

Savannah returns from her phone call right as the doctor comes out.

He explains that Eli finished his CT scan, and they're going to do some additional testing, but he's alert and receiving fluids. "He's back in his room if you'd like to see him, he's asking for Randy and then Heather."

"I'll be brief." He smiles and then follows the doctor through the double doors.

Relief floods my veins now that we've confirmed he's going to be fine. I close my eyes and say a silent prayer to Stephanie. I feel her here. This hospital was where we spent so much time together. Days of testing that turned into overnights because of her exhaustion. So many nights I slept in that God-awful chair that they said was a bed, hoping her pain would subside.

I hoped it would be a long time before I walked these halls again.

Randy returns to the waiting room not even ten minutes later.

"He's waiting for you." He smiles. "We have to get back to the kids, but if you need anything, just call, okay? I'll come back tomorrow to check on things."

Savannah pulls me in and kisses my cheek. "I'll call you tomorrow as well, okay?"

"Of course."

I make my way to Eli's room and knock softly. The door creaks and his eyes meet mine. All at once, my emotions burst forward. Relief that he's okay, fear that it could've gone another way, happiness that he looks a little like himself, guilt that I wasn't there, and most of all . . . love for this man.

"Eli," I say as a prayer. I move forward, and he pulls me to his chest. "God, I was so scared."

His arms are tight, and I breathe him in. "I'm going to be fine, baby."

I lift my head and touch his face. "You scared me."

He closes his eyes. "I was stupid."

"Stupid?"

Eli takes my hands in his. "I should've never pushed myself."

"What happened?" I ask, but the nurse enters.

"Hi, Mr. Walsh, I'm your nurse, Shera," she smiles. "I'm going to start the Solu-Medrol in the IV, and then I'll take your vitals again."

"Thank you," he says.

I know that drug.

I don't know why, but I swear I've heard it before.

I rack my brain to remember why the hell it sounds so familiar.

Then it hits me.

Solu-Medrol is what they gave Stephanie when her nerve pain flared. It's a drug she had several times to reduce the inflammation, and it's only used for severe conditions.

My eyes meet Eli's, and the floor drops out from beneath me.

CHAPTER TWENTY-FIVE
ELI

I see the storms roll through her brown eyes. I watch the confliction without saying a word. There's nothing I'm going to be able to say to explain this.

I've been lying to her.

The nurse takes her time as the tension fills the room. I almost want her to stay, any second to prolong the inevitable, I'll take.

There were so many times I could've said something. Randy laid into me pretty hard, and I deserved every word.

He has no idea the guilt I've felt for keeping my illness from her. The nights I lie awake with her in my arms, hating myself because I'm a pussy and couldn't let her go. I'm a selfish prick. I know this, but for the first time, I didn't care.

"All right, I'll be back to check on you in an hour," Shera explains and pats my arm. "I'm a big fan, Mr. Walsh. We'll take good care of you."

The knot in my throat doesn't allow me to speak. My gaze turns back to Heather, and I wait.

A single tear rolls down her perfect cheek. I watch as it lands on her lips, ones I know I'll never feel again, and my heart breaks. I wonder if this could've been different. If I'd told her I was sick, would she have stayed? I'll never know.

"You're sick." Her soft voice is filled with pain.

"Yes."

Heather's hands shake as she tries to wipe her face. "Do you have Huntington's disease?"

"No, I have relapsing-remitting multiple sclerosis."

Her lips part, and I watch her face fall. Fear beams from her eyes before another tear descends. "Are—" She clears her throat. "Are you okay?"

Agony like I've never felt before spreads through my body. Not because I'm actually in pain, but because even though she knows I've been hiding my condition, she's still worried about me.

I'm a fucking piece of shit.

I don't deserve her.

"I haven't been symptomatic in a while. I usually take medication that helps keep things under control."

She nods slowly while twisting her hands. "I see. And you're not taking them now?"

I've been reckless with my body the last few months. On tour, I didn't take the infusions regularly. Then I met Heather, and I thought I could be free for a little while. I didn't know we'd have something like this. Yes, I had feelings for her, but I truly thought they would fade, not intensify. My time with Heather has been the first time I felt warmth in my life, and I know the darkness will be that much deeper when she leaves.

"Not like I should."

Her gaze moves to where her hands are laced tightly together in her lap. "Okay. How long have you known you have MS?"

Her calm tone scares me more than if she were yelling.

"I had my first symptom ten years ago."

"Right. Ten years."

There's no anger in her voice, only resignation. She keeps her eyes down, leaving me no indication of what she's thinking. She has no idea how much guilt I've grappled with. But my need for her won out. Self-preservation came before anything else. I had to have her. I needed to keep her.

"I wanted to tell you," I admit.

"But you didn't."

Because I'm a fucking pussy. "I couldn't."

Her eyes lift, a mix of hurt and anger fill her gaze. "And you thought lying to me about it was the better option?"

"I couldn't tell you. I tried, but I couldn't do it."

She clutches her stomach and drops her head.

My chest aches and dread spreads through me. She's going to leave, just like Penelope. As soon as she found out I wasn't the perfect man, that I was damaged, she took off. When Heather returns her gaze to me, I see the same goodbye in her eyes, exactly like all those years ago.

"You kept the fact that you were sick from me. You . . . hid this." She chokes on the words. "Even knowing everything I went through? How could you do this to me? How could you make me believe that we were building a future together, when all the while you were keeping something so serious from me? How, Eli, how?" Her voice cracks at the end, and I curse myself for being weak.

Weakness in my heart. Weakness in my body.

I can't go to her. I can't grab her and force her to hear me out. Even though, I have nothing but excuses. Dread fills the room, weaving its way around my broken heart, squeezing tighter as I prepare for her to leave me.

"I've hated myself for it. I wanted you to see me, know me, love me, and then I was going to tell you. I know it's fucked up. But when you told me about your sister, I couldn't tell you. Then the day I was finally going to tell you, Stephanie died. After that, there was no way I could say it."

"And what about all the time since then?"

"Each day I kept it in, it became harder to tell you. I was afraid if I did, you were going to leave."

"What?" She turns with a mix of anger and shock. "You thought if I knew you were sick, that I'd walk away from you? You think that's who I am?"

"I think it's easy to love a man who isn't falling apart."

"And you think I'm that shallow? Do you know me at all? I would never have left you because you were sick!"

"I couldn't know that!"

Heather stands and moves toward my bed and tears fill her eyes as she touches my cheek. I want to relish in her touch, but I won't allow myself any of it. "You didn't give me a chance to show you."

"If you're going to go, then go," I spit the words.

She shakes her head, opening and closing her mouth before she collapses in the chair. Heather's body sings of defeat. I've broken her.

Anger toward myself builds like blocks. Each stacking higher and higher until I can't see over the wall. I punch my way through, each blow causing my panic to rise. She's going to leave me, and I won't be able to stop her.

"I want to fucking stand and come over to you," I say, hoping she is still listening. "I want to take you in my arms and be the man that you thought you had. But my fucking legs won't work. I can't walk, Heather. I can't fucking walk. I screwed up every goddamn chance I had with you. I know this. I hate myself for it, and I won't hurt you."

Her head lifts, and she wipes the tears with the back of her hand. "What do you mean your legs won't work?"

"I had shooting pain up and down my legs earlier. They're now numb."

Her lips part and she sucks in a breath. "Is that how you fell?"

"Yes, I knew it was happening, but I tried to pretend it wasn't."

Heather doesn't say a word. She watches me with her gorgeous eyes. Eyes that I know each speck of gold, each tiny piece of light brown, and every darker spot by memory. Eyes in which I've found everything I've ever wanted. She's loved me because I've been the man she needed. Because of my MS, I'm now broken, weak, and a liar.

I decide she needs to hear the entire ugly story. Let her get a glimpse into the hell my body is stirring. "My hand has occasionally been going numb over the last week."

Awareness flashes and she gasps. "Like when you dropped your phone?"

"Today, I was in the bathroom and realized I'd left my phone on the table in the bedroom. My foot started to tingle and there was shooting pain up my legs. I sat at the tub, thinking I could rub my legs enough to make it stop, which it did enough that I thought I could get to my phone." I look over, wanting to see her face when she hears it all. Heather is a statue, she doesn't move or even breathe, so I lay it out. "I took one step before I went down. My head slammed on the side of the counter."

"Eli," she gasps.

I lift my palm to stop her. "I don't think I passed out then, and I knew I was bleeding. But I couldn't feel my legs." Her hand covers her mouth as another tear falls. "I couldn't move, and all I could think about was disappointing you. I knew you needed me, but I couldn't get to you. I was lying on that floor, refusing to fail you. So, I used every fucking scrap of strength I had and clawed my way out of there. Using only my arms, I pulled, pushed, and struggled to gain each goddamn inch. Knowing that this was going to be how it went." She moves to my side, and I brush away her tears. I touch her blonde hair, memorizing the way it feels in my grasp. I touch her face, wishing I could go back in time. "I couldn't get far before my arms started to ache. My hands weren't closing like I wanted them to. I was weak, because that's what this disease has made me."

"You're not weak," her feathery voice rebuts. "All of this could've been avoided, Eli. Tonight could've been so much easier if you told me you were having symptoms instead of lying to me."

"You only knew me as Eli Walsh, the singer, actor, and man who could give you the world. I've lived this scene before, Heather. I watched it with Penelope, so go ahead and make your exit so we can go back to our lives!"

"No." The single word is steel, and it stops my pity party in its tracks. "Don't you dare make me out to be like your ex. I'm not her. I'm not running away. I'm still sitting right here, trying to understand!"

"Why?" I yell. "Why bother?"

"Because I love you!" She's on her feet at my side. "That's what you do when you love someone!"

I shake my head and smother the hope that tries to claw its way through. "What if I don't love you?"

I push the lie out of my mouth, needing her to have a seed of doubt.

Heather's eyes narrow, and she grips my face in her hands. "Say it to me again, Ellington. Tell me you don't love me. Look me in the eyes and tell me that."

One tear falls from her beautiful eyes, and it kills me. No matter what happens from this moment forward, I won't lie to her. I can't hurt her like that, because it would be like cutting out my own heart.

"I can't."

Her hands move from my face to cover her own. "You can't lie to me anymore, Eli. If we're going to do this together, we have to be honest."

"Do what?" I ask.

"If we're going to fight this. I need to know what all of your disease means."

I had so many brilliant reasons why I should keep this from her, but all of them seem ridiculous now, except this last one. The one I feared more than anything, that she'd look at me like this. Heather's eyes are no longer filled with fear or anger, now it's resolve. It's the same way she looked at her sister.

I love her more than anything in this world, and I won't be another thing she has to care for.

She's done it her whole life, and it won't be how we live.

"I won't do this," I say. "I won't become a patient to you. I can't."

"What?" she gasps.

MS doesn't have a guidebook. I don't get to predict my outcome, and I won't burden her. I knew the day I found out about her sister that I should've stopped pursuing her, but I've never been able to stay away. She needs to know the truth of what this means for us, but I cannot be the man she pities.

"I'm not your sister, Heather. Don't you get it? Don't you see that I want to be the one who takes care of you!" I yell, frustration rolling off me. Her body goes ramrod straight. I watch the anguish spread across her face, her shoulders slump, and her jaw drop. I say the dumbest thing I could. "Just leave."

Her eyes meet mine, and then Heather does the one thing I both wanted to happen and prayed wouldn't . . . she turns and walks out the door without a word.

I've just lost her.

Agony like I've never felt before engulfs me, and I fucking deserve every last bit of it.

CHAPTER TWENTY-SIX
HEATHER

I lean against the wall outside his door, struggling to catch my breath. I can't believe he said that. Of all the things that have come out of his mouth, nothing has ever hurt me like him bringing up my sister.

I've never looked at him like that. I loved my sister, I cared for my sister, and it's only been a few weeks since I lost her. I didn't need him to draw the comparison—I already had, and I was coming to terms with how different this is. He has no idea how much he hurt me. Not just because of the comment, either. I've shared everything with him. There's nothing I keep from him, and yet, he keeps vital things from me.

Anger sears my veins, and I fight the urge to go back in there and rip into him. Explain how things in an adult relationship are supposed to work, but I don't move.

"You okay?" Shera, the nurse assigned to Eli's room, asks.

I rub my eyes, hoping I don't look like a crazy person before righting myself. "Yeah, sorry. I just . . . I need a few minutes."

She rubs my arm. "Okay, honey. We'll keep an eye on him. Don't you worry. He's going to be okay, you'll see, the IV will help, and he'll be good as new."

Yeah, but what will we be? How do we move on from here when he's pushing me away? I don't voice that to her, I attempt a smile and nod. "Thanks."

My head falls back against the wall, and I close my eyes, trying to think through everything that happened. He had to know what he said would break my heart. Mentioning Stephanie like that was a low blow that I felt in the depths of my soul. She was my entire world, and I never pitied her, I did whatever I could to lift her up. How dare he wound me so deeply?

But Eli's never been callous, he's always been . . . perfect.

Perfection is an illusion we create to convince the soul to trust. Now that the curtain has fallen, I see how stupid I was. The thing is, I don't need perfect. I need real because Matt was perfect until shit hit the fan. Then he was gone. But this hurts so much more than that did.

I need air. I need to think and get control, because if I go back in there, I'm going to lose my shit.

I make my way toward the front of the hospital while my mind runs in circles. Tears roll down my cheeks as the warm air hits my face. I inhale, hoping to get some clarity, but I find something much worse.

"Ms. Covey!" My name is being called by a crowd of people all rushing toward me. Flashes of lights go off so fast I can't see anything around me. Over and over they blind me and create a circle so I can't move. They scream my name and bark out questions while I try to find a way out of their enclosure. "Is Eli okay? What happened? Is it true he collapsed? Ms. Covey, over here!" There is no time to answer even if I wanted to. "Are you still together? Are you crying? Can you tell us if there were drugs involved?"

My heart pounds too hard in my chest as I push through them without saying a word. I get back in the safety of the waiting room and release a heavy breath. One more thing to deal with today. God only knows what those photos will look like.

My phone pings, and I pull it from my pocket.

NICOLE

Hey, don't want to bother you, just checking in. Are things okay there?

> No, things are definitely not okay. He's fine, but relationship wise . . . not so much.

NICOLE

I'm sorry. Need me to kick his ass?

> I think I got this. We'll figure it out or we can both kick his ass.

NICOLE

Regulators . . . Mount up!

I burst out laughing as I hear her doing her best Warren G impersonation. Nothing like Nicole to bring some humor in when I feel like I'm drowning.

I dial her number, and she answers on the first ring. "You're so not okay if you're calling me."

"I need you to remind me that I can handle this."

Nicole goes quiet and then clears her throat. "I don't know what happened to make you question yourself."

I tell her about what happened tonight. Nicole listens and allows me to spill my heart. I'm so hurt and angry. I'm also disappointed because I thought we were great. I didn't know he'd been lying to me and hoping I wouldn't find out. I'm angry because he hid his symptoms from me, which led to me finding him collapsed in his bedroom.

"I can't even get some air because I was assaulted by fucking photographers," I complain and sink into the chair.

"Do you want me to come kick some asses? I'll handle the

paparazzi, and then I'll fuck Eli up for being a douche. I figure you're done with him so you won't be upset."

"I know what you're doing," I grumble.

"Either you're going to do it or I need to come and end it for you."

She's insane to think I'd let her handle this. "Stop being an asshole."

She lets out a cough that sounds more like a laugh. "You should talk. You're on the phone with me instead of in there fighting for him. Guys like Eli don't come around often, and if you're dumb enough to let him go, then you're not the fierce woman I've admired."

"I feel betrayed," I admit. "Him keeping this from me is a big deal, and then to be so cruel by bringing up Steph."

"You should feel that way and be sure to let him know that. But remember what happened to you not even two minutes ago, babe. Eli deals with that day in and day out, he has to protect himself, too. More than anything, you have to decide right now if you're willing to end things. If the answer is no, then get your tiny ass back in there and fix it."

She's right. I need to let him know exactly how I feel. I knew when I walked out of that room, I'd walk back in. He isn't the man I'm willing to watch leave my life. When Matt left, there was sadness but also relief. The idea of not having Eli causes my heart to drop.

I sigh and get to my feet. "I need to go."

I'm a strong woman who knows exactly what I want, and it's him. I'm going to tell him exactly how this is going to work. He doesn't get to decide this alone, it's as much my choice as it's his.

"I knew you'd do this," Nicole says with pride. "God help him, because my friend is a badass who doesn't take shit from anyone. Love you, call me if you need me."

"I will. Love you, too."

He isn't going to know what hit him. My life has always been a series of misfortunes, but I've never allowed it to define me. I may feel like I don't have a say in how things go, but I can decide how to deal with them. I'm a fighter, and I won't let anything stand in my way of the prize.

After a few deep breaths and an idea of what to say, I stand straight, crack my neck, and march to his room.

The door opens, and our eyes connect. Eli shifts slightly, and I clench my fists.

"You talked before, now you're going to listen," I demand. I'm determined for him to hear me. I move to the side of his bed and touch my finger to his chest. Our eyes stay on each other's, and I refuse to break away. "First, you will never use my sister against me. It was a dick move to do after everything I've been through the last few weeks. I will never allow you to hurt me like that again."

"I didn't—"

"No." I push my finger harder, silencing him. "You don't get to talk this time, got it?" I ask.

Eli nods and puts his hands up.

"Good." I ease back a little, still standing, needing the height to make me feel stronger. As much as I try to convince myself I'm going to just say what I need to, the truth is that I'm terrified this could end very different from how I hope it will.

Eli may decide that he doesn't want to be with me, and there's nothing I can do if that's his choice. However, I'm not going to allow myself to focus on that. I'm steeling myself for the outcome I desire, which is us moving forward—together.

My eyes close, and once I have my composure back, I continue on, "This situation is nothing like it was with Stephanie. I know you're not her, but it seems you don't get that. She was my sister, but she became my entire life when my parents died."

"I can't have you look at me like that again, Heather." He interrupts, and my eyes open.

The pain on his face causes me to let him have his say. I'm lost. I have no idea what he's talking about. During that entire thing, I wanted to make sense of it. All of it. I was focusing on not losing my shit on him, which I clearly didn't do a great job of. However, I can't recall whatever he says he saw.

"I didn't look at you like anything."

He sighs and glances at the ceiling. "You looked at me like you had to take care of me. I know right now my body is a mess, but I'll work through it. Usually, when you look at me, it's like you become bright and hopeful." He pauses. "When you were in here before, it was gone. Instead, I was a problem for you to solve. I watched your eyes go from days in the sun to doctor visits and hospitals. I know your sister was your life, but it was the same way you looked at her."

He couldn't be more wrong. That was not it at all. The fact that he feels that way sends a wave of fresh hurt through me. Why are men so stupid?

"First of all," I sit on the bed and rest my hand on his chest. "She was my responsibility. I was her parent for all intents and purposes, not to mention she was practically still a kid when she was diagnosed. I *had* to be the adult. It's not anything like that here. You're a grown ass man with a family that loves and supports you. I was her everything, Eli. There was no family or support system, I was it for her. So, yes, my entire life revolved around fixing or making things better for her. But us . . ." I sigh "It isn't that way. I want to be your partner. I want you to lean on me and then hold me up when I'm falling. That's not pity, that's love. Don't ever make this a parallel to Steph, because it's not."

He lifts his hand, touches my lips and releases a deep breath. "I'm so sorry, Heather. I never wanted to hurt you like that."

I believe him. Eli and I both have a lot of shit in our pasts that will be our demise if we don't work through it.

"I don't think you meant to hurt me, but it did, which is why I needed to walk away before I said something I'd regret."

"I thought you left," he admits with dejection laced in his voice. "I didn't think you were coming back and that I lost you because of this . . ."

I shake my head, partially in disbelief and partially in frustration. After all that we've endured, I don't know how he thinks I would be the girl to leave him because he's sick. There is no choice for me when it comes to him. The day Eli Walsh showed up at my door, he became a part of my world. I fought it, and failed. He's the other half of me, and there's no way that I could ever walk away from him.

Which brings me to my next part of this discussion. He has to see the distinctions in how we are from our pasts.

"I'm glad you bring that up." I lean back so we're not touching. I tend to think more clearly when we have a little distance. "I am not my ex-husband or your ex-girlfriend. I get that you have issues, and I do, too, but it's completely unfair to expect me to behave like them. Not only did you compare me to Penelope but also you made me Matt in the same breath. I hate her for what she did to you, and if you don't see the differences, then we should end things now."

People like her and Matt don't deserve a love like ours. Eli has given me more joy in our time together than anyone was able to give me in years.

Our relationship will be tested, but he has to know I'm not going anywhere. He's assured me of that more times than I can count. Not only in his words but also in what he's shown me. Now, I need to give him the same assurances.

Eli stays silent for a few seconds, and regret rolls off him. "Jesus, I'm just fucking up left and right. I know you're not her or him. I was pissed off at myself, and I needed to give you the reason to walk away."

"Is that what you want?" I ask.

His fingers wrap around my wrist and he tightens his grip. "No."

"I'm glad, because I have no intention of going anywhere. Even if you act like an ass sometimes. I'm not some fan who loves you because I have this idealistic dream of who you are. Love isn't some word to me, it's everything. I shared my heart with you, not because I want perfect, but because I want you. When I look at you, I see a life together. And no matter what life throws at us, I'm going to fight for you and with you, Ellington."

"Am I allowed to talk?" he asks.

"No, I have one last thing." He fights a smile, but it's probably the most important point we've yet to cover. "Don't ever lie to me again. This entire thing could've been avoided if you had talked to me. No lies between us. Ever."

"Okay," he replies, releasing my wrist only to take my hand in his. "I'll never lie to you again."

"You're going to share with me, Eli. You're going to have to let me carry your burdens just like I let you shoulder mine. But I'm not going to run from us. I've done that before, and you caught me."

Eli grips the back of my head and pulls me close so we're nose to nose. "I'm glad you say that, because as soon as I got control of my legs, I was going to hunt you down, and you weren't getting away again."

No matter what the future throws at us, I want to walk through it with him. I need him so much it's not even normal.

"I don't think you would've had to go far," I admit. "I never left the hospital grounds. I couldn't do it even though I was pissed."

Eli releases me. "Lay with me."

"Are you sure?"

He winces as he moves his legs over, making room. "Come on, I need to hold you."

I get on my side, nestling myself against his chest. I rest my chin on my hand and look at him. He smirks. "What are you smiling at?" For the first time, I can't help but laugh a little. He's too damn adorable.

"That you love me and couldn't leave. I'm glad I made you fall deep."

I roll my eyes. "Whatever, you're just as bad."

His smile fades, and Eli takes my face in his hands. "I'm far deeper than you even know. My life didn't make sense until that night at the concert. I thought I knew what love was, I didn't have a clue until you. I've never been more broken than when I watched you close that door. The pain I felt in that moment isn't something I ever want to feel again." Eli brushes his thumb against my cheek. "You're the strongest, most beautiful thing I've ever seen. I promise that there is nothing I won't do to prove how much I love you. Forgive me, Heather."

I kiss his lips and then rest my forehead against his, knowing we can face the storms ahead of us together. "I forgive you."

"I told you before that we could only own tonight, but that was bullshit."

My eyes meet his with confusion.

"I'm going to own all of our days, nights, and every tomorrow."

He presses his mouth to mine, and I melt into his touch. The weight that was sitting on my heart is lifted, and I know we're going to be okay.

"Are you sure you want to do this?" I ask him as we park in my driveway.

"You baked me a cake, and I'm going to eat it."

Eli was released from the hospital today, and he basically demanded we go straight to my house. He regained feeling in his legs after the first day, and he's able to walk now with his walker. His doctors reiterated how important it is to stay on track with his medications and infusions, and he claims he understands.

We've spent the last few days making plans and trying hard not to focus on his condition. Matt granted me another week off work, and I'm going to New York with Eli.

I help him from the car, and he grumbles when I bring the walker out.

"Don't gripe, you know you have to use it, Gramps."

"You do realize in a week, I could be perfectly normal and be able to kick your ass for that comment."

I smile, "I like my chances on outrunning you."

He huffs and pushes the walker toward the house. "Thinks she's all badass because she's a cop, I'll show her."

I've missed this playful, smartass, and horny-as-hell side of him. However, I swear, he tried to get me to blow him in the hospital. That was a fun fight, where I did actually help him a little, however I was not on board with hospital blow jobs. He threatened that if I didn't, he'd find a nurse to give him a sponge bath.

No one in that hospital was touching his junk but me.

We enter the house, and he sits on the couch. "You okay?" he asks for the millionth time. I don't need to even bother asking what he's referring to.

Tomorrow, Eli will hold a press conference to announce his condition along with our relationship. His publicist pretty much demanded we take control of the situation. They took thousands of photos of me coming in and out of the hospital. The constant barrage of questions was out of control. Eli was livid and demanded Sharon get here and handle things.

"Stop asking me that. I'm fine." For the most part. "Am I excited about this? No, but it's what has to be done. Honestly, I'm glad we had time before people figured it out."

Eli pulls me to his side and kisses the top of my head. "You're going to be great. You don't have to talk, just stand there and look pretty."

He's ridiculous. His publicist, Sharon, is a lunatic. I swear, she's her own brand of energy. She talks a mile a minute, has a Bluetooth constantly attached to her ear, and can carry on at least four conversations at once. She scares me—a lot.

"Sharon said they're going to hound me more if I refuse to speak. She practically demanded I answer questions."

"Baby, they're going to hound you no matter what. It's part of their game, but the beginning will be the worst. After that, some asshole will do something stupid, and they'll move on."

I look at him and grin. "Basically, we should hope for a celebrity shit show?"

"Pretty much. Give them a real juicy story, and they'll all flock to that."

This world is a little odd. I've never understood the appeal of stalking celebrities. Nicole tried to explain it to me once, but it was as if she were trying to explain quantum physics to a rock. I just didn't get it.

"Your life is bizarre," I muse while enjoying his warmth.

"And yours isn't?"

I sit up with my jaw open. "Umm, how is my life weird?"

He chuckles. "Let's see, you chase after criminals. People with guns."

"Yeah, bad people who need to be in jail."

"Even worse!" Eli laughs as his voice raises. "You're nuts."

"Oh, I see, now you're just an actor again?" I nudge him. Not so long ago, Eli was claiming he was practically a cop, I guess he forgets that.

Recognition dawns on his face, and he rolls his eyes. "I'm a man who is dying for some cake." He winks.

Smooth.

I kiss his cheek and get to my feet. I don't even know if the cake survived, but if I know Kristin, she wrapped it up and put it in the fridge for me.

I, on the other hand, would've just tossed it. I will never be the class mom or the wife who organizes some big event. It's not my style.

"You know," Eli yells from the living room. "I could skip the cake and go for a sponge bath."

"I bet you could, but I'm good, thanks." I laugh as I open the fridge.

Sure enough, the cake is wrapped in plastic wrap and aluminum foil, which is something I'm going to need to ask her about. Especially if it preserves cake for longer, that's a good tip.

Cake is always a good thing.

"Killjoy! Did you find the cake?" he asks.

I walk out with the whole thing and two forks.

"It looks great. Is it edible?" he jokes.

I move around to the couch and sit next to him. "Ass. I'm not sure, but since it's your birthday cake, you should totally have the first bite."

He eyes the cake and then looks back at me. Then, he dips his finger in the icing and moves it to his mouth. His green eyes move back to mine before he smears it on my chest. I go to jump up, but he grabs my wrist, holding me down. "Stay there," he instructs. "I want some extra sugar with my cake."

His lips kiss a trail down to my neck, and then his tongue slides across my skin. Heat pools in my center at the feel of him on my skin. Eli takes his time, licking the frosting from my chest. I've missed his touch. My fingers glide through his thick hair, and his longer-than-normal scruff scratches in the best possible way.

I make a mental note to tell him to keep it for a while.

"I think the cake is perfect," he muses.

"Yeah?"

"Oh, most definitely."

I dip my finger in and then pop the sugary goodness in my mouth. "Mmm," I moan. "It's good, but I think maybe it's missing something."

He takes a bigger swipe and places the frosting on my thigh. Eli grips my calves, pulling so I fall backward. "I need another taste," he explains.

"Well, by all means." I'm not going to stop him. Eli is the fire that I never want to extinguish. When he's around, I'm alive, and I never want to go back. I'm beautiful, special, and precious to him.

His tongue moves higher and higher up my leg before he stops. "Eli," I groan, wanting him to keep going.

He leans back, fire blazing in his eyes, and I know this cake is going to be eaten very creatively.

———

"MR. WALSH WILL READ a brief statement, and then we'll allow a few questions at the end," Sharon says as we stand in front of a crowd of reporters.

Eli squeezes my hand before releasing it. I hate this for him. I hate this for me, too, but he's the one talking. Hours before, Sharon explained the importance of the wording and our body language before making us review each possible way to handle any questions. When she was satisfied we wouldn't screw it up, she berated me for another fifteen minutes about my outfit. After she finally found a black pants suit, red heels, and jewelry that she found adequate, we were on our way.

Now, it's really happening.

My heart races in my chest when Eli clears his throat. I wish this weren't necessary. He's kept his condition a secret for years, and today, he's going to tell the world.

"Good afternoon. I'd first like to take a moment and thank you all for the get-well messages. The staff at Tampa General Hospital is truly phenomenal, and I received the best care while I was there." Eli clenches his hand and then flattens it. "Six days ago, I was in my home where I fell and hit my head. Thankfully, I didn't sustain any lasting damage from the concussion, and my face is fine, so no worries about filming." He winks at the camera before tossing a smile to the reporters. "However, my fall was due to a condition I was diagnosed with ten years ago. I have relapsing-remitting multiple sclerosis and have been able to manage my disease with a fantastic team of doctors and regular medication."

The faces of the reporters vary from shock to worry. I

listen as he explains more about his MS and how it affects him. He speaks about his medication, the fact that he wasn't symptomatic, and what it means going forward.

I wish I could take this for him and handle it, but a swell of relief washes over me at how well he's doing. Eli didn't need me to do anything but be by his side. We talked about how to deal with the press in regards to me, and we agreed as a couple that I wouldn't speak today.

Eventually, we got Sharon to agree to it, but we had to give her something in return. So, as soon as he's finished with this, he'll head outside where there are barricades to keep the fans at bay. Sharon thought it would be good for him to sign autographs and appear normal after he tells them about his illness. I thought he should get rest, but I was pretty much overruled.

"My girlfriend, Heather Covey, has been by my side through the entire week." Immediately, the press get to their feet, hands are raised, and people are calling his name, but Eli doesn't flinch. He gives them a second and just smiles. "I'm going to give you all the run down so hopefully you won't have any questions by the time I'm done. Although, I'm sure that won't happen." Eli laughs as a few of them do as well.

After he tells them a very abridged version of our relationship and who I am, I can breathe a little. My heart is still going a mile a minute, but he commands the entirety of their attention. He's truly in his element right now, and it's downright sexy.

He finishes, draws a deep breath, and asks, "Any questions?"

"Are you saying you're officially off the market?" A young reporter asks.

Eli rocks back on his heels with a grin. "Yes. I'm very much off the market."

He points to the next person with their hand up. "Do you plan to move back to Tampa?"

"I plan to fulfill my obligations to *A Thin Blue Line* and make time for my relationship as well. Does that mean I'll be in Tampa a lot more? Yes." I watch in awe as he takes each question with ease.

"Any plans to get married?"

My eyes widen at the leap from being off the market to marriage. We both love each other immensely, but Jesus.

Eli chuckles. "We're taking things day by day right now."

"So, it isn't serious?" The same reporter asks.

I can almost feel Eli's mood shift from amusement to anger. "If it weren't serious, I wouldn't be here, Joe. In the last ten plus years, when have you heard me talk about a girlfriend?" Eli challenges him. "It's serious."

Joe doesn't respond, and Eli moves to the next hand. It goes on with the same variations of questions, all centered around our relationship, none about his multiple sclerosis. Which is baffling since that's what the point of this was.

I stand one step behind Eli as he moves to the next question.

"Ms. Covey." She looks at me and a flash of fear hits me. "Do you plan to quit your job as a Tampa Police Officer?"

Eli starts to speak, but I touch his arm as I get closer to the microphone. I don't know how I got here, but my feet somehow moved toward him. "I don't. I love serving this city, and I'll continue to do so." I slide my hand down his arm and rest it on top of his hand. The smile on Eli's face is full of pride. He laces his fingers with mine, and I'm not afraid. He's up here taking the hits and standing strong.

I can do this because together, we're unrelenting.

"Is it true you were married before?"

I watch Eli's knuckles turn white from gripping the side of the table he's holding with his other hand. I squeeze my fingers and take a page from his book. "Yes, I've been divorced for five years. Eli is aware of my previous marriage."

Sharon moves to the other side of Eli and pulls the microphone out. "That's all we have time for today."

Sharon ushers us to a private room, where Eli takes a seat. He refused to use the walker today. I didn't even attempt to convince him otherwise. However, it's clear that it took a great amount of energy for him to stay on his feet and perform.

"You did great," I say, wiping his forehead.

"You weren't so bad yourself." He smiles and takes my hand in his.

"Yes, yes, you both were great," Sharon says as she types on her phone. "We need to get you out there as quickly as possible. They all need to believe you're the epitome of health."

I'm suddenly thinking this meet and autograph thing was genuinely a bad idea.

I roll my eyes and fight back the urge to slap her. "Are you good?" I ask him.

"I've got this, baby."

The instinct to protect him rises, but I repress the urge. I have to trust him, which means not trying to control the situation. It's so much easier said than done. I'm a cop. I thrive on being in control. It's who I am, but I also know that it's his greatest fear within our relationship.

Instead of doing what I really want to do, I smile. "Okay."

Eli bursts out laughing and pulls me on his lap. "You're such a shitty liar."

"Don't laugh at me." I smack his chest.

"You should see your face. Don't ever go into acting."

Whatever.

"Let's go, Eli." Sharon claps her hand. "I want you to go for as long as you can."

I glare at her. "Don't you think you should be a little concerned for him?"

"I'm concerned for his career, which is my job." Sharon doesn't even look at me. She goes back to her phone and huffs. "I'll meet you out there. Don't take long."

I get to my feet once she leaves the room. "I'm pretty sure she's Satan's daughter."

He chuckles. "Makes me glad she's on our team then."

Eli pulls me into his arms, and I wrap mine around his waist. "I love you," I tell him.

"I love you."

He drops his lips to mine, and I couldn't give a shit less about his fans waiting or Sharon, who is probably ready to butcher me. Right now, I have him all to myself. I love how centered he makes me feel. I never worry where his mind is. When we're together, it's on us.

"You should go," I mumble against his mouth. "And be careful, those women are crazy and will try to kidnap you."

He pulls back. "Don't worry, we have police protection."

"What?" I ask.

Eli shrugs. "I know you're able to take care of yourself, but this is a new set of rules. You're in my world now, and I'm going to do what I can to protect you."

I'm still not understanding. What the hell does any of this have to do with police protection?

He waits a second, and it hits me.

"Oh my God! You have people here to protect me? Other cops? I am a cop, Eli. I don't need protection." There's no freaking way this is going to work for me. I'm not getting other cops to shadow me. A lot of us do it part time. It's great money when the celebrities are in town. I've done it, and over my dead body will I become one of *those*.

"You have no idea what the hell crazy fans are like, I do. We do this my way, baby. No room for discussion, at least in the beginning. I have a bunch of off duty guys who will stay with me and some will stay with you."

My eyes narrow. There are so many damn things to say to him, but the worry in his eyes makes me swallow every single one of them. He's truly afraid and doing what he can to ease his own fears.

"We'll talk later. Right now, you need to go." I table the discussion.

His brow raises, but he doesn't say anything. We both know what this means . . . one hell of an argument followed by some fantastic sex.

We exit the room, and I see a bunch of my squad leaning against the wall.

"Hey! Look who it is, our very own celebrity officer!" Whitman laughs and looks around.

"Look, it's my over-aged security detail." I smile. "I've missed you jackasses!"

And I have. I've been off work since Stephanie passed away, and I've been itching to get back on the road. This squad is part of my family. We may give each other a hard time, but I would literally take a bullet for them. They're my brothers, and I don't forget how lucky I am to have these kinds of people in my life.

Whitman and Vincenzo pull me in for a hug. "It's good to see you with a smile."

"Yeah, it's all thanks to this guy. Boys, this is Eli Walsh."

"Eli, this is Whitman and Vincenzo." I point to each in turn. "They were who responded to your fall."

"Oh, wow." Eli shakes their hands. "Thank you, guys. I'm really grateful."

"We're glad we could help." They both brush it off. And in all honesty, it's our job. Being praised for doing what we took an oath to do is sometimes weird. I always feel awkward because I love it. I want to help others. I like the calls where I get to make a difference, and those two did so much—for Eli and for me.

"I'm glad Heather had someone she knew there to help," Eli says and then kisses the side of my head.

Federico coughs, and I glare at him before finishing the introductions. "You know Brody. This dumbass is Federico, that's Jones, and—" I stare into the eyes of one man I didn't think I'd see here. I don't know why I never thought it was a possibility, but it's happening. "My lieutenant, Matt Jamerson."

"Nice to meet you guys." Eli shakes all their hands and then wraps his arm around my waist when he reaches out to grab Matt's hand. "I appreciate the help with the crowd."

I look to Brody and purse my lips, using my mind to yell at him about not warning me. In a weird way, he seems to understand my internal screaming and has enough sense to look contrite.

This is going to be so damn awkward.

"Well, we all love Heather and don't want anyone to hurt her," Federico says, as if I don't know they bitched about it.

"Yes, we do," Matt says in agreement.

Is he unhinged? Eli's hand constricts against my side. "Good to know."

Matt steps closer. "She's one of us. We protect our own."

I feel as if I'm having an out-of-body experience. I must be dreaming, because there's no way my boyfriend and my ex-asshole are having this discussion, right? I've had some weird shit go down in the last few days, but this isn't real.

"I completely understand," Eli says smoothly. I look up, slightly confused by how he managed to miss the hidden meaning in Matt's words. I'm not a guy and I get it. "It's why I hired you all. Heather's safety is paramount. I always take care of what's *mine*."

And there it is.

"She wouldn't need protection normally."

"When she fell in love with me, things changed. However, I clearly have all intentions of taking care of her . . . in every way. I don't walk away from my responsibilities, especially when it comes to people I love."

This conversation is going to get out of hand real quick. I look to Brody, who is about two seconds away from popping popcorn, and the rest of the guys are grinning. Matt is a good cop, but no one likes him as a person.

Time to end this.

"You guys about done?" I ask. "Want to measure who is bigger? Although, I already know the answer to that."

Matt huffs and shakes his head. "I've got paperwork to fill out, I'm sure you'll be fine with Brody."

I watch the man I thought I loved for so long walk away. Someone I made vows to, and would still probably be with if he hadn't left, and I wonder how I was so blind.

Matt would never have hired a bunch of police officers if my safety was at risk. He'd tell me I was being stupid. He wouldn't go out of his way to make me feel comfortable or just take my hand for no reason.

Eli does all of those things and more.

I turn back to Eli, who has his chest puffed out, his smile is ridiculously bright, and is probably two seconds away from him pounding his chest like a caveman.

"You're that happy with yourself, huh?"

He grins at me. "You're welcome."

I roll my eyes and drop my forehead to his chest. "You're a mess."

Eli's arms encompass me. "Your ex-husband is an idiot."

"I'm well aware."

"I'll handle him if he becomes a problem."

I'm not sure what he'll do, considering Matt's my boss, but I'll never tire of his desire to care for me. It's nice having someone there for me. We're truly partners in every sense of the word.

I lift my gaze back to his with my hand on his chest.

We don't say anything, we don't have to.

The depth of Eli's love is soul shattering, and I feel it in my bones. He gives me things I didn't even know I needed. He looks at me as if I'm the only thing that matters. It's the kind of love I saw in my father's eyes when he looked at my mother.

We could've fallen apart last week, but we didn't. We stand here, stronger and even more secure than before.

"Thank you," I say.

He takes my hands in his and smiles. "I should be thanking your ex."

"Huh?"

"I've never been more grateful than I am right now. If he weren't such a dick, I wouldn't be able to do this." He drops lower and kisses my lips. "And this." He places a kiss on my forehead. "Or this," he says before he cups my face and kisses me deeply. His tongue slides against mine, and I forget where we are. My hands grip his shoulders as I kiss him back.

I hear someone clear their throat, and we both pull back. Shit.

Brody stands there with a shit-eating grin. "Now that was some funny shit. Glad someone finally told him what a piece of shit he is."

"He's lucky I'm recovering or I would've kicked his ass," Eli concurs.

Oh, dear God.

I scowl at Brody and then look back to Eli. "Go be the famous hot guy who everyone loves."

He dips his head, giving me a sweet, short kiss. "Good thing I only love one person."

"Good thing she loves you back."

Eli smiles and taps my nose. "Once in a lifetime," he says before he heads out of the room.

I lean against the door, grateful that Kristin was in the Four Blocks Down fanclub. Otherwise, this chance would've passed us by, and *that* would've been a tragedy.

CHAPTER TWENTY-EIGHT
HEATHER

~ TWO YEARS LATER ~

"This is so exciting!" Danni jumps up and down as we get escorted to our seats.

"Dude," Nicole grumbles. "FBD is totally not as fun as the last time we were here."

I laugh. "Why because you know them all now?"

She rolls her eyes and huffs. "Duh! I swear, your boyfriend isn't even cute anymore."

"You're so full of shit." I smack her arm.

Eli Walsh is still a very sexy man, and she knows it. He's like a fine wine that only gets better with age. He's been on tour the last few months, and once again, he's doing his final show in Tampa. I spent two weeks with him jumping to St. Louis, Nashville, Chicago, Indianapolis, St. Paul, and Little Rock before I booked a flight home. Hell no was I doing that again.

They're all slobs.

I much prefer his apartment in New York than being cramped on the bus with the guys.

It's been a whirlwind the last few years. One that I'm

sometimes amazed we've endured so well. The media responded well when I said I wasn't leaving my job, and I think being a cop shielded me a lot.

I'm clearly not after his money, even though he practically throws it at me.

The lights dim and déjà vu hits me like a Mack truck to the face.

Kristin grabs my hands, squeezing tight. "I'm so glad Eli hooked us up with these seats."

"Well, I didn't give him much choice." My smile is wide as she giggles.

"This is true. Still, I'm so grateful."

As much as this is like the first time we attended the concert, so much has changed. Kristin left her husband and now lives in my old home with her two kids. Danielle and Peter are actually doing extremely well after having a second honeymoon. And Nicole is still the same, having random sexcapades and God only knows how many threesomes. I stopped asking after it started giving Eli ideas.

I'm now permanently living in Eli's Tampa house. Though, at first it wasn't entirely by choice. Eli practically moved my stuff out of my place and into his the day after our press conference. My home was swarmed with photographers, and he wasn't having it.

I was exceedingly against it, we fought, and then did a lot of making up—in our new home.

The silhouettes of the band members are visible now, and the crowd roars. Lights come on and the concert begins.

I watch Eli the entire time. The way his dark brown hair catches the light, his green eyes meet mine every time he's close, and the way he only gives me his cocky smirk that makes my heart melt. I love him more each day, even on the days I'd like to wring his neck.

He dances around, and I study his movements, watching

for any sign of his hands bothering him. He told me they were tingling after his last show. Today, he looks great.

The music shifts, and my adrenalin starts to thump. Anytime I hear this song, I can't help but smile. "I've got someone very special in the audience tonight," Eli says.

Oh, no. No, no, no. He promised. I try to move, but Nicole grabs me. "You're so going up there."

"My girlfriend is here tonight, and if you don't know, this exact concert a little over two years ago, was where I met her." He gazes at me and winks. "I'd like to bring her back up tonight and remind her just how much she loves me. So, come on Heather, get up here."

My lips purse, and he gets the meanest stink eye I can muster. But what does he do? Laughs. The asshole laughs.

The bouncer extends his hand. Eli watches me, and I mouth *I hate you* to him.

As soon as I'm on stage, he pulls me close and plants his lips on mine as the crowd goes crazy. "You love me," he says against my ear.

"Not for long."

"Randy," Eli calls his brother over. "Heather might need a little support for this number."

Randy laughs. "I see you're going to lay it on thick?"

"She is my once in a lifetime girl . . . she needs to feel it in her bones!" Eli yells.

Dear God this can't be my life. Here I sit, on stage while my boyfriend, Shaun, PJ, and Randy have fun at my expense. I'm going to kill Eli, and then I'm going to have Savannah kill Randy.

Damn Walsh brothers.

The music keys in, and Eli begins to sing.

After the first chorus of him being totally over the top, he stops.

He pulls me to my feet and sings to me. The audience

disappears while he holds me close. We sway to the music, and suddenly, I don't care about the people or the lights. My embarrassment fades into the distance, and I pretend we're alone at home. Eli and I are in our kitchen as he tells me the words of the song.

I look out at the crowd and see the lights from the cell-phones filling the room. It's like a million twinkling stars shine just for us.

My fingers rub the back of his neck, and I kiss his cheek when the song ends.

"My once in a lifetime . . ." He extends his hand.

Eli pulls me back to his chest and kisses me again. "Come backstage after the show. I've got another memory I want to recreate."

I shake my head and laugh. "I love you, Eli."

"I love you more."

Just like the first time, my friends all smile and are lost in the fanfare.

"What did he whisper?" Kristin asks.

"To go backstage," I say through a laugh.

"I totally thought he was going to propose," Danni says offhandedly. "I'm a little disappointed he hasn't."

My eyes widen, and my heart skips. I hadn't thought of that. I mean, I did, but he made a comment the other night that he was really happy that we're where we are. I've been married already, so it isn't like I need a ring, but there's a part of me that wants to be his completely.

Until now, I didn't even give it more thought, but having her say it, makes me a little sad.

Nicole smacks her arm and then comes in front of me. "You guys are happy, honey. Really happy, you don't need a ring to prove it."

I expel the rush of disappointment that hit me hard. I don't need it, and whenever Eli wants to propose, that's when it'll happen. I'd rather have him than anything else. "I was being dumb."

Nicole nods. "Trust me, there isn't a woman in this arena who doesn't hate you right now. Eli kissed you, sang to you, and then invited you backstage. If he proposed, we'd have to put you in protective custody."

I burst out laughing and agree. My press life with Eli is always . . . bizarre. When he was nominated for an Emmy, it was like nothing I'd ever seen before. People calling our names, taking so many photos I thought my face was going to be stuck with a smile. Not all the fans were awesome, though. Some were completely awful toward me. Not to mention the media picking apart our outfits, hair, makeup, everything . . . all for entertainment. If Eli draws attention to us, it only gets worse. It's why I prefer our happy little bubble in Tampa.

Not that he's here that much, but we've found a way to make it work, exactly like he promised.

We enjoy the rest of the show and then head backstage. The boys come out, and I hug them all. Shaun and PJ are always the first ones to enter the party. I swear, they have alcohol running through their veins instead of blood.

Then I see him, his perfect face and gorgeous smile heads right toward me. Eli's arms are around my waist and he lifts me, spinning around. "Hi, gorgeous."

"Hi there, sexy. I'm mad at you."

"You know I had to do it," Eli explains.

"Uh-huh."

Eli sets me down and kisses my nose. "Let's go somewhere private."

I hit his arm. "We are *not* having sex on the bus."

He tugs me against his chest and grins. "Oh, yes we are."

I start to protest, but he squats before tossing me over his shoulder. "Eli!"

"I told you, we're heading to the bus!" he yells as he spins around to face the party. "We'll be done in a few hours. I'm going to make my girlfriend scream for a bit."

"Oh my God!" I slap his ass. "You're a dead man."

I hear the door to the bus open, and he slides me down the front of his body. "I think you'll let me live," he says against my lips.

"Don't be so sure."

Eli climbs the stairs backward, and my eyes take everything in. The bus is filled with candles and red roses. Dozens and dozens of flowers fill the space. There's no surface untouched by soft delicate petals and warm candlelight. I spin around, my eyes filling with tears as I see how absolutely gorgeous it looks. The floor has a line of petals leading to the bedroom. I turn back around to Eli and my breath hitches.

This isn't happening.

"What are you doing?" He's on one knee before me.

"I'm doing what I've wanted to do for a long time."

My hand covers my mouth as he pulls the lid back on the black box. "Heather Covey, I've spent a lifetime waiting for the woman I'd want to share my heart with. We met at this concert, we made love on this bus, and you're the only person I want by my side. I know we've said we were happy with how things are, but—"

"Yes!" I scream out, unable to hold it in any longer.

"I wasn't done yet," he complains with a laugh.

I get on my knees with him and giggle with tears in my eyes.

"I want it all, baby. I want you to be my wife. I want us to share everything. I need to give you my name just as I've given you my heart. So . . . will you marry me?"

I launch myself into his arms and kiss him hard. "Yes, yes, yes!" I say and then kiss him again. "I love you so much."

"Good." He kisses my tears of happiness.

Then I watch as he puts the stunning princess cut

diamond on my finger. I stare at it shimmering in the candle-light. I'm going to be his wife. Our lives have fit together seamlessly. We find true happiness in each other like I've never known. My eyes meet his again, and I touch his cheek.

"I don't know how I ever lived before you." I rub my thumb against his stubble. "I love you so very much."

Eli stands and then pulls me to my feet. His arms cinch around me, and we hold on to each other. "I wasn't living before you. I was waiting."

"No more waiting." I smile, remembering the same words I spoke to him years ago.

His eyes meet mine, and there's so much love in his gaze, it takes my breath away. "I'd wait forever if it meant I found you."

I can't wait another second to kiss him, so I do. Eli leads us to the bedroom where we make another memory. This time, there will be no running away after.

I lie in his arms, loving the way we fit together. After some time, my mind fills with a pinch of sadness. My first wedding was a justice of the peace deal, but with Eli, I know he'll want it all. My sister isn't here to see us get married, and I have no one to give me away.

"Hey, what's wrong?" he asks.

He can always tell when my feelings go dark. I seriously need to work on hiding that.

"I wish Stephanie could be here, and my parents. I know my dad would hate you, but my mom would be completely over the moon."

His arms tighten. "I wish I could give you that, but it's the one thing I can't."

"I know, and I know if you could, you would."

"There's nothing I won't do for you," Eli promises. "And wait, what do you mean, your dad would hate me?"

I sit up, smiling as I think about my daddy. "No one was

good enough for his little girls. Also, he didn't like you. He had to hear all about how I loved you and how amazing you were. On top of that, he had to listen to all your songs—he wasn't impressed. He told me to avoid dating any musicians. Clearly, I didn't listen."

When Four Blocks Down came out, I was obsessed and told my father one day I would marry Eli. My father told me boys were all stupid and I should stay away, but boys in a boy band were the ones I should run from. I want to believe he'd have changed his tune after meeting Eli. Regardless, it would've been funny to watch.

Eli moves so we're eye to eye and smiles. "I would've won him over."

I touch his cheek; the diamond on my finger catching the light and sparkling. "Daddy would've seen that you weren't a spoiled, self-centered, egotistical jerk who uses girls and leaves them."

"That's what he thought?"

I laugh. "Probably."

He moves quickly, pulling me beneath him. "Well, in a few weeks you'll be my wife."

"Weeks?"

He nods. "Weeks. Three to be exact."

"Wait!" I push him off me. "You want to get married in three weeks? I don't have a dress or anything! We can't get married in three weeks!"

Eli is always doing this to me, like the trip he surprised me with to Antigua. He came home, told me to pack, and took me away four hours later. He even had Brody get my time off cleared, he's crazy. And yet, he's everything.

"The date is set, everyone knows."

"Everyone knows?" I push his chest. "You just asked me! We haven't left the bus, how the hell did you plan a wedding?"

He shrugs and then gives me a smug grin. "I knew you'd say yes."

I groan and flop back on the bed. I'm not angry, but he kills me. "Okay, I'll bite, when is our wedding?"

My life is filled with love and a crazy man who plans a wedding before he gets the bride.

He tells me all the details while I stare at him with a stunned expression. He actually planned the entire damn thing. I'm not sure if I should jump his bones or beat the crap out of him. Eli said it was more because of his schedule. He's starting a movie in Vancouver in a month, so he wants to tie the knot before he leaves.

"You really want us to get married on a boat?" I ask.

This is the one detail I don't understand.

Eli climbs over me and pushes my hair back. "This is for many reasons," he explains. "Number one being that I can control the security and guest list. Number two is because I like boats and our first date was on one." I smile at that one. "Number three is that there's nowhere for you to run."

"Run?"

"Yeah, there are no fences for you to climb if you get cold feet. I'll have you right where I want you, right next to me —forever."

Holy crap. I'm getting married today.

I stand in front of the full-length mirror in the master bedroom, stunned. The day after our engagement, I met my wedding planner, Kennedy. She arrived with a van packed with options. I thought his publicist was scary, but she could learn a thing or two from Kennedy.

In two days, I had a dress, flowers, colors, bridesmaid dresses, and the menu selected. It's amazing what you can get done with a woman who doesn't understand the word "no" and an unlimited budget. When a vendor said they couldn't do it, she told them they didn't have a choice.

"Oh, Heather." Nicole enters and her eyes fill with tears. "You look gorgeous."

My eyes go back to the mirror, and I take it all in. The hairdresser arranged my hair to be mostly up with tendrils of blonde hanging around my face. My makeup is flawless. It's soft but still slightly dramatic. However, the dress . . . I still can't believe it's me in it.

"You think?"

She stands behind me in the aqua-colored dress I chose

and places her hands on my shoulders. "Yes, honey. You're breathtaking."

I glide my hands against the satin fabric, loving how perfectly it fits me. Nicole and Kennedy argued over their top choices for what I should wear, and Nic demanded I try on her choice. The scoop neck shows off the right amount of cleavage and is skin tight through the bodice before it trumpets out at the bottom. It's classic, elegant, and I love every inch of it.

"I can't believe he planned all this," I muse, still looking myself over.

"Lucky bitch." She snorts, and we both laugh.

I know I'm lucky. Each time I look at my ridiculously sexy fiancé, I remember how special what we have is. Sure, we have our ups and downs and things are never always easy, but he's worth it all.

Kristin peeks her head in. "You guys ready? We need to get to the dock and send the limo to the park."

I roll my eyes at the lengths he's gone to, but he said he refuses to let one photo be leaked. Therefore, there are fake limos, and he rented out the park we went to before Steph passed away.

Kristin, Danielle, Nicole, Savannah, and I climb into the other limousine and head to the boat. The wedding is only immediate family and friends, we want to be surrounded by those we love without any fanfare.

"Are you ready?" Savannah asks as we pull up.

Our relationship has become incredibly close. She's been there each step of the way, helping me find my footing in this crazy public life. I'm so grateful to her, and I'm excited to become sisters-in-law.

"I really am."

"I'm so happy for you guys," she takes my hand.

Kennedy opens the door and ushers everyone out. "Let's

go. So far, we've evaded any possible press, so let's get you out to sea before that changes." When we don't move fast enough she claps her hands. "I'm not kidding ladies, let's move your butts."

We all glance at each other, and I stifle a laugh.

Once safely aboard, we head to the first level, where there's a plush living room type area. The boat is magnificent. It has a dining area with a dance floor, a bathroom that doesn't make me cringe, and even a few bedrooms. It's basically a miniature cruise ship.

"Do you think he's nervous?" I ask the girls.

"I'm sure he's being restrained by Randy so he can't come find you." Savannah laughs. "Eli isn't known for his patience."

"No shit," Nicole agrees. "Who the hell plans a wedding before asking the bride?"

"I think it's romantic." Kristin grins.

I agree with Kristin. On one hand, he's crazy, but on the other, he's sweet. "Well, he does leave for filming soon, so we either did it now or waited a few months."

After a bit, Kennedy comes in and instructs us where to go. She fusses over each of my girls, getting their dresses perfect.

Nicole turns to me and pulls me close. "He's the one, Heather. The one who deserves you." She pulls a note from her freaking cleavage, and I know what that is. "I wanted to do this before we left, but I forgot until now. Stephanie said this was only to be given to you on your wedding day to a man who truly deserved you."

My hand reaches out, shaking as I take the paper. "I can't read this," I admit.

"Do you want me to read it to you?"

"No," I sigh. "I just mean I'm going to lose it."

She touches my hand. "I'll hold Kennedy back. Take your time."

Nicole makes good on her promise, informing Kennedy that she'll make her walk the plank if she comes in here. I sit on the chair and open the note. My sister is always with me, and today has been tough, but I pray this won't wreck me.

HEATHER,

I really hope you get to read this, and for real, don't cry!

You were meant to be loved by someone special. You have given yourself to everyone around you, and I hope you've found a man who will finally fill you up. I don't remember Mom and Dad's marriage like you do, but from what you've told me, I pray you've found that kind of love. I hope the other half of your soul is a fraction as wonderful as you are.

While I can't be there, know that when you finally open this note, I'm smiling down on you. If it's sunny, it's because I'm shining. If it's raining, it's because I wanted to make your makeup run, because that's what sisters do. However, if it's a hurricane, then Daddy is probably trying to send you a message or you just have really shitty luck.

I hope you're happy today. I want you to smile all day, even when you miss me. I'm never far from you because you're a part of me. I love you so much. I wish I could tell you how special and beautiful you are right now, but this letter will have to do.

Last, let him know if he messes up, I probably have other ghost friends by now, and I'll make sure he never sleeps again.

I love you.

Stephanie

P.S. You get the next letter when you either have a kid or turn fifty. Either way, I'll be back . . .

I TUCK the letter into my bouquet of flowers so she's with me down the aisle and look out at the now coral-and-purple sky with a smile. She's such a turd, even from the grave she still messes with me.

My sister would've loved this. I can imagine her giving me crap about the color dresses, the flavor of cake, and pretty much anything else she could make a fuss about. The way she would've gone to war with Kennedy and then with Nicole. She would've loved Eli. They only met a few times, and I know she'd be completely on his side. He has this way about him that she wouldn't have been able to resist. It's annoying how charming he is.

There's a soft knock on the door, and I open it.

"Ready?" Brody asks with a smile.

"I'm ready." I loop my arm in his.

Brody kisses my cheek, and we start to walk. "I'm happy for you. Eli's a good dude."

I chuckle. "He is."

"You doing okay after the letter?"

"I actually am. I miss her. I miss her so much, but she's with me all the time."

Brody stops me at the bottom of the stairs. "She would be so proud of you."

Now the tears start to come. I look up, fanning my eyes and hoping to keep them until at least the vows. "Damn it." I laugh. "No more talking. I'm not crying before the wedding."

"All right, let's focus on you not tripping."

"Agreed."

We make it to the upper deck, and nerves have me gripping Brody's elbow a bit tighter. I think about how different my life is. I'm not afraid anymore, and that's all thanks to Eli. I don't sit and wait for the floor to drop out, I dance on it, enjoying what we do have. He's been there each step of the way, always holding out a hand for me to hold. When he wanted to leave his show, we talked about it. He wanted me to quit my job, and we talked through my staying. I'm there by his side at his doctor appointments, but I'm not the one running it all. There may come a time when things will change for us, but that's okay. If it does, we'll do it together.

Kennedy makes her way over and fixes my veil. "Here we go."

The double doors open, and I continue to cling to Brody's arm so I don't falter in my steps. The space is more stunning than I could have imagined. There are blue and green flowers, beautiful white chairs, and twinkling lights fill the space. It's absolutely perfect.

The music cues, and the room no longer is what I see. The man I love more than life comes into view, and I melt. His black tuxedo frames his body, showing off his broad shoulders and trim waist. Our eyes connect, and he smiles. My chest clenches, and I fight the urge to run toward him. Suddenly, I can't wait.

I start to move, but Brody holds me steady.

Each step I take eases the tightness around my ribs. The closer we get, the easier I can breathe.

We reach the end, and Brody places my hand in Eli's as a tear falls. I look at my best friend who has been a brother to me. He winks and kisses my cheek. "You have a new partner now."

Another tear drops, and I nod. "Thank you."

"Be good to her," Brody says as Eli shakes his hand.

"Always."

The minister calls attention to us all, and I feel the greatest sense of calm. Here, surrounded by our family and friends, we confess our love. Eli slips a diamond eternity band on my finger, and I place a titanium ring on his. When we picked out our rings, Eli said my ring was to be wrapped with no break in stones. I chose one that was the strongest metal.

"Ellington and Heather have decided to write their own vows," the minister explains. "Heather, you're first."

I take a deep breath and confess what's in my heart. "I never believed in fate. My world was exactly what I made it to be. I felt that by believing there was something else controlling the things around me, it meant I wasn't worthy of much because my life was a mess. Therefore, I controlled anything possible. And then I met you. A day that was a way for my friends to force me out of the house for a good time, became my future. I didn't know that one instant could alter everything I ever believed in, but you did that. You showed me that it was okay to take chances. You gave me a safe haven through the storm. You give me the ability and the strength to believe in tomorrow." A tear rolls down his face, and I swipe it away like he's done for me so many times. I take his hand in mine and squeeze hard. I want him to know how much I believe in us. "I promise that I'll never run from you, not even if you push me outside my comfort zone. I promise that even when our lives feel like they're crumbling, I'll stand beside you. I will be your strength when you need it. I promise you will never have to wonder if I love you because I'll show you in every way. You are the other half of me. You are my belief in fate. You're my reason for going on. You're my salvation, and I love you so much. I give you my heart, my soul, and my life from this day forward."

I release a shaky breath and try not to cry, but I fail. Nicole hands me a tissue, but Eli wipes it away before it falls. We smile at each other and the minister nods at him.

"Love wasn't something I was ever looking for. I didn't seek it out or hope it would come along, but then I found you. Through a sea of people, my eyes met yours. I suddenly didn't know how to breathe. All I wanted to do was talk to you, touch you, know you, and I had to find a way. I had no idea that moment would flip my entire world upside down. That the words to that song would be exactly what you are, my once in a lifetime. I had no way of knowing that one night could alter every tomorrow. Knowing that you're with me gives me all I need. Heather, I would chase you over a thousand more fences if it meant I had the next day beside you." I giggle through the tears, and he grins. "I won't ever give up on us. I'll fight every darkness that threatens to blind our love. I'll never let you feel alone because you'll always have me. On my bad days, I promise to come to you and lean on you for support. On your bad days, I promise to be your rock. I will love you through every doubt, fear, laugh, cry, and emotion that you may have. When we're apart, I will love you through the distance. From this day forward, I promise that you'll be my day, night, and my tomorrow."

Tears of happiness fall down my cheek, and all I want to do is kiss him. The minister speaks but I don't focus on him, all I see is Eli. He steps closer and brings his hands up to cup my face. Before the minister is finished declaring us man and wife, Eli's lips are on mine, sealing all our promises until the end of time.

First, thank you for reading. We Own Tonight materialized from four best friends who went to their childhood boy band and acted like fools. The fence story is real (although not from that concert) .

As I intended, this book would be just this ... one. However, I don't seem to know how to do that. I hope decide to read the beautiful love story for Kristin. Divorce isn't easy, but ... well ... there's always a second time around, right?

Read One Last Time Free in Kindle Unlimited!

I have a special bonus for you! Just a little more Eli Walsh! Keep swiping for exclusive access to a never before seen Eli POV!

BONUS SCENE

Dear Reader,

I hope you enjoyed We Own Tonight! Do you want more Eli Walsh? If so, sign up for my newsletter and you'll get an exclusive bonus chapter that you can't get anywhere else!

http://www.subscribepage.com/BonusWOT

BOOKS BY CORINNE MICHAELS

The Salvation Series

Beloved

Beholden

Consolation

Conviction

Defenseless

Evermore: A 1001 Dark Night Novella

Indefinite

Infinite

The Hennington Brothers

Say You'll Stay

Say You Want Me

Say I'm Yours

Say You Won't Let Go: A Return to Me/Masters and Mercenaries
Novella

Second Time Around Series

We Own Tonight

One Last Time

Not Until You

If I Only Knew

The Arrowood Brothers

Come Back for Me

Fight for Me

The One for Me

Stay for Me

Willow Creek Valley Series

Return to Us

Could Have Been Us

A Moment for Us

A Chance for Us

Rose Canyon Series

Help Me Remember

Give Me Love

Keep This Promise

Whitlock Family Series (Coming 2023-2024)

Forbidden Hearts

Broken Dreams

Tempting Promises

Forgotten Desires

Co-Written with Melanie Harlow

Hold You Close

Imperfect Match

Standalone Novels

All I Ask

You Loved Me Once

ABOUT THE AUTHOR

Corinne Michaels is a *New York Times*, *USA Today*, *and Wall Street Journal* bestselling author of romance novels. Her stories are chock full of emotion, humor, and unrelenting love, and she enjoys putting her characters through intense heartbreak before finding a way to heal them through their struggles.

Corinne is a former Navy wife and happily married to the man of her dreams. She began her writing career after spending months away from her husband while he was deployed—reading and writing were her escape from the loneliness. Corinne now lives in Virginia with her husband and is the emotional, witty, sarcastic, and fun-loving mom of two beautiful children.